A Man's Worth

Horse Doctor Adventures

Elizabeth Woolsey

Elizabeth Woolsey Horse Doctor Press

ISBN: 979-8-9869111-4-4

A Man's Worth I Did My Best is a work of fiction. Any similarities

to places or. persons, living or dead, is coincidental.

Cover artist Jan Dappen https://jandappen.com/

Published in the United States

ewoolseydvm@gmail.com

https://elizabethwoolsey.com/

For my veterinary colleagues past and present
including my father:
Dr. Jack Woolsey
To my fishing buddies
Dr. John Mitchell
Dr. Larry Smith
Dr. Charlie Vail
You men have made my transition to American soil and
rivers with trout so delightful
For Dr. Sharon Spier
My sister from another mister
And finally,
For the real Bill O'Neal of Birmingham, Alabama

Chapter 1

One more ring, and I knew my call would go to voice mail. My sister finally answered. "What?"

"Hey, it's me, your favorite sister." Crap, I didn't think of the time zone. "Sorry, did I wake you up?"

"No. Oh hell, who am I kidding? Of course you did. Unless Mom or Dad lied, you're my only sister. Call back in an hour."

She's pissed. Not a great way to ask for a favor. "Okay, but I need a ride from the airport tomorrow. I'll text you the details later."

"Is it over? Are you finally coming back?" I heard the disdain in her voice.

"Yeah, go back to bed. We can talk later."

"I'll call you when I'm awake." Control was my sister's weapon of choice. I accepted it and her need to one-up me on every occasion.

I packed my bags and prepared to leave his house. His children will arrive tomorrow for the funeral, and I will be gone before they come. The funeral will only be for his children. I wasn't invited. It didn't matter. We said our goodbyes days ago before he slipped into a coma.

I knew my sister was calling when the phone rang three hours later. No one else would call me at this hour. "What time?"

"Ten-thirty. I'll call you when the plane lands."

"Two years, Hayles. I hope he was worth it."

Two years earlier: "Hayley? Is that you?" There was no mistaking the voice. It was my boss from over twenty years ago.

"Hey, Doc. How are you? I haven't heard from you in how many years?"

"I called you last Christmas. Don't you remember?" Doc's voice was as strong as ever.

"Uh, no. Must have been one of your other girlfriends."

He laughed. "I have a proposition for you. How would you like to come and work for me?"

"Gee, I'm honored, but I've retired. I thought you had as well."

Doc hired me straight out of school to work in his equine vet clinic. I worked for him for ten years until I met my husband and moved to Georgia, where I lived and worked until I retired. Doc was fifteen years older than me and had retired only a few years ago.

"Are you still married to that idiot?" Typical and to the point, my former boss is laying it on the line.

"No, I divorced the idiot twenty years ago. How about you? How's Myrna?"

"Off with the fairies. I've got her in a home. I tried to keep her here, but the damn kids took her away. It got to be a bit much. I'll tell you about it when you get here."

"I'm sorry, I had no idea." I felt profound sorrow for the man. I knew how much he loved her. Still, what was my role in his plan?

"Life goes on, Hayley. I've adjusted."

I wasn't convinced. "Doc, I can't just come out at the drop of a hat. I have a life. I have kids and grandkids."

"Hayley, don't lie to me. Your kids are no more family than mine. I talked to Ted the other day. He says you're sitting on your ass all day. I need help with a project. You're the one who can help me. Do you need money for a plane ticket?"

"You talked to Ted? How is he? The last time I saw Ted was at his funeral. You do know he died a few years ago, don't you?"

Doc snorted. "Bullshit. Are you sure about Ted Gregory? Damn, no one told me. Now, get your sorry ass and your typewriter out here. We can't waste any time."

"Doc, let me think about it. What kind of help?" *Was this man losing his marbles?* Ted worked with me when I began my career at Doc's clinic. We had a brief fling, and then he left the practice and started a vet clinic in Arizona.

Doc didn't wait for a reply. The phone went dead. What did he want? Maybe he's writing something and needs help? Why was I even considering this? I loved my life. I wrote articles for veterinary journals and novels, fished, and... But what was the "and" these days? The kids had moved to Texas to join one of the many burgeoning tech companies. We talked once a week. My dog, Little Miss

Bossy Boots, died three months ago. I hadn't even contemplated replacing her. I wanted some time to travel without worrying about a dog.

I texted him. *How long and how soon?*

Now, and I don't know but not long, he responded.

I called the vacation rental company I had used before and arranged to lease my house for a month. I'd done it many times. It was easy. My personal possessions could be put into one room which I could lock. I called the airline and made reservations.

I made my final text for the day. *Arrival ten-forty-five, Thursday.*

I sat down and made a list of what I needed to do before I left and went down to the creek to fish one more time. The water was getting hot, and fishing in my stream would end soon. It was too stressful on my trout when the oxygen levels dropped in the heat. At least I could fish in Doc's lake.

***

I opened my phone as I landed. Doc had sent a text message.

Look for a red Ford F-250 and a very handsome driver. I'll be behind it in the next red truck.

I laughed. He still had a great sense of humor. I hadn't seen him in twenty years, but he was good-looking in his youth. *Weren't we all?*

I saw a red F-250 and waved. The driver signaled back and then proceeded to drive on past. It wasn't him, and I felt foolish. This was like high school when I had a crush on Darren McMasters and waved to him when he smiled at me. Thankfully, Darren didn't notice me as he smiled at Candy Petersen standing behind me.

Several minutes later, a second older red truck pulled up. Doc appeared pale and thin. I held out my thumb, hoisted my bag into the back seat of the dual cab, and climbed in. He reached over and kissed me. He smelled the same—Old Spice and cigars. There was a cigar butt in the ashtray.

I couldn't help myself. "You know those things will kill you."

"Too late. I'm on my way out but not from smoking." He stared straight ahead, as many elderly drivers do.

Shocked, I glanced at him and then looked away. "I'm guessing you aren't joking."

"You guessed right—lymphoma. But that's not public knowledge. Only my doctor knows. You hungry?"

I was starving. "No, I can wait. Do we need to stop at the store before heading out?"

"That depends. You still a gin drinker and meat-eater?" He gripped the steering wheel like an older driver. Doc had aged.

"I don't eat as much meat as I used to, but I'm easy with whatever you want to eat." I glanced at him again. He was eighty-two by my reckoning and still appeared vigorous, but his hair had thinned, and his tan had faded. "You want to tell me why I'm here?"

"Can you wait until we get to the house? We're stopping at *the home,* so I can see the inmates. You'll have to stay in the truck. I can leave the AC on if you like. I'll only be a minute. I like to check up on her and make sure she's getting what she needs. You can't trust these people."

An hour later and an elevation rise enough to give me a nosebleed, we were in my old stomping grounds. The town was twice the size of what I remembered. The aged care home, Greenbriar, needed paint but appeared to be in reasonable shape. People came and went through the glass doors, and they seemed happy. *How could you tell, though?*

I rolled down the window. "I'm good. Stay as long as you want."

"It's the 'want' that's the killer. I never want to come here. They need to change the wedding vows. Till death or dementia do us part. I'll be quick. There's more. I'll explain later."

He stepped out of the truck, and I could see his unsure stride. We'd both aged, but we weren't ready for *the home*. I wasn't the young girl when we met over how many years ago? As he emerged from the facility, he shook his head. He climbed into the truck and, without a word, drove to a small diner.

"Last chance for a decent meal, kid." He smiled and placed his hand on the small of my back as he guided me through the restaurant's door.

"Hi, Doc." The greeter knew him and pointed to a booth. "Coffee?"

"Yes, please, Sal. This is Hayley. She's one of my former employees. She's here to help me with a project."

Sal acknowledged me. She cocked her head, waiting for me to give her my drink order.

Knowing I needed to maintain hydration at this elevation, I replied, "Just water, thanks."

We sat at a booth, and Doc folded his hands and leaned forward. "I usually get the breakfast special, but it's almost lunch, so have what you want. By the way, you look great."

"Thanks, and one small detail—why the hell am I here?"

The waitress arrived with coffee and water and asked if we were ready to order. "I'll have what Doc is having."

She smiled. "Easy done. It'll just be a sec." She turned to the counter and held up two fingers.

"I liked the book you wrote." He smiled and placed his hand on mine.

"Which one? I thought you were a classics kind of guy."

"The one about fishing. We can fish when we get to the house. I want to explain what I have in mind, and I need to show you something first. Do you mind waiting until after dinner?"

I was dubious. I felt there must be something he wasn't telling me. "All right. Have you fished lately?"

"No. That's part of the reason you're here. My kids don't like me fishing alone, and I promised Myrna that I would outlive her. It's a bit of a race to the end." He sighed and searched for Sal. "What's taking them so long?"

Our food came, we ate, Doc paid the bill and tip, and we drove into the hills and went in through a private gated entrance to his house. The gate was open and appeared to have been disabled.

"Jesus, it's magnificent. How long have you lived here?" The house was a single story with many-windowed rooms facing the lakeshore. The structure stood several feet above the waterline with a large veranda skirting the entire house. The modern and light theme carried from the living room into the kitchen. The clear, expansive view from the living room peered over the lake and the small floating dock anchored to the sandy shoreline. A separate three-bay garage sat behind the home.

He insisted on carrying my bag to my room. After placing it on the bed, he pointed to the dresser. "Yes, some have confused me with Jesus, but since I retired, I don't confuse anyone anymore. I built it shortly after you left. Myrna announced that if she was going to be a vet's widow, she wanted to live in a place where she was happy living alone. Get your fishing gear on, sweetheart. I have needs."

A kayak sat tethered to a nearby tree stump. Doc told me to get in, then he pushed it out over the water and joined me. He appeared to be strong, and I could see his mood lift. He indicated we were going to a cove down the way. A few other homes were along the lake, and a woman waved from her deck as we passed their house. Why did his family ask him not to fish alone?

We entered the cove, and Doc used his paddle to nudge me in the back. He had already selected flies for us to use. "You first, Hayles." I let out some line, and after two false casts, I let the fly land near the bank. The strike was immediate. That was how the afternoon went. After catching two fish, I watched Doc cast and land another good-sized trout.

"This lake is stocked. How about a trout dinner?"

"I won't say no." I glanced around. "Yep, the coast is clear. No purists around to admonish us for not releasing the little buggers."

We returned to the house, and Doc cleaned and placed the fish in the fridge.

"Power nap, old man. The time zone change is killing me."

Doc pointed to the recliner. "Knock yourself out."

"Pun intended and accepted. I'll only be a few minutes."

But I wasn't. An hour later, Doc gently shook my shoulder. "Rise and shine, sleeping beauty. Dinner is on the table. Red or white?"

"White, but don't open a bottle for me. You still a whiskey man?"

"Sit down and let an old man spoil you. You can start working it off tomorrow."

The dinner was delicious and actually appeared to be healthy. I knew the reason for my summons was coming. "Want to tell me why I'm here? I know you've always wanted to get me into the sack, but my guess is I'm here for another reason." *Oops, too much wine.* He never indicated he was anything but faithful to Myrna.

"Funny, but I did want to." He sighed. "You never showed me any indication. Well, that's in the past. I've asked you here for far more than..." Another pause. "I want you to write a book about me." We both knew he never had any interest in me or anyone other than Myrna. I sat up.

"The books I write are fiction. You want a biographer." This was a mistake. He brought me all the way here for something I could not do. *Damn!* My house had been rented for a month. Where the heck was I going to go? I had been so lucky to get a quick renter, but now I regretted that decision.

"You can write it. I read all your books. You talk my talk, and you've walked my walk. You're a vet, and you know what it's really like. You feel like I feel, and you've agonized just like I have over your life choices and decisions. Just write the damn book and stop making excuses. I should have given you more wine before I started this conversation."

"But you're famous. I'll bet several authors could write your story and would pay for the privilege. I think you need a man anyway."

"Hayles, we're a dying breed. We're the last of the old-school vets. The young ones don't understand. In ten years, we'll be gone, and those that follow will not know why we did what we did, and someone will write about us as they write about native Americans with their personal slant on the *whats* and *whys*. Nope, I want you to write it. You're the one person who I can trust. You talk like I talk, and you think Iike I think."

He picked up a cigar and studied it for a minute. "I'm not long for this world, and I want to leave a legacy. How about if I promise not to smoke a cigar ever again?"

"Do you promise to wear the Old Spice, though?"

"Scouts honor, and I'll pay you. Name your price."

"I'll let you know tomorrow. I want to walk down to the lake before I retire. Is it safe?"

He handed me a can of bear spray.

"Thanks." I opened the front door leading to the veranda.

"Lock the door when you return, sweetheart. There are worse things than bears around these days."

"Doc, how much time have we got?" He knew what I was asking.

"Piece of string, but my oncologist says a few months at best. I finished the last of the chemo two weeks ago."

"Sweet dreams, Doc."

CHAPTER 2

I was up early. I was still on Eastern time and had two hours to write. The early mornings were my golden time. I found some instant coffee and sat with my computer on the couch. I stared at the screen. Was there Wi-Fi here? I couldn't find a link. I prayed it was simply turned off. The view from the front window showed the moon's reflection on the lake. It would set in the next few minutes.

I took the can of bear spray, threw on one of Doc's jackets, and walked down to his pier on the lake. I sat on the bench and watched the moon disappear over the forest surrounding the lake. I saw lights that dotted the shore and counted at least twenty homes. Doc's oversized jacket covered my folded legs. I heard an owl and possibly a hawk. I drank my coffee as I watched the increasing light.

I'd made up my mind. I would tell Doc when he woke and be on my way. I felt terrible for letting him down, but I would not do justice to this man's footprint on this earth.

So much had been written about him. He'd worked hard and far longer than any other veterinarian I had known. I would find the perfect biographer for his project.

Several minutes later, I watched the sun begin to hit the lake. With that, I saw and heard the splash of trout jumping in the early morning feeding frenzy. I was mesmerized by nature's display. I didn't hear Doc approach the bench as he carried two cups of coffee. He didn't speak but handed me a cup. Mine had grown cold an hour ago. We silently acknowledged each other as he sat down next to me.

After we had finished our coffee, he put his arm around my shoulder. "'Going to the mountains is like going home.' Do you know who said that?"

"Dolly Parton?"

He punched me with his hand that enveloped my shoulder. "No, but she sure as hell sang it. You reminded me of the game you all played at work. No matter what quote I would give you guys, you would come up with some ridiculous suggestion about who said it. I think the best was when you all replied to a quote, and I don't even remember which one, but your answer was Buck Owens. You all set me up."

"It was who said, 'The biggest fool to hit the big time, and all I've got to do is act naturally?'"

Now Doc put me in a headlock. "John Muir."

"No, I'm sure it was John Denver. Hey, old man, should you be out here? It's cold, and you don't have your jacket on."

He pulled on the collar of the jacket I wore. "Gee, I wonder why."

"Do you have Wi-Fi in the house?" My resolve to leave was dissolving, and he knew it.

"So, you changed your mind?"

"Maybe. What makes you think I'd decided?"

"You didn't unpack your suitcase. I turned off the internet last night so you would go out and see what nature has for you here in the mountains."

"Two months won't be enough. We're starting on the Dr. William O'Neal health plan for extended living—no cigars, one glass of alcohol a day, and unlimited power naps."

"I don't nap." He stood up, pulling me up and into his arms. He briefly kissed the top of my head and let me go.

"I do." I extended my hand. "Shake on it." We did.

He put his arm around my shoulder as we headed to the house. "Hayley?"

"Yes, sir?"

"Two things. One is the money, and the second is I haven't smoked in six months. You were set up, and you fell for it. So much to teach you."

I finished the phrase we young vets had often heard at his clinic. "'And so little time.' Now let's go find something good and nutritious for breakfast." *This is going to kill me. I only want a bear claw.* "I'll decide on my fee after seeing how it goes today. I did learn a few things from you."

"Maybe I taught you too well." He paused and turned toward the lake. "Hayley, you should know something. You were always my favorite. I would have liked to…" He didn't have to finish the sentence. I knew what he meant.

"Doc, I have one question. How many other people did you ask to do this for you?"

"Ten. Maybe twenty. More coffee?"

Was he kidding? I expected two or three. My eyes stung. He saw my reaction. "Okay, only two. Dolly flat out said no, and well, we both know Buck Owens is not around anymore. So gullible. You are the only one I wanted to help me. I swear."

CHAPTER 3

I placed my laptop on a long table in Doc's office where I could see the lake. He sat next to me with a collection of picture albums and documents he wanted to consider for his project.

"Okay, what are the rules?" I knew parts of his life would not be put on paper. God knows there are large chunks of my life that aren't for public consumption.

"Rules?" He sipped his coffee and stared at me.

"I think you know what I mean. The truth or the kinda truth? What's in and what's out?"

"Yeah, let me think about that." He closed his eyes.

"Okay, so where do you want to start? Your birth, further back? Family or no family? Just vet stuff?"

He stared out the window for some time while I Googled his name. I found at least twenty entries. I began to open and read them when he touched my shoulder. "Rule one, let's start without any past published material. You can use that after I'm..." Again, another unfinished sentence. "Anything bad about Myrna or the kids is out."

"Is there anything bad?" I thought she was a goddess—the perfect trophy wife, mother, and life partner.

"It was my fault. I was gone too much. Myrna was lonely." He glanced at a picture of Myrna that hung on the wall. Next to it was the couple's wedding picture. They were so happy and so beautiful—movie star gorgeous. With Myrna in her blond, curly bob and Bill in his thick brown hair, blue eyes, and prominent chin, either could have made it in the film industry.

"Oh, we work together until two, then I go to Greenbriar, the extended care home, and at four, we fish, your damn naps aside. Evenings will be dedicated to me educating you in the classics. For God's sake, no more Doc or Dr. O'Neal. I'm Bill."

"Yes, sir." I had an outline by lunchtime. I asked him to list events and animals he wanted to include in the book. He'd already made several notes about cases and events, and I would enter the details as he told me his stories.

After a short break for lunch and my first power nap, which was only a few minutes, we were back at it. We started with Bill's family history.

I initially wrote in the first person and said we could always change it if he didn't like the format. I used my phone to record what Bill recounted of his family's history.

Bill leaned back in his chair with his hands clasped behind his head.

My family had roots in Montana. It was a miserable existence, and all my grandparents knew each other. They hated one another. My father's parents raised sheep, and my mother's family grew crops and had cattle. My father was far too poor for the likes of my mother's parents. My mom and dad attended school together and fought daily. No one knew that they secretly loved each other, and despite the public display, they began meeting privately at night. Three guesses.

My brother was the firstborn. He was surprisingly premature, but despite his prematurity, he was big and strong. He took over the ranch when my father died. My sister was born a year after my brother. She was the opposite of my brother and died in infancy of rheumatic fever. I was born shortly after my sister's death. My mother had what they called melancholy. Today, it would be called postnatal depression. But it really was depression from losing her beautiful daughter.

Two years after me, she had my sister Olivia. I became the middle child. My mother tried to love me, but she struggled for years with off-and-on mental health issues. My big brother, Clive, was all the son that my father ever wanted.

Today, I would be labeled as a product of middle child syndrome—what a bunch of BS. I had a great childhood. I visited my grandparents, where my maternal grandmother taught me to read and introduced me to the classics. My grandfathers taught me how to care for animals, and I was driving a tractor before I was nine. I never had an idle moment. I was sent to each grandfather as their needs arose. I drove a horse team in the snow to feed the livestock. I learned to bale and buck hay by the time I was twelve. I had read Chaucer, Shakespeare, and Dickens before I even thought of attending school. I hardly ever stayed with my parents. They didn't care, and neither did I.

I made notes as I recorded the story. "Do you have pictures? Are either your brother or sister alive?"

Bill paused and sighed as he thumbed through the photo albums. "My brother was shot in the Korean War. He was never the same. He lost his leg and returned to the farm. He ran it and kind of barely eked out a living. My parents died in their early seventies, and my brother died on his sixty-fifth birthday. He never married, and the farm was left to Myrna and me. My younger sister was the spoiled child my grandparents all knew she would become. One day she announced she was moving to Hollywood. After Olivia arrived in California, she wrote two letters to my mother asking for money. There was none to give in those days, and we never heard from her until we received a death notice when she died from a heroin overdose."

"I'm guessing we will leave that out of the book?" I turned off the recording app on my phone.

"Nothing about my sister's troubles—maybe a mention of their deaths. You know I still own the farm. I lease it out to a family that raises sheep. I don't think they even live there. I thought I would be buried there with my family, but Myrna wants our ashes spread in the lake. I'll let the kids decide. I don't give a damn."

"When was the last time you visited the farm?"

"A couple of years ago." Bill was getting ready for a trip to town. He poked his head into the office and suggested I look through the top album for pictures to use in the book.

"Any desire to visit it before you—"

But he interrupted me. "Croak? We don't have time. Hey, I forgot. I have a doctor's appointment after I see Myrna. Why don't you take the kayak out and do some fishing?"

"I have a lot to do, but if I finish, I might. Do you want me to cook dinner? What time will you be back?"

"We can eat later. Go catch a fish." He walked out of the house, and I saw him go into a shed next to the house. He threw something onto the porch.

"Hey, Hayley?" He stood at the window.

"Yeah?" I shouted through the window.

"Wear a life jacket. I want this to continue for as long as I have left."

I raised my hand in acknowledgment.

"I'm serious."

"Yes, I know. Drive carefully. The same goes for you."

CHAPTER 4

After I picked out a few pictures and edited the first chapter of Bill's book, I went to the kitchen. I searched for something filling and unhealthy. I ate some stale corn chips and sipped a soft drink.

I took my rod from the porch and laid it in the kayak. I pulled the kayak out into the water and remembered the life jacket. I ran back to the porch, grabbed the jacket, returned to the water, slipped into the vessel, and paddled out to the cove where we fished yesterday. Today the woman who lives down the way was spin fishing in a small kayak. I waved. I ensured I was well away from her kayak and began to cast my fly where we caught fish along the bank.

I wasn't having much luck, so I stopped and replaced the dry fly with a streamer. That brought me some action, and I brought in two small trout. I moved down farther into the cove and tried again. This time I successfully caught a nice-sized hen. I guessed that this trout was a native. I put her back into the water. The woman waved again, and I observed she was having no luck.

She raised her paddle to get my attention. "Do you mind if I come over?"

I waved her over and paddled in her direction to meet her halfway. "No luck with the spinner?"

"Not today. I'm Lorna. I saw you out with Bill yesterday. Are you a relative?"

"No, ma'am, I used to work for Dr. O'Neal many years ago. I'm just visiting and helping him with a project. You sure have a beautiful place up here."

"Oh, well, so are you here for a while, then? How's Myrna? I'm guessing you know about her. Such a shame. Just when they were finally beginning to enjoy his retirement. I'm guessing you were a nurse or a secretary. He's had so many over the years."

"Yeah, something like that. I can give you a fly that will work on your spinning rod if you want to try it. I would try over where I was just fishing." I pointed to the shore where I could see a deep channel off the small peninsula. "It seems to be where the buggers like to hang out."

The woman took the fly and stared at it. "I don't know how to tie it on. Can you do that for me? Did you tell me your name?"

"I'm Hayley. Point your rod over to me." I removed the spinner lure and replaced it with a streamer similar to my own but with a weighted head. "You won't be able to get it out as far as with the spinner. It's not as heavy, but if you move closer to shore, you should get some action."

She paddled closer to the shoreline and sent the weighted fly toward the water's edge. She retrieved it and had no takers. I could see she needed to give her bait some animation. "Try giving your line some jerking motions as you retrieve the fly."

On the second cast, I saw her rod tip dip and knew she had a fish on her line. I watched as she brought in a nice fish. She smiled and gave me a thumbs up. I paddled away and leaned back in the kayak to enjoy some sun. My eyes were closed, but I heard her approach in her kayak. I pretended to ignore her.

"Hayley, you're probably a nice woman, and I know you don't know me, but I just want to give you some advice. You know I was, no, still am, Myrna's closest friend. She means the world to me. I would hate to see anything happen to their marriage before..." Lorna coughed to get my attention. "Well, you know. He'll never choose you over Myrna. I would hate to see you get a reputation. I know Bill's lonely, and you're probably filling a void, but in the end, you're just one in a string of dalliances."

I wanted to smack her. Any denial would be admission in her eyes. I didn't respond other than to say, "Hope you catch more fish."

I paddled back to shore. Bill was standing on his dock and waved. I returned the wave and drove the kayak into the sandy shore next to the pier. Bill wore a short-sleeved shirt, and I observed a bandage on his elbow. He must have had blood drawn.

"How was it? I saw you talking to my neighbor." He took the line and tethered the kayak to the post buried on the shore.

"The fishing wasn't as good as yesterday, but it was still early. I did switch flies and caught a couple. It was nice to just get on the water." I didn't mention my conversation with Lorna. "How are things?" I pointed to the tape that covered his needle stick.

"I'll know the day after tomorrow. As for Myrna, well. I suspect Lorna gave you an ear full?"

I laughed. "And then some."

Bill took my vest. "She's a loyal friend. She means well."

"If you say so." I retrieved my rod from the boat and slipped on the sandals I had left on the bank. "Would you like me to cook the dinner?" I silently prayed he would say no. I liked to cook, but it was never as fun as fishing. I knew in a short time that I would assume domestic responsibilities when he was unable.

"It's already in the oven. My doctor says I need to maintain my weight. We're having pasta tonight. Gin and tonic? I have some guacamole and corn chips."

"No thanks on the gin, but I'll take some tonic. Does the Hayley Alexander classics education program start tonight?" On the rare times I rode with Bill in his truck, I remembered Bill reciting poetry and discussing the authors he loved. He made them sound interesting.

"Sure does. How did the editing go today? Do you mind if I read it?"

"Bill, it's all yours. You can read it anytime. It would be good, and then we could correct anything you don't like. It's only the first chapter, and we may want to expand on your memories. I use a program to edit, but I'm no fool. Once I'm satisfied with my manuscript, I send it to a professional editor. On average, she finds a thousand ways to improve the book."

We went into the kitchen, and he took some tonic out of the fridge, poured it over ice, and cut a sliver of lime. He poured himself some juice. "Why don't we agree on four nonalcohol nights a week? Alcohol isn't going to kill me, but I want to be able to teach you, and I know you fall asleep when you drink."

We clinked glasses, and he went to our office. He returned with a printed copy of today's work. I dreaded his evaluation. He handed me a copy of a book of poetry from the 1800s and sat down on the couch. He made a few marks on the pages and didn't say anything. After two poems, I was asleep on the couch.

"Hey, dinner is served. Girl, you are going to be hard work. I can't even keep you awake. How am I going to educate you?"

I should have been embarrassed, but I simply grinned and shrugged. "It's a genetic thing. You know it's a compliment. I feel comfortable in your house."

"More like an insult. Here I am, a virile, good-looking man and all you do is sleep around me."

"According to your neighbor, sleeping around you would be okay, but it's the sleeping with you that she objects to."

Bill sprayed out his pasta as he coughed. "What the hell?"

I shrugged. "I got a lesson in propriety from Lorna today. Don't worry. She's on to you and your 'dalliances,' as she calls them."

"Hayles, I..."

I held up my hand. "Bill, your personal life is none of my business. I'm here to do a job—nothing more. You're a good man. You care for your wife as best as you can.

You've served the equine community and the world to the highest degree. I have nothing but respect for you. No one is perfect. Can you pass me the salt and pepper? Your culinary skills are lacking." I gave him a sealed lip grin and reached for more salad.

He sat opened mouthed and just stared at me. I thought his reaction was somewhere from furious to shocked. Maybe this was where I would get the boot, and perhaps he thought I would jump into the sack with him after he wowed me with his knowledge of poetry or literature. I was sure he was too ill for that. I would be the one woman who didn't fall under his spell. If I had to be truthful, that horse bolted from the door over thirty years ago.

"I'll do the dishes, Hayles."

I stood to return to the living room, and Bill's phone rang. I half-listened to the conversation. It was hard not to hear Bill even from the other room.

"Hi darlin', how are you? How are the kids? Yes, I have someone staying with me. You wouldn't remember her, but she worked for me a long time ago. As a vet. No, she's helping me with a project. No, I saw your mom today as usual. Jessie, I don't know where this is going, but she's here helping me. I don't know how long. It's a long project."

I returned to the kitchen. Lorna had obviously talked to one of Bill's kids, and my presence did not amuse his daughter. I didn't want to be the cause of any family rifts. I sat down to read some more poems. He was still on the phone. I heard him say Greenbriar was calling, and he needed to see what was happening. He said he would call her if it were anything important.

A minute later, he entered the front room. "Hey, it seems Myrna is having a bit of a turn, and I'm going to have to go into town to see if I can settle her down." It was still light out, but it would be dark when he returned. I offered to go, but he said no. He apologized and said that my cultural lessons would have to be postponed. "I should be back in an hour, but if not, lock the door. I have a key. I have ice cream in the freezer. I'm really sorry."

"I'm so sorry, Bill. If it would help, I could go stay in town."

"I have a better idea." He pointed toward his bedroom. We laughed, but he was flustered and embarrassed.

"Drive carefully. See you in a bit."

After he left, I picked up the printed transcript and searched for his notes. There were two spelling errors he picked up, and one line crossed out. He replaced it with his own wording. There were two paragraphs where he wrote the word "more" and one where he wrote "good."

I could fix a few of the changes he wanted, but I would have to wait until tomorrow to fill in the blanks. I went out to watch the sunset over the mountains above the lake. It was a warm night. I could see a few people on the lake fishing. I was quickly chased back into the house by the mosquitos. The poems and book for tonight's lesson were from Ralph Waldo Emerson. I researched Emerson's history and found enough information to, hopefully, not make a complete fool of myself tomorrow.

Then I remembered a quote for the introduction to his book. I raced to the computer and entered it. Along with the corrections, I added the quotation which I knew was the perfect start of his book.

***

Dr. William Tyler O'Neal
Horse Doctor

The master in the art of living makes little distinction between his work and his play, his labor and his leisure, his mind and his body, his information and his recreation, his love and his religion. He hardly knows which is which. He simply pursues his vision of excellence at whatever he does, leaving others to decide whether he is working or playing. To him he's always doing both.

James A Michener

***

I quickly reprinted the first chapter with the title with the Michener quote. I placed it on the table where he would see it. Oh, how I wanted this assignment.

CHAPTER 5

I rose, showered early, and made coffee. I noticed that the newest copy of the initial chapter was not on the table. I wondered if this would make Bill consider paying me more. We still hadn't settled on an amount. I laughed to myself. I could easily see this conversation ending with me agreeing to pay him for the privilege of writing his biography. I took a cup out to the lake and sat on my bench to watch the fish feed and play in the dawn's light.

He didn't join me, and I suspected we'd been observed yesterday morning. Probably his neighbor, Lorna, had seen us together and had reported it to Bill's daughter. When the morning rise ended, I returned to the house. Bill was making a few notes on the work from yesterday. His hand was bandaged, and he sported a bruise on his cheek. I noticed his hand was shaking.

"Morning, Mrs. Michener." He had a plate of eggs and toast, which he removed from the oven. There was fresh mixed fruit in cups on the table. I stared at his face, which reddened.

"Bar fight. You should see the other guy." He handed me the salt, knowing my penchant for the condiment.

"If you say so." I sat, trying not to look at his face. I ate, rinsed my dishes, and went to the office. *What the hell had happened?* When he entered the office, he sat facing the window and the lake. He had a fresh cup of coffee.

"Bill, I do my best work between four and eight in the morning. I need the internet turned on to research and edit what I write. I promise to look at the lake at dawn."

Bill let out a deep breath. "Thank God. I thought you might be leaving."

"Are you serious? My life has been so dull in the last ten years. During the previous twenty-four hours, I've been admonished for transgressions I have yet to commit." *Not that it hasn't crossed my mind.* "I've heard you take a verbal bashing from your daughter. Now I suspect someone assaulted you for God knows what. I learned twelve fun facts about Ralph Waldo Emerson to impress an old geezer who is only giving me the pleasure of his company for two effing months before he leaves me high and dry. I don't think so, mister. So, let's get cracking. I want to hear the rest of the story."

"Hayley?"

"Yeah?" I held my breath.

"Most days, Myrna doesn't know who I am. When she does, she hates me. She fell in love with the builder. I begged her to come back. She eventually did, and she has regretted it ever since. There's a bite from Myrna under this bandage, and she swung and hit my cheek last night. The kids don't know, and they will never hear this from me. They think their mom is a saint. She loved them unconditionally and did the hard yards. At the same time, I got to work, grow my business, and have exciting adventures. I didn't have a sliver of the warmth and caring from my mother as Myrna gave our children. She sacrificed everything for them. So, the story is that an unruly patient in the facility did this to me last night."

"Okay." I wanted to hold and comfort him, but I opened my laptop to continue writing his story. "Five thousand."

"That's not enough. My story is worth more."

"It's all I can afford."

He realized I was offering to pay him to write his story and not the reverse.

"How did I get so lucky to get you?" He leaned over and hugged me.

"You should have tried harder with Dolly."

He loved his kids, and he loved Myrna. Thankfully we only had a short time before he would be gone. Phew, I could fall for this guy.

"Okay, so do you want to expand in the area where you said 'more,' or do you want to work on something else? We haven't even touched any vet medicine."

Bill reached for the transcript and flipped the pages. "Oh, yeah. This is important. This is where things changed for me."

I turned on my voice recorder.

I had a lot of free time to myself as I grew older, probably too much. It didn't take long to realize that I had three homes, and I moved from one to the other depending on the heat. If I had chores, it was a given that I would help where needed.

But there were times when I was left on my own. That's when I would take off, and no one even knew I was gone.

My grandparents each thought I was with the other, or my mother and father thought I was with one of the grandparents. Our families never socialized or even spoke to one another unless it was calving or lambing season or we were baling hay. I spent my days following creeks, or I would go to a secret place in the mountains to read my books.

I found an old cabin up there that shepherds must have built in the 1800s. It was in the national forest. The government had taken over large tracts of land during the great depression when people left to work on the railroads and canals. This cabin had aged well. I could see that it was used by the forest service on their trips to the mountains to inspect the livestock. Use of the forest for cattle and sheep grazing had ceased by the time I was a boy. I had a place I could hide my books and personal items, so no one ever knew I had come there for several years.

Well, that was until I was about fourteen. A ranger showed up early one morning when I had finished cleaning the fireplace. I walked out of the cabin with a bucket of ashes, and there he was with his pack team. We faced each other without a word for what seemed like a lifetime. It was probably just a few seconds.

He smiled at me and dismounted. "I knew someone was a regular up here. I thought it might be a hobo, but you're the O'Neal boy, aren't you?"

"Yes, sir." I could barely speak. He was short, thin, and had a large shock of blond hair protruding from his hat. He had blue eyes that bore right through me.

"I think you forgot this the last time you were here." He pulled out a book on the care of farm animals. The man walked toward me and handed me the book.

"Thanks." I thought I'd lost it, and I was desperate to replace it. My grandfather was after me to find it. He thought I had taken it home or to my other grandparents' farm. Grandpa O'Neal had me working it off.

"How often do you come up here? I'm always looking for conversation and a second pair of eyes."

I didn't answer at first. I was afraid I was in trouble, and the ranger was baiting me.

The ranger stood and cocked his head. "I don't bite, and as long as you aren't poaching and starting fires, you can come here whenever you want. My name's Jasper Mason, and I went to school with your parents. They were ahead of me in school. Your dad was a hell of a football player. I try to get here every month and spend the night. I'd appreciate it if you would leave a book once in a while. I have some as well. I was going to leave a couple and a message. I figured whoever was here was a bit older. So, there are a couple that I won't leave." He smiled and nodded.

I finally got the courage to talk. I told the ranger my name and said I was happy to read whatever he had. He laughed and said that was probably true, but he said not unless I was willing to share the reading material with my father. I got the drift and realized the books might be a bit risqué for a fourteen-year-old. Damn, I wanted those books. There was an old Merck Manual and another on the care of horses. One book was written in the 1890s. I would kill for that book now. Anyway, we became friends, and the following summer, he rode up to our house and asked my father to lend me to the *forest service for the summer. My father figured it was like sending his son to the enemy, but my mother was glad to have one less responsibility.*

He would employ me and send me home for the haying season. That was where I discovered my love of horses. Jasper Mason set me on my course to learn as much as possible about their diseases and care. I spent three summers with him. We rode all over the national forest. We fixed trails, found lost hikers, and removed cattle that mysteriously moved from ranches to the forest. We discovered a band of wild horses that somehow eked out a life in the high mountains.

My last year before high school graduation was the end of my forest ranger career. Jasper was shot and killed when he came upon some poachers. It was early in the season before I was to join him. He had no wife or children, and his small bank account and a library were to be used to help students to further their education. I received a three-hundred-dollar scholarship for my first year of college. It was a fortune.

I went through Jasper's library with the school librarian. I found Jasper's stash of risqué books. That started me on my other path of interest. Until I read those books, I was a slow starter.

I turned off the recorder. "I'll bet Jasper had a nice send-off. Did they get who did it?"

"No. There was talk that it was one of the ranchers. Hell, it could have been my family. The rangers were hated for not allowing the cattle into the mountains. If I had started my summer work a few weeks earlier, I would have been dead as well. There may have been five of us at the funeral. He was not liked in the town."

I sat for a minute. "Well, this book will give him a page in history."

Bill stared at a picture of his family in an old photo album he had opened. "Hayley, he's probably my sister's father. Thank God he died before she left. It would have killed him."

"Are you sure? Did your father know? Did she know?"

Bill looked out toward the lake and sat without speaking. He sat forward and prepared to rise from his chair. "I don't think anyone knows but me. My mother would have known. I never told Myrna. It's not for publication. There was a letter I found in one of his books."

"No, of course not. Lunch is on me. Tuna or peanut butter?" I laughed as I stood to head toward the kitchen.

"I need a beer. I have enchiladas that we can heat."

"We have two months. If you can't tell me your story because you wallow in your past and drink yourself to death, I'll make it up, and you won't like it."

"You can't make this crap up." Bill rose to leave the room.

"Try me." *Nope, he's right. His family is eleven on the ten-scale of dysfunctionality.*

CHAPTER 6

Bill's phone rang. His blood results were back, and the doctor wanted to see him at once. He stared at me and asked me if I wanted to come with him.

"Sure. You know I don't even know what kind of lymphoma you have. Have you had it for a while?"

"Years. It's been in remission. I've never told anyone ever. I don't know why I didn't tell Myrna, but I think deep down she would have liked to see me dead so she could go be with that bastard."

I remained silent. Remaining neutral was my gift. I usually side with the wife, but once in a very great while, I might side with the husband. The jury was out. I had not forgotten the neighbor mentioning Bill's dalliances. Where did the truth lay?

We arrived at the doctor's office, and the receptionist asked us to sit in the waiting room. Bill thumbed through a Field and Stream while I checked my phone for messages. There were two from my son. He and the family were going to Europe for a holiday. I was invited. There was no doubt my presence was a ploy to get me to babysit the kids.

Bill was summoned into the oncologist's office. He stood, and it was clear he expected me to join him. I was introduced to Dr. Jill Wheastone. She was in her fifties and immediately took Bill to a table and palpated his external lymph nodes.

"Huh?" Dr. Wheatstone took forever to examine Bill. "I don't know who the hell you are, but you aren't the man I last examined."

I watched Bill's face and saw no emotions that told me what was going on. She listened to his chest and examined the sclera of his eyes.

Bill finally asked her what the results of the last test showed. I braced myself for the bad news. Bill pulled his jersey back over his head and sat without comment. The doctor returned to her computer and appeared to be scrolling through images of scans.

"Bill, we did your last scan two weeks ago, and the one before was two months ago?"

"Something like that. Is there a problem? I promised Hayley that I would give her two months of my time. Please don't tell her I won't be able to live up to my end of our bargain."

I knew that he would not live as long as he thought. He'd returned to the chair next to mine, and I took his hand. Dr. Wheatstone kept staring at her computer and then excused herself. I put my arm around Bill's back as he leaned forward.

"Jesus, I don't feel bad. In fact, I feel a lot better."

"You look kind of pinker, but maybe that's from your bar fight last night." I stared ahead and purposely didn't look for any reaction.

We sat in silence until Dr. Wheatstone returned. "Dr. O'Neal, Bill, I…" She looked back at her computer.

Bill squeezed my hand as we waited for the revelation. I braced myself. I had cared for my father when he was dying. I had some idea about what was to come. I had only hoped it would be after Bill and I had written his book, and he had some closure. I hated that stupid term, 'closure'—as if.

"Bill, I hate to give you misinformation. I feel like an idiot, but there is no mistaking what's happening, and the nice thing is that it's good news. It seems you're going into some form of remission. That's not to say…"

"Am I cured?" Bill let my hand go, got up, and walked over to the computer. He adjusted his glasses and stared at the monitor. His last two scans were side by side, and the illuminated masses were significantly smaller in the most recent scans. "Did you mix up the dates?"

"That's what I went to check. I won't say remission, but your tumors have shrunk. I need to caution you. It won't last, but when and how long is an unknown. I have seen this a time or two, but I know how important it is for you to finish your project. You may have more time. Your blood count has improved too. I'd planned to start transfusions. Now I may be using your blood to treat others." Dr. Wheatstone smiled.

"I think I'll go plant a redwood tree. I always wanted one in the backyard." He thanked her, and we left her office. He drove to the aged care facility and left me in the car. He was only there for a few minutes. Myrna was asleep.

We drove back to the lake house, and Bill asked for some time to be alone. He made a phone call, emerged from the porch, and said he was headed back into town. Bill went to his room and returned in a sports shirt and smelling of an aftershave that was not Old Spice. He asked me not to wait up for him and pointed to the kayak. "Take the rest of the day off. We can begin again in the morning."

Bill handed me a book with several bookmarks. It was a book of poems on death and dying. "Totally irrelevant." He laughed and went out to his truck.

He drove away but returned a few minutes later. I was in shock, sitting at my computer and attempting to edit the work from today. He knocked before he entered the room. "Hayles?"

"Yeah?" I didn't turn or look at him. I was trying to edit a passage that didn't sound right.

"Myrna's car is in the shed if you need anything in town. The keys are in the top drawer in the laundry. I hope you get some fishing in. We may be getting a storm tonight."

"Sure thing. Have a good time." Whatever you're doing. "Be safe."

He left, and I stared at the computer and wiped away tears. I am such an idiot. Lorna was right. He had his dalliances. He brought me here only so I could write his story. Get real, Alexander, you are a scribe, and all you have is an execution delay.

I closed my laptop, reached for my fishing vest and rod, and headed for the lake. The life jacket was still in the kayak. I removed my shoes and pushed off from the shore. There was another inlet farther along the lake, and I decided to explore it. A man sat in a single small boat with an outboard motor. He was fishing with a spinning rig. I went past him and waved. When I was a reasonable distance where I would not disturb him, I cast a fly toward the shore. I had no luck, but a large trout jumped near my fly. I changed to a grasshopper and tried again without success.

I sat for a minute and then put on a Parachute Adams knockoff. That did the trick. I brought in a moderately sized rainbow and let it go. I brought in two more and then looked toward the man in his boat. He waved and pointed to the clouds that were building. I nodded, set my rod in the kayak's fishing rod holder, and paddled toward the lake body and Bill's house.

I said hi as I passed him. He was preparing to leave the inlet, had retrieved his line, and was stowing the rod. "Looks like we might be in for a drenching. Best to get to shore if you know what's good for you."

"Thanks. Any luck?" I didn't want to talk to anyone, but I didn't want to seem to be rude.

"Yes, earlier I got two nice ones." He held them up and replaced them in an icebox.

"Lucky you. Someone's going to have a nice dinner."

"You and Bill are welcome to join me." He must know Bill.

"Thanks. Bill's away, and I'm not really hungry. I'm Hayley, by the way."

"Martin." He began to start his outboard motor, but it wouldn't engage. He appeared to be embarrassed. "This damn engine is going to be the death of me."

"Can I help?" Other than dragging his boat, I had no idea what I could do. "Do you have a paddle?"

He held up a small paddle that would have only reached the water. He would have to work to get back to shore. "Throw me your tow rope."

I could help tow his boat. We had plenty of time to get to shore before the rain hit, but I couldn't leave him. He tossed me the line, and I tied it to the back of the kayak and began to paddle back to Bill's house. I observed that he was still attempting to start the engine and was not paddling. Progress was slow, but he appeared old, and I thought maybe the exertion of leaning over and paddling with the short paddle was too much for him.

"Where's your dock?" I had to shout as the wind picked up.

"I'm two doors down on the right." He pointed to his house, which was halfway between Bill and Lorna's lakefront houses.

I reached it, got out, and pulled him onto the shore. The waves made the approach to the rocking dock a challenge, and I knew it was best not to risk crashing his boat into the wooden pier. I got back into the kayak and quickly paddled over to Bill's, secured the vessel to the post, and ran into the house as the rain hit.

I was hot and sweaty despite the chill coming over the area. I showered and put on a fresh shirt and shorts. I decided to wash some of my clothes, and when I returned from the laundry, I heard a knock on the door. It was raining heavily, but the veranda's roof was extensive, protecting the entrance. There was Martin, the man I had pulled to shore. He held a covered plate. I greeted him with, "Bill's not here right now." I was reluctant to invite him in.

"Good. I brought you some cooked trout. You don't have to share it then." Martin extended his offering.

Martin had dressed in a blue checked, pressed shirt and tan shorts. He was probably in his late seventies, and his full head of hair was white. Not a ten, but definitely an eight on the ten scale for old geezers.

I relented. "Please come in. I'm afraid I don't have much to add. I only have leftovers, but could I offer you some wine?"

"Bill has some good wines. Anything open?" Martin didn't wait to be asked twice.

"There's plenty around. Bill won't mind." Bill had mentioned he wouldn't have enough time left in his life to drink what he had accumulated over the years. Maybe he'll have enough time now that his cancer was in remission.

"So, you're kind of famous around here. Funny you don't look like the devil incarnate." Martin cocked his head and pretended to study me.

"Well, I am. At least in a few people's eyes. And how about you?" I pursed my lips and looked skyward.

Martin walked into the kitchen without hesitation. "The devil in me left years ago. You don't have to worry. I'm the secret keeper. Your evil deeds and thoughts are safe with me." He had a kind smile. He probably was telling the truth. But then again, my ability to judge people had taken a severe hit tonight when Bill left to spend the night with someone else.

I laughed. "If I have either of those, I'll remember your offer. I think my reputation might be overstated and undeserved. So how about you? What lurks behind those kind eyes and smile?" I opened the foil that covered the trout.

Martin opened the cupboard and retrieved a plate. "Who me? Not much. I'm the new kid on the block. I moved in about twelve years ago. I was just about to be accepted until I found myself sticking up for that hussy who sits and canoodles openly on the shorefront of our lake with a married man."

I laughed so hard that I sprayed my wine. "Oh, sorry." I mopped up the wine remnant off his shirt. "Bill and I go back a long way. I worked for him when I first graduated from vet school. We worked together for ten years until I met my husband and left the practice. He needed some assistance with some publications he's working on, and I write books, so he asked me to come and help. If he hadn't promised me access to some spectacular trout, I can assure you, I would not be here."

"Oh, a writer? What is your genre?" Martin sipped his wine.

"Fiction and veterinary medical journals. So, Martin?"

He knew what I was asking. "Psychology. I worked for years with abused women and children. Do you need any psychotherapy? I'm a little rusty, but I can point you in the right direction if you want to talk to someone."

"Maybe just get Lorna off the warpath." I poured the last of the wine.

"Uh, well, I'm not that good. Lorna's a passionate friend of Myrna's, and she'll protect Myrna's interests to the end."

"Good for her. I admire loyalty. She has no issues with me." And after Bill went to the arms of another woman this evening when he finally had some good news, she never will have any issues with me.

"Bill and I are fishing buddies. He's a good man. No one is perfect. I have no idea why he invited you, but he asked me to ensure that Lorna doesn't kill you. It's a tough ask, but I owe him one or two."

"So, did he ask you to come over tonight?" Maybe Martin did know about Bill and his illness.

"No. I knew the truck was gone, but until I saw you fishing, I thought you two would be out together. I think you saved my life. I pulled a muscle in my back, trying to get the damn motor running. Paddling was killing me. I'd have spent the night on the water, and you saw the storm."

"You better get a new motor before you go out again. I try to help one old geezer at a time. I don't have time for two."

"Yeah, I better get back anyway. Lou is going to be frantic."

Oh, so he has a wife. "I'd like to meet her if she hasn't gone to the dark side and joined Lorna."

Martin smiled and shook his head. "Lou is my terrier. She's been on the dark side all her life."

Martin left, and I sat down and read the poems that Bill had marked in his book. I took the book to bed and noted Walt Whitman's O' Captain! My Captain and others.

I made a note, but this is the one I thought he might like in his book.

<u>Let Me Go</u>
Author Unknown
We've known lots of pleasure,
At times endured pain,
We've lived in the sunshine
And walked in the rain.

But now we're separated
And for a time apart,
But I am not alone-
You're forever in my heart.

Death always seems so sudden,
And it is always sure,
But what is oft' forgotten-
It is not without a cure.

There may be times you miss me,
I sort of hope you do,
But smile when you think of me,
For I'll be waiting for you.

Now there's many things for you to do,
And lots of ways to grow,
So get busy, be happy, and live your life,
Miss me, but let me go.

~

And
<u>His Journey's Just Begun</u>
By Ellen Brenneman
Don't think of him as gone away
His journey's just begun,
life holds so many facets
this earth is only one.
Just think of him as resting
from the sorrows and the tears
in a place of warmth and comfort
where there are no days and years.
Think how he must be wishing
that we could know today
how nothing but our sadness
can really pass away.
And think of him as living
in the hearts of those he touched...
for nothing loved is ever lost
and he was loved so much.

CHAPTER 7

I woke at four as I usually did. I reached for the book of poems, but it was gone. I looked on the floor where I'd left it, and it had not fallen off the bed. Bill must have returned. It was alarming as I had not heard or awakened, and he had entered my room. I went to the kitchen and found a note for me to pack my bags. I had been fired. The message only said, *pack your bags*, but the implication was clear.

I made my coffee and sat staring at the window. It was still dark, and I could only see my reflection in the glass pane. I opened my computer and searched for places to visit while my house was unavailable. I thought the most manageable plan might be to head south to Arizona or New Mexico. I almost went over to Martin's house to ask for a ride, but it was only five in the morning.

I would have preferred never to see Bill again. Yes, he was a brilliant vet who started me on my journey as a recent graduate. Yes, he did bring a small amount of "cultcha," as us young vets who worked under him used to say, but he had gone off the rails. I had always suspected he had strayed as Lorna had indicated. I didn't care when I was a young, new vet. I simply wanted to learn from the man. I thought this journey would be a learning experience. I was going to learn how to die. Course correction—I was now going to learn how to live.

I walked outside to experience my last dawn on the beautiful lake. This time I had my rod. I walked along the shore and cast out toward where the fish rose and only caught one. The morning insect hatch and trout feeding frenzy ended abruptly, and I turned to the house and observed Bill standing off to the side. He sipped a cup of coffee and smiled when he knew I was staring at him.

We silently walked back to the house, and when I entered, I smelled pancakes and bacon. He pulled a plate out from the oven. "Hurry up. I don't have all day."

What a jerk. "It won't take all day. Just drive me to town, and I'll take it from there." I finished the pancakes, washed my plate, and went to my room. I took my sheets and headed to the laundry.

"What the hell are you doing?" Bill blocked my way.

"You asked me to leave. I'm leaving. Take me to the closest car rental place, and I am out of your life." I was firm, and I was direct. No tears and no chances of arguing the point. "If it's too inconvenient, I have a new bestie here on the lake. I'm sure Martin will take me."

Bill looked incredulous. He stood in the hallway and would not budge. "I asked you to leave? What the hell are you talking about?"

"Well, you were gone to see someone last night, and I saw the message to pack my bags. I didn't arrive here on a turnip truck. I'm leaving, and someone else is coming in."

"Oh, boy. You sure as hell did arrive on a turnip truck. Hayley Alexander, you are so out of your depth on this one. I'm not taking you to the airport or a car rental. Not that I don't have a mind to. We're going to Montana. I want to visit my family's homestead. Jesus, you're exasperating. You haven't changed in over thirty years. You were a smartass then, and you still think you know more than anyone. Get your sorry butt into the truck. We're going on a road trip."

"But I…" I was furious but probably more embarrassed and relieved.

Bill had his suitcase and fishing gear. He stood in the hallway. "I'm assuming you honor your contractual obligations whether there is a written or oral contract?"

I turned away. I had to control my embarrassment, guilt, anger, and tears. I took my bags and fishing rod case and threw them in the back seat of Bill's truck. I put on my sunglasses and sat with my face turned away from Bill. We drove to town, and he refilled his vehicle, and we headed north.

After several hours without conversation, Bill pulled over at a rest stop. We both went to the restroom. As we approached the truck, he handed me the keys. "Your turn. Wake me up when we get to Jackson Hole."

We each adjusted our seats, and I took off down the road. Bill immediately fell asleep. When he woke up, he turned to me. "Until last night, you, Dr. Hotstuff, and my GP were the only ones who knew about my impending death. Once

I knew I might outlive Myrna, I decided it was time to tell the rest of my family.

"Both my son and daughter live in New Mexico. I called my son and asked him to come to my daughter's home north of Albuquerque. It's a five-hour drive each way. I met them there and told them the truth about my condition and why you're staying with me."

"How did they take it?" I was mortified and relieved.

"You know they were almost sympathetic. They know their beloved mother will likely not survive another year, and they expect me to care for Myrna until she passes. After that, I think they're happy to have me live out my remaining time as I wish."

I stared ahead as I drove. "You know what I was thinking when you left."

"I did this morning when I returned. You know you're kinda cute when you get riled up. You can't cast a fly for shit, though."

"When did you take up swearing? You never swore when I worked for you."

"Knowing you're going to die soon is kind of liberating. I won't swear anymore."

"I think you know where I stand on swearing. The F-word and C-word are a no-go but otherwise, knock yourself out."

I drove on for a few minutes. "Bill, you know I haven't asked for any money?"

"Yeah? I knew this was coming." He straightened and looked up toward the sky.

"Any chance we can spend the night at the Wort Hotel?" I might as well go for the gold.

"Jesus, I was a horse vet. Not a plastic surgeon." He put his hand to his forehead.

"Never mind. I'm pretty sure Jesus would be considered a swear word, but what the hell? You can damn well do as you want." It wouldn't matter where we stayed. I was going to the Teton National Park.

"I made a reservation there last night. So, you know the place?"

"The Wort and I have some history." I smiled, remembering.

"Will we be allowed in when they know it's you?" Bill lowered his seat and attempted to return to sleep.

"Time will tell." I accelerated, and the red truck did what all red cars do—went faster.

"Not if we get killed with your speeding. By the way, you drive like an old lady. Sit back and don't try to strangle the steering wheel." I laughed inwardly, remembering this was what I observed about his driving a few days ago.

CHAPTER 8

We arrived at the Wort around four, and each took a bag into the foyer. Bill was greeted with a familiarity that made me understand he was known to the staff. He took a single key, turned to me, and pointed to the elevator. My heart was racing. There was no way I was going from zero to one hundred on the sleeping arrangements after the emotional turmoil I had been through over the last twenty-four hours. He's too sick anyway. At least it would be two beds, but when we entered the room, there was a single bed.

Bill set his bag on the counter and lay down on the bed. He pointed to the door, which I thought led to the bathroom. "Your room awaits. Wake me up in thirty, and we can go down and hit the Silver Dollar Bar." It was a well-known bar in Jackson Hole.

I went through the door and into an adjoining bedroom. On the table were flowers. There was a note. Dr. Michener-Anon-Brenneman. Great choices. Picking you to write my story was a wonderful option. Thank you, your friend Bill.

I did cry, and order was restored. We're all in our places with bright shiny faces.

I felt a pillow hit my head. "I give you one job, and you can't even do that." Bill was standing by my bed. It was dark, and we'd both overslept. I realized it was well past the power nap acceptable range. I looked at the clock next to the bed. It was eight, and we'd slept for three hours. I groaned, knowing a night of insomnia would follow.

We were escorted into a dining room, where a table was set with champagne resting on ice. Bill apologized to the maître d'. He winked at Bill, and we both laughed at his assumption. We ordered dinner, and the waiter popped the cork and poured each of us a glass.

We toasted Bill on his recent escape from an impending death sentence. "To life."

Bill rolled his eyes as our dinner was served. He smiled and held out his glass once again. "To old friends and new beginnings, and all you have to do is act naturally."

I spilled my glass as I laughed, recalling the Buck Owens song.

"Mama Cass," I said as I remembered the credits at the end of The Proposal movie. The character, Ramon, started to sing, "God Bless America." He then attributed the song to Cass Elliot of the Mamas and Papas.

Bill looked quizzical. "Mama Cass?"

"You haven't seen that movie? Bill, Bill, Bill. It's one of my favs. I will have to start the Bill O'Neal, Hayley Alexander's greatest hits educational program. It has Betty White and Ryan Reynolds."

"Really?" Bill shook his head. "What's it about?"

I explained the premise, and he still shook his head.

"It has Sandra Bullock?"

"Okay, now you're talking." He pretended to care, but I knew he was being kind.

As we ate, a middle-aged couple came up to the table and introduced themselves. "Dr. O'Neal, you took care of our horse many years ago. We saw you sitting here with your daughter, and we just wanted to say hi and thank you once again for what you did."

I laughed and received a kick under the table while listening to their story about that colicky horse. Bill remembered and even said the horse's name, which impressed them. I was amazed as I rarely remembered the names of the horses I treated over the years. Bill certainly had all his marbles.

We returned to our rooms. I opened my computer and suggested we do a vet story before retiring. Bill said he was too tired, and we needed to leave early.

"Why early? You have the rest of your life." Bill didn't laugh. Note to self: no more end-of-life jokes.

"What's the name of the movie you like?" I flipped on his television and found The Proposal and headed to my room, but Bill patted the bed, so I lay down next to him. I woke up hours later. The television was off, and Bill was asleep and snoring. I slipped off the bed and headed to my room, trying not to disturb him. As I closed the door, Bill turned and said, "Well, you're a lot of fun in bed. Pleasant dreams, Hayles."

We ate breakfast and returned to the truck. Bill drove to a fly shop, parked the car, and told me to get our fishing gear. He had booked a drift trip on the Snake River. "You're kidding! OMG, the perks of being your scribe never end."

We spent the morning floating down the Snake near the Grand Tetons. Bill outfished me and never seemed to tire. I had fished here before and knew of a few good spots. The guide showed me some techniques and flies that worked well on this river. When we finished for the morning, we entered the parking lot. I hugged Bill. "Lunch is on me, Billie Boy."

We went back into Jackson and had a salad, and Bill had a beer while I had a soft drink. Before we continued our journey, Bill went into a store and bought some gum. I waited outside and watched the tourists. We returned to the truck where Bill opened a small box and showed me a beautiful ring. I was shocked and slightly uncomfortable.

"Do you think Myrna will like it?"

Just for a moment, I thought the ring was for me. That was a jolt back to reality.

"She'll love it. I'm sure." Check yourself, Alexander, and remember your role.

We headed out of Jackson, and Bill wanted to drive through the park. I suspected he thought this was the last time he would observe this beautiful place.

"Okay, let's not waste time while driving this afternoon. Tell me about vet school."

I turned on my recorder as we drove through The Grand Teton and Yellowstone National Parks. We stopped and took pictures of the Tetons, and while attempting a selfie, a man walked up and offered to take a picture of us. Bill put his arm around me.

"Pretend you love me, Hayles."

Bill took back his phone and glanced at the picture of us with the Tetons in the background. "I want this one in the book."

"Back to reality, my friend. Let's get cracking on that project. I need to earn my living. Tell me about vet school. How did you get in? Was it difficult to be accepted to the program back then?"

My grandmother paid for my education. I suspect she may have committed minor larceny to sock funds away. I never knew for sure, but I overheard my parents discussing the possibility. With her savings and the money from Jasper, I was off to university. I studied and worked in the cow barn of the Ag department. I wouldn't say it was a struggle, but times were tough for us all.

That's where I met Myrna, and so began the love affair that I thought would last me a lifetime.

Bill winced as he said it.

Myrna was the most sought-after girl on campus. I was a country bumpkin, and my presence was not a blip on her radar. She was a year older, a former high school prom queen, and came from the city.

Myrna was studying to be a lawyer. She was intelligent, ambitious, and a hard worker. She belonged to a sorority, and I would never be asked to join a frat. I lived for a year in a bungalow on one of the extension farms owned by the university. I paid my way by attending the lambing and shepherding at the sheep farm.

Myrna came to the farm on a windy day with a photographer. She was the model for a photo story about a wool processing company. She held lambs and posed with some men wearing wool suits and shirts. I was assigned to keep the lambs until the last minute when the photographer would take the picture.

Myrna was not touching any live lamb until the very last minute. The couple would pose, I would hand her the lamb and step away, the photographer would take a picture, and then she would immediately hand back the lamb. I was in ecstasy and Myrna was not. She did thank me for my help, but an hour later, the photographer and the models left.

I didn't see her again for months. The veterinary school was scouting for a student to work in the pathology department. They needed a part-time student to clean the autopsy room in the evening. I applied, and now I had free accommodation and a small salary. The classes and studying were easy. I was a good student, and I loved science.

When I had free time, I began to hang around the farrier employed by the large animal clinic. Mr. Kersling taught me how to shoe horses, and I was there when the instructors brought over their lameness cases. I was in the background, soaking up anything I could. That was the beginning of my veterinary education. I had a year's experience before I was even allowed into the school.

That was the easy part. Courting Myrna was the hard part. She was in the liberal arts program, and I was tracking the prerequisites for veterinary medicine. Our paths rarely crossed. I began dating a girl who was in Myrna's sorority. I liked the girl, but I was her stepping stone to a vet student, and after a month or two, I was left high and dry.

I did see Myrna at one sorority social. She smiled and called me "sheep boy." My heart was racing, but I corrected her. "Shepherd, Miss Myrna."

I knew my face was red, and I had gone over the line with an older sorority girl. I took my date, and we danced until my date disappeared. I could not find her, and one of the sorority sisters saw me searching and said she had left the party. I'd been dumped, but I didn't care. Myrna had recognized me and talked to me.

I stayed at school over the holidays, and through my work in the pathology room, I met a professor who began to show me interesting cases. He knew I was fascinated with horses, so he started to save specimens and would show me tissues and cadavers after work. Dr. Kennedy invited me to Christmas dinner with his wife and daughter.

I had a wonderful time. I drank wine, played cards, and sang Christmas carols. I was invited to attend a late-night church service with the family. Dr. Kennedy's daughter was only sixteen, but we had a delightful time together.

As we sat in a pew, Myrna walked in with an older student. She was dressed in the red wool outfit used in the photo shoot. She sat in the pew in front of the Kennedys and me. She turned and said, "Merry Christmas, Shepard Boy."

I smiled and returned the greeting. I tried to ignore her, but my heart was racing. The service began, but we didn't interact again that evening. She clung to her date's arm throughout the service.

At the end of the first year, I received a letter saying I was accepted into veterinary school. I was to make financial arrangements to ensure I would complete the four-year program. That was the best letter I ever received. I still have it. The second best was a letter offering me a full scholarship if I agreed to live at the veterinary school. It was two doors down from the sorority where Myrna resided.

I studied anatomy, histology, and physiology. At night I cleaned the large animal clinic. I was handy with a tractor, and I was occasionally called to remove dead horses from the surgical suite. This interested me, and the surgeons began to tease me that I was not to enter the surgical theater as they thought I was only there hoping to drive the tractor.

The instructor who taught anesthesia was young and loved experimenting with new anesthetics. He loved succinylcholine. That drug paralyzed the horse and did nothing to control pain. It was handy when the horse would wake up during a procedure to keep the horse from walking off the table, but to me, it was cruel. I'm glad those days are gone.

One of the surgeons found several vials of succinylcholine and other narcotics missing during the school holidays. As I was the primary suspect, my room was searched. I was scared to death. I was escorted to the dean's office. The campus police, the dean, and the surgical staff were all present. The only person missing was the anesthesia instructor. The dean sent his secretary to get him. She returned with tears and reported the anesthesia instructor was slumped over his desk and appeared to be dead. He must have overdosed on the stolen items.

I saw the dean in the hall several days later. He apologized once again and asked me to come to lunch with him and the head of the large animal surgery. I was offered an internship and asked to stay for one more year. I would do the anesthesia at night and during the school breaks and perform the duties of an intern. It was a fantastic opportunity, and so I stayed on.

I only returned to my family once a year. My grandparents were getting old, and my brother had returned from war. With his leg amputation, he could not handle more than my father's property. So, my grandparents each sold their farms to a large cattle company that had taken over much of the ranching properties in the area. I was expected to return home and begin practicing rural veterinary medicine. My family reminded me that they had sacrificed to get me through veterinary school. Adding an extra year for an internship was a waste of time.

By now, Myrna was in the law program. She had one more year to complete her studies, and we would finish and leave the following year. Since we lived within a small area, I occasionally saw her at the cafeteria next to the veterinary school. She was always with her friends and never spoke to me.

One day, when I was eating dinner, she approached me and sat down directly across from me. I was reading a book, and she noticed it was a book on the lameness in horses. She asked if we vet students ever got our noses out of a textbook. I reached into my satchel and pulled out The Heart is a Lonely Hunter. Hook, line, and sinker.

I turned off my recorder. But who was the quarry?

CHAPTER 9

We pulled into the town of Emigrant, Montana, and I reached down and turned off the map app on my phone. This time there was no question about accommodations. Bill ordered two rooms. The hotel owner knew him. Everyone in town greeted the returning prodigal son. Our dinner was interrupted several times when friends would stop by our booth.

There was no mistaking their interest in the woman Bill had brought to their small town. He explained he was writing a story about the area for an equestrian magazine. He needed images and access to the backcountry behind his property. By the time we finished dinner, Bill had arranged for horses and a packer to take us up into the National Forest.

I returned to my room to type up the notes and stories from today, and Bill stayed on and went to the bar with his ancient friends. An hour later, there was a knock at my door. Chain secured, I partially opened the door to find a young muscled-up motorcycle guy with tattoos and chains attached to his leather jacket.

"Hey, are you a friend of Bill?" He put his foot in the door, and I could not close the door.

"What can I do for you?"

"Bill's down the street at the pub, and he isn't looking too good. He asked me to get you." The man would not move his toe pressed on the bottom of the door.

"You don't look like Bill's friend. Why should I trust you?"

"Yeah, he said you would say that." The man looked down the aisle and then said, "Here he comes. You can ask him yourself." I heard a commotion and saw two men supporting Bill coming toward his room. The man stepped away, and I shut the door to release the chain, then helped the men carry Bill to his room and bed. Bill was pale and shaking. He smiled weakly and mumbled something about food poisoning.

Bill turned onto his side, and I grabbed the wastebasket in time to catch the vomit. He vomited for several minutes and then said he needed to go. I helped him into the bathroom, and Bill glared at me and told me to get out. I went down the hall to get ice and returned just as he emerged from the bathroom. I took a towel, cleaned his face, and placed an ice-filled washcloth on his forehead. He smiled wanly and then fell asleep.

Hours later, I felt Bill tossing back and forth as I lay at the end of the bed. I rose and touched his forehead. The fever had broken, but he was soaked with sweat. I sponged him, helped him dry, and changed his clothes. He was still verging on delirium, but I was now sure he would survive. I stayed for several hours, but by early morning, I returned to my room and attempted to sleep. This was a trial. If I could do this, I knew I was capable of helping him when his time would come.

I slept for a few hours and then dressed and wandered down to the diner to get a sweet roll and coffee. I was perusing the local newspaper when Bill staggered into the shop and sat across from me in my booth. "I'm so, so sorry. I don't know what I ate, but I thought I would take an early curtain call on life last night. Did I make a fool of myself?"

With everything I had, I kept a straight face. I gave Bill a closed-lip grin, raised my forehead, and stared directly into his eyes. "Bill, no way. You were wonderful. I might even say magnificent. I came three times. You should be proud. Can you pass me the salt?"

Bill's face reddened. "Did you?"

"Yep, I saw you naked as a jaybird. I want to see your birth certificate. There's no way you're eighty-two." I immediately went back to the newspaper, hiding my glee.

The waitress arrived to refill my coffee cup. She looked at Bill and shook her head. He put his hand over the cup and declined the coffee.

"Hi, Minnie. How's your mom? I'll have a single piece of toast with no butter and weak tea, thanks."

"Mom's a hell of a lot better than you today, and she's been dead for two years." Minnie turned and went to place the order. She shouted back to Bill. "One piece of toast? Can you afford it?"

I peered over the edge of the newspaper, still trying not to laugh. "I'm guessing we're delaying the trip into the back-country today? When was the last time you rode a horse?

I'll be in my room working on yesterday's manuscript. So, Myrna's a lawyer? Wow, I never knew."

Bill shook his head. I would wait for that story. I went to the counter to pay, and Bill called out. "Minnie, her money's no good."

Minnie smiled and shook her head, pointing to the door. I walked down the street and noticed a museum. That might be an excellent place to get some photos of the town and people who would have been influential in Bill's life. I returned to my room and opened my computer. I made edits and a few notes to remind myself to get more info on events such as Jasper's death. Bill didn't have any pictures of his early mentor, and I planned to include a picture of the man who was so crucial in Bill's early life.

I decided to nap and was awakened at noon by Bill entering my room. I was sure I had locked the door. Bill waved a key and told me to get going. His vitality was returning. He wanted to head up to the homestead. He'd packed lunches for us both.

We drove for several minutes and came to a gate. Bill motioned for me to open it, and I slipped out and did the honors. I closed the gate after Bill's truck passed through. Cattle were grazing along the driveway. We drove down the narrow path and arrived at an old wooden barn leaning to one side propped by long two-by-four rails. The house stood by a large tree that had dropped branches onto the roof. The door was ajar. The paint was peeling, and the siding was warped and decaying.

"How long since anyone lived here?" I glanced over at Bill, who seemed dismayed at what he saw.

"Years. No one's lived here since my brother died. The family that leases the property uses it for grazing their stock in the summer. I didn't know it was this bad. The last person to visit was Myrna. Did I tell you she came up here every summer with the kids? A city girl no less, and she would bring the kids to get a taste of rural life."

"Your parents were still alive then?"

"Yep, I brought her up shortly after our marriage and took her into the backcountry. My brother had returned from the Korean War and lived in a bungalow next to the house. It burned down after my parents died. The kids were only little, and they loved to come and visit their Uncle Clive. They would stay for weeks." Bill entered the house and was surprised to see evidence that someone had recently been in the kitchen. There were dishes with cereal and cups of desiccated coffee. "Probably one of the shepherds is using it during lambing season."

"What would Myrna do all day? I can't imagine her wanting to stay here."

"She fished and rode horses and went into the backcountry on her own. My parents loved her. They would care for the kids while she took her annual trip to the cabin. She wrote and painted and swam in the creek. She said it was the best part of her life. She looked forward to it all year long."

"Did you come and join them?"

"Once in a while. I was finishing my residency, and then I built the clinic. We were so poor. I had to work. I didn't take much time off." He gazed at the kitchen window. "I should have come more often. I never had any great attachment to the ranch. I stayed more with my grandparents. As I mentioned, those ranches were sold while I was in vet school. We can visit those as well."

"Bill, what did Myrna see in this place? Sorry, but why would a city girl return every summer when she complained of her loneliness back home? Why didn't she visit her parents? Didn't they live near the ocean?"

"Her parents never accepted me and wanted nothing to do with the kids. Myrna rarely spoke to them. When they died, they left her a small stipend and gave the bulk of their estate to her brother and sister."

"Oh, are her siblings still alive?"

"I don't know. Myrna never communicated with them after her parents died. I know her brother and sister have children, so our kids have cousins. They never discuss it." He opened the door to the laundry, and we walked out to the back of the garden. We walked up a short rise, and there were the markers of four graves. Bill's parents, sister, and brother were buried up here.

"I guess it's legal?" I speculated this was done before laws were passed only allowing burials in cemeteries.

"It is. The truth is my brother wasn't allowed to be buried here. Myrna insisted they put a marker. He was cremated, and his ashes were spread up in the mountains."

"It was nice that Myrna stood up for him. At least he had one friend in life. Sounds like he led a lonely existence."

"I hardly knew him. He and I never got on well. He hated me for leaving the family and not returning when I finished vet school. Oh, heck, he hated me for everything."

Bill cleared the graves, and I took a picture of the headstones. I turned and realized the burial plot had a marvelous view of the valley and stream that flowed through this property.

I didn't have to ask if Bill wanted to be buried here. That was a firm "no." He walked away and never looked back. He had no affinity for this land.

"Hayley?"

"I know. Nothing in the book that's negative—I got it. Bill, what do you miss about this place? I mean, there has to be something."

"I miss the smells of the hay harvest, the pines, and the aspen in the mountains. The smell of wet soil as it's tilled, the first snow in the autumn, and the ice melting on our creek in the spring. The taste of fresh, wild, fried trout and not much else." We returned to the truck and drove across the valley to a large entrance gate to the Harrogate Cattle company. The Harrogate Cattle Company bought my grandparents' farms and still owns them. He stopped at the gate and decided to turn around. He pointed to a house at the end of the valley. "That's where my father's parents lived. I rode my horse from my house to theirs and then down the road to the other grandparents. We'll go past here tomorrow when we head into the backcountry."

He drove to a turnout next to the creek where the water flowed through the valley. There were hayfields on either side of the basin, dissected by this small creek. Aspen rose near the creek. I took a photograph of the picturesque valley.

"Let's eat." We walked down to the creek and sat on a bench near the water's edge.

He was sweating. I leaned over and felt his forehead. "I think you're going to live. You did give me cause to wonder last night."

Bill blushed and began to eat the sandwich he'd purchased from the deli. We sat without speaking for several minutes.

"Only three times? Hayles, I'm slipping." He smiled, and I could see the old Bill I knew over twenty years ago returning.

Myrna didn't finish law school. She resigned as soon as we were engaged. We were married a month after our fateful meeting in the cafeteria. It was the best time of my life. I was allowed two weeks off from my internship.

We went out, and I met her parents. They were furious that Myrna was quitting law school. They blamed me. I tried to tell them that I wanted her to continue, but Myrna asked me not to discuss it. She said it was futile for me to plead her case. She said the only reason to continue law school was if she was going to be a spinster. She wanted to get pregnant as soon as we could.

Bill laughed out loud.

I was all for that. After the wedding, I took Myrna to meet my parents. They had declined to travel to the wedding. If they ever left the state, it would be news to me. We spent the day at my parents' house, and she met my family, including my brother. We had a party at the Grange Hall, and then she and I took horses and went up to the cabin where we stayed for a week. Two weeks later, she told me she thought she was pregnant.

I wasn't surprised. I knew Bill and Myrna had their children early in their marriage. "That was Richard?"

"Yes. Richard was premature." Bill gazed over at a bald eagle sitting in a nest on the other side of the valley. "Very premature. I never asked, and I never discussed it. I knew my friends and coworkers thought we were, as they like to say now, 'active,' before the wedding, but we weren't."

There was a long silence. Bill didn't need to expand on that, and I knew it would not go into the book. I continued to eat without comment.

"One of Myrna's law professors came to the house a few times with the excuse of returning books or just checking in on Myrna. He always brought Richard a present. I never said anything to Myrna. I loved and cared for Richard as any father would."

Bill stood up and went around the corner to relieve himself. I did the same, and we returned to the truck.

"Hayley, only four people know this, including you, and I think the professor may be dead. I worry that Myrna might accidentally tell Richard. She has no filters anymore."

"Does she even know who Richard is? Wouldn't he think she was simply delusional in her demented state? I don't think you have any worries. You know I won't tell anyone. Of course, my fee for doing the book has risen substantially in the last few minutes."

Bill turned and put me in a headlock. "Do you want me to tell anyone about how I caught you and Ted in the hay barn?"

"Truce. You have my silence. That was a little awkward. At least we weren't doing it."

I remembered I sat in Ted's lap with his hands in a very compromising place under my shirt. Bill walked in and stayed while we stood and tried to pretend it was something other than what it was.

"Well, it gave me hope. I thought you were impenetrable." He released me.

"Okay, back to my original offer. I'll pay five thou, but no more to do the story. And you need to up the Old Spice. You're a bit pungent today."

Bill raised his arm and smelled himself. I quickly stood so he could not put me in another headlock.

"Bill, for sure no one else knows?"

"You mean about you and Ted? The whole clinic knew." He snorted and shook his head. "As far as Richard, I never even discussed this with Myrna. She thought I was so besotted and naïve that I thought he was mine. For Richard's sake, I never let on. For my sake, I was so in love with Myrna and Richard. I would never confront her."

We drove to town in silence. Bill parked in front of the museum. "Let's see if we can find a picture of Jasper, then let's call it a day."

CHAPTER 10

The museum displayed the county's history from the mid-eighteen hundreds to the present. Artifacts found in the area from indigenous tribes, old farming implements, and a room with photographs from the early 1900s were displayed in the room.

A small room had photographs from the past rodeos and prints from some of the men employed as forest rangers. Bill identified two pictures of Jasper. In one image, he had on chaps and a large cowboy hat. He had a walrus mustache and had his arm draped over a woman with a sash that said Rodeo Queen. "Was he a bit of a ladies' man?"

"Oh yeah, and then some. He wasn't tall, but Jasper was good-looking, and that mustache was an attention-getter for sure. I tried to grow one, but that was a big failure."

I didn't mention Bill's suspicion that Jasper might be his sister's father in the museum. I was afraid of being overheard. I did ask where we could get the news reports of Jasper's death. Bill whispered that as far as he knew, there was only one report, which would be in the sheriff's department in the neighboring town. Bill was a suspect, as was any man who resided in the township. All were questioned and cleared. Bill was in school, and no one was found to be responsible for Jasper's death.

Bill showed me more of the town, and then he asked to go back to the hotel. He was tired from the events of last night. I asked to borrow the truck, and I went to the sheriff's department in the county seat.

The current sheriff was helpful and had looked into the case when he became the head of the department. This murder and one other, which took place twenty years later, were the only unsolved cases in the county. He showed me the entire file, which only had four or five pages and no forensic evidence.

The sheriff did not need to explain why there was so little evidence or sworn statements. The murder took place in the 1940s. I photocopied the notes and returned to my room at the hotel.

Bill was rested and feeling much better when we went to dinner. Once again, we were the center of attention at the diner. The men taking us up into the backcountry stopped by our dinner table and announced we were all set for an early morning start. They would pick us up at seven, and we needed warm clothes and any fishing gear we wanted to take. They had protective slickers for us to use if it rained.

Bill and I returned to the hotel. I opened my computer and reviewed the photocopies of the case report when Bill knocked and asked to come in.

"Enter at your peril, Billy Boy."

"Do you mind if I examine the sheriff's report?"

I handed it to him, and he quickly read through the notes and placed them on the table. He was surprised that his parents had been interviewed. He didn't know that they were involved at the time. Bill then asked if he could read what I had written so far. He made some suggestions and closed the computer.

"I can't thank you enough for what you're doing. You don't have to be a super-sleuth to see my marriage was not what I wanted. Myrna was not the saint everyone believes she was. I'm not the fool that you must think of me. I know the love I gave her—no, still give her—was not returned in total, but despite my kidding with you, I have been a faithful husband. I was wondering what your story is. You never talk about your life. I want to know more about you."

"My life has had its ups and downs, like any life. I have had two great relationships and a few not-so-great ones. I have no regrets. I admire your faithfulness in your marriage, but that is not me. How about we talk more at the cabin? This trip is about you. I would love to get a work story."

Bill left the room and returned with two beers. He set them down on the bedside table and stretched out on my bed.

"Oh, thanks."

"Hayles, did you think one was for you? Sorry." However, he opened both bottles and set one on the table near me. Bill sat in the chair next to a small table near the window and began his next story.

Okay, well, this is one that happened during my residency. I finished my internship. I had just started my surgical residency when a horse was brought to the teaching hospital with an unusual lameness. It appeared to have a neurological component. The surgery and internal medicine departments examined the horse, but we still couldn't pinpoint the source of the lameness. This horse was hospitalized for further assessment.

A student was assigned to each hospitalized horse. Jimmy Ledbetter was given this case. Jimmy did the vitals and wrote up the SOAP. Remember that: subjective, observation, assessment, and plan.

Bill stopped and took a sip of his beer. He shook his head. We both had discussed this method of writing up cases. We hated it.

Jimmy was a character. He was not going into large animals. This rotation was something he would endure and then return to his love, feline medicine. Jimmy was unusual in that he only wanted to see cats. These days that's not unusual, but back then, Jimmy was an odd duck.

Two days after the horse arrived, the gelding spiked a fever. Of course, the clinic had an outbreak of salmonella the previous year, so everyone was on high alert. Fecal cultures were sent to the lab along with hematology and chemistries. Nothing was unusual. The fever disappeared, and the horse began to act normally, but the lameness persisted. I checked the student's SOAPs and laughed as I flipped open the chart on this horse and found a list of twenty differentials Jimmy had written in the horse's file. I would have had three or four.

Our powerful x-ray machine was not working, and it was supposed to be ready in a day or so. I asked Jimmy to get the horse out for another lameness examination. Jimmy and another student ran the horse up and down the lane.

Damned if the horse didn't fall. This case was beginning to appear more and more like a neurological problem.

The following morning, at grand rounds, Jimmy was scheduled to present his case. Once again, the horse had a fever, and so Jimmy outlined the history and gave his assessment. The head of surgery was a bastard, and he loved mocking students. I still can hear him ask Jimmy to give his differentials. This time he asked him to put them in order of most to least likely. Jimmy put tuberculosis of the spine at number three. The entire surgical team laughed and told Jimmy to go back and read his textbook. This was a wobbler, and tomorrow everyone was sure we would prove it when the x-ray machine was up and running.

The machine was not ready for use the next day, so we kept the horse over the weekend. His temperature waxed and waned. On Monday, the head surgeon again made Jimmy feel like an idiot and proclaimed, "If this horse has TB, I'll eat my hat. If he doesn't have it or something like it, you will go through all the files we have and find all the neurological cases for a paper I'm writing. Mr. Ledbetter, you can take this bet or leave it."

As cool as a cucumber, Jimmy replied, "Sir, I would advise wearing an edible hat."

The horse was taken to the surgical suite and anesthetized for the radiographic examination—three guesses on the diagnosis. There was a mass that had eaten into the cervical vertebrae. After the horse was euthanized, a culture was submitted. Yep, it was TB. Jimmy had read the intake notes, which included a history from the referring vet and owner, who was not present as he was undergoing treatment for tuberculosis.

The entire treatment crew, students, and veterinarians that attended the horse were tested multiple times. The following day Jimmy presented the head of surgery with a hat he fashioned from Rice Krispies and marshmallows. I became friends with Jimmy and followed his career until he died of HIV.

CHAPTER 11

"Hayley Alexander, will you get out here? The men and horses are here, and we need to leave."

I was in the shower and realized I was running late. I quickly finished and yelled that I was on my way. He didn't hear me, and with the key he obtained yesterday, he opened the door. I was naked, and he saw me as I searched for the riding pants I planned to wear. He quickly closed the door and stood outside my room.

"Sorry. Well, not really. Turn around is fair play, as they say. Now how can I help?"

"I'm on my way. Can you grab me some coffee, and I'll be down in a minute?"

As I entered the back seat of the dual-cab truck, I was handed some coffee and a bear claw.

Bill sat in front with the wrangler who was taking us up to the trailhead. "Don't you just love the scenery?" I knew what he was inferring.

"Sure do," I said as I peered down at three young wranglers climbing into a truck that would follow us to assist in packing the mules and horses to take us up into the National Forest. "Beautiful." Our wrangler laughed as I was sure he knew what we both inferred.

An hour later, we were at the trailhead. I had the clothes I took in a small duffel bag the men had provided the day before. They quickly had the horses saddled, the panniers adjusted, and mounted on the mules. There was enough food for a week, but we would only stay four nights. There were mounting blocks that made it easy to climb into the saddle. I needed it more than Bill. His vitality seemed to be increasing daily, one food poisoning aside. Tuck Henshaw turned and asked if we were comfortable. We nodded, Bill grinned like a teenager, and then we were off to the mountains and Bill's beloved cabin.

Tuck turned, clicked to his horse, and pulled the rope leading the mule. There was a brief moment when the mule thought better of this arrangement, but Tuck persisted.

I was riding a sorrel gelding whose red mane glistened as it fell to one side. Bill rode a buckskin gelding. Before we left the compound, he handed his camera to the youngest wrangler and asked that he take a few pictures of us all and then just me and Bill. It was digital, and Bill looked at the last shot and thanked the young man.

We rode through a lush green meadow surrounded on one side by aspens and the other pine trees. Bill and the wrangler talked and pointed out some changes made on the trail that Bill had ridden so many times in his youth. We crossed rivulets and then began to climb up a rocky path for another hour.

Bill was ahead of me, and he turned and smiled. "You okay back there?"

I nodded and gave him a thumbs up. "Magnificent." I wondered if he caught the reference to the night he was ill, and I teased him about sleeping with him.

"Do you know how old these mountains are, Hayles? Despite their age, they're a thing of beauty."

"Couldn't agree more," I grinned, knowing what he implied.

We rode for another hour and descended into a valley with a river running through the grassy meadow. When we were at the bottom, we stopped to let the horses rest and adjust the pack on the mule. Bill had his fly rod tied onto the back of his saddle. He quickly assembled it and handed me a fly, and I tied it onto the leader. I handed it back.

"Nope, the first one's yours." This trip was for Bill, and it was probably his last, but ever the gentleman, he was calling the shots.

Tuck took the horses away after letting them drink. I climbed a rock and watched to see if I could find a fish. The water was too rapid, and I blindly cast as Bill stood down at the water's edge. After three more casts, Bill joined me and stood directly behind me and took my arm. "Relax, let me do the work. And on three." The line sailed across the river and landed in a large pool I could not reach alone. The strike was immediate, and Bill stepped back and cocked his camera.

I landed the fish. Bill took the obligatory photo, and the fish was returned to the water. Bill took the rod and fished and caught two cutthroat trout. I had his camera, and I took a picture of him landing and holding a very nice-sized trout before he let it go.

As we climbed out of the valley, Tuck pointed to the north. There was a small band of maybe six horses. "Wild bunch. That's a small offshoot of the main herd."

Bill quickly changed to a telephoto lens and took several pictures. He glanced at his screen and nodded. I was getting sore. I usually rode with a friend for a few hours weekly, but this was challenging. I wondered how Bill was holding up. I didn't want to embarrass him, so I rode on without comment.

We stopped to eat as we came over the last rise and saw the cabin on the opposite side of the valley. "I can see why the ranchers wanted to continue to use the grass up here." At this elevation, I saw snow on the peaks of the distant mountains and then the granite below, which eventually supported trees. Farther down the slope was a dense forest that merged into the valley. Running through the valley was a stream large enough to support trout but not as big as the river we had crossed after fishing.

"Bill, how did you travel so far when you were a kid?" I could not imagine a boy on his own traveling this far.

"This is the long way to the cabin. I wanted you to see the backcountry. See that mountain pass to the right?" Bill pointed to a much lower route at the end of the valley where the cabin sat. "My grandfather's ranch was over on the other side. This little adventure allows you to see where and how I lived."

We reached the cabin within the hour. The panniers, the large baskets evenly weighted and tied to the mule's pack saddle, were left inside the hut. We had a beer with Tuck and asked him not to forget us up here. He said he would try. Bill was amused and suggested that if Tuck was late by a day or two, it wouldn't be the world's end.

The cabin was one room with two single beds separated by a curtain. There was a wood stove, and the last person here had left plenty of wood. Tuck said he would replace the wood when he came to get us. "Just enjoy yourselves, Doc, and catch some fish for me to take back to the missus. She loves her mountain trout."

I searched through the panniers and found all the food we would need for several days. I didn't see any bear spray. I was not amused. The chances of cooking food and living here for three days without bear interactions were remote. Bill had gone down to the creek and was sitting on a rock. He looked lonely. I stood on the porch and observed him. He would look up toward the clouds when one would go over him. Otherwise, he stared at the mountains and the pass he usually traversed from his grandparents' ranch.

I took a picture with his camera using the telephoto lens. I began some cleanup of the cabin. It didn't appear to have been occupied this season. There were two steaks in our package, and I decided tonight was the night to consume those. I struggled to start a fire in the wood-burning stove, but eventually, it ignited. I needed water for some string beans and had to interrupt Bill. He smiled as I came into view. I brought the camera, and as I approached the water, I turned and took a picture of Bill with the cabin in the background. The light was perfect, and I checked the image to ensure I had captured the light and Bill as I saw it. He was not movie-star material anymore, but he was close.

He patted the log, indicating I should join him. "Rest a minute, old girl." He pointed across the creek where he saw some antelope grazing.

Bill put his arm over my shoulder and pulled me into him. "I have you to thank for this."

"Or your oncologist." At which we both laughed.

"Seriously, Hayley, I would never have done this by myself. I'd forgotten how much I loved this spot. I think you can see why even a city girl like Myrna loved to come here."

I'm sure he could feel me tense when he mentioned her name. I felt sorry for him. His entire life was spent loving a woman that even a blind person could see, did not return the love. If we were both young, I would have tried to get him to see the light. He was a brilliant veterinarian, admired and respected by people worldwide. Yet, as far as I could see, he received no love at home from either the woman he loved or even his children.

"Bill, I wouldn't mind having my ashes left here." I was only giving him an option that might give him some comfort.

"Hayles, if you go first, I'll make sure it gets done."

"You never know. As far as I can see, we have no bear spray or protection. We may both have our bones spread here this week anyway."

Bill squeezed my shoulder. "I could think of worse ways to be returned to the earth. I'm sure there's an old shotgun left in the cabin. Did you climb up in the loft?"

"No, we can only hope. How's steak, beans, and a baked potato sound for dinner?" I stood and took the pail and scooped up some water. "I'm assuming we need to boil the water before drinking it?"

"Yeah, I think I'm immune, but you better not take a chance. I'll be up in a few minutes. Can you leave the camera with me?"

"I'll have dinner ready in less than an hour. I might study the inside of my eyelids while the potatoes bake. Have you checked the privy? I don't mind spiders, but snakes are a different issue."

"Snakes are rare up here. I'm waiting for you to go in there. I don't like spiders."

"You are such a wuss, I swear, men!" I returned to the cabin and took a broom to the outhouse. I saw no snakes or spiders, but a Playboy magazine from 1973 sat next to the hole. I perused the contents. No displays of pubic hair in those days. I laughed, remembering my son thought it was called "public hair."

Returning to the cabin, I put more wood into the stove and placed two potatoes wrapped in foil into the oven. I lay down on one of the beds and dosed until I heard Bill enter the cabin. He came over to me and sat on the bed. He leaned over and kissed me full on the lips. That was different? What brought that on?

"That picture you took of me with the cabin in the background needs to be on the book's cover."

I sat up and hugged him. "Done deal, let me get the beans going, and then we eat. The steaks won't take long."

The sun was setting when we finished dinner. We went out onto the porch to watch the sunset. Bill patted the bench where he sat. I joined him, and once again, he put his arm around me. "Thanks for the day, old girl." He leaned over and kissed the top of my head. I knew he would give the world if he could replace me with Myrna, but that would never happen except in his dreams. "Hayley?"

Oh, boy. What now? "Yeah?"

"What about you?" He turned and peered at me with a look that commanded an answer.

"What about me?" What was he asking, the immediate me, the future me, or me in the past?

"So far, all we've talked about is my life story. I want to know about you. What happened after you left?"

"You know, the usual. I got married, had two kids, started my own clinic, got divorced, had a couple of short-term relationships, got bored, and began to write books."

"I'm only going to say this once. Fill in the damn blanks." Bill crossed his arms.

"Not going to take no for an answer?"

"Nope." He was not going to back down. I'd seen this look a time or two when I worked for him. Something had gone wrong at work, and he was going to get to the bottom of where things had deviated from standard procedure. There was no retreating from the man sitting next to me with his folded arms and steely gaze.

"Roger and I had a great relationship. He was a doting father, and the kids adored him. Roger allowed me the freedom to work. He never asked me to come home early or sacrifice my passion for veterinary medicine for our family. I was there and attended all the school events. I hosted all the kid's parties and took them on calls until they were old enough to be on their own. I thought three years of age was old enough. They could open the fridge by then."

Bill smiled and replied, "No way, four was more appropriate."

"Anyway, all that time, Roger was seeing two other women. I know what you're thinking—not a clue. He was home every night, and he worked and earned a good wage or so I thought. We kept our finances separate, and I never knew he wasn't actually working. I kind of think, like you, I was in love and never questioned his love or loyalty.

"My clinic was at our farm, so I had staff who would watch the kids after school. I took them to school most days and picked them up as Roger's job was too far away to do those things. He was nine-to-five. I was happy and in love.

"Then, one day, I received a call that changed everything. A woman called to tell me she was in labor and couldn't find Roger. She said he promised to be there when his baby was born. Of course, I laughed. 'Sorry, you have the wrong number.' Well, she didn't. It was not pretty. He'd never worked, and he had no bank account.

"A year later, the judge awarded him half of our assets and access to the kids, who were now in their teens. The kids have no idea about their father's antics. He never married that woman, but he married the second one the day after the divorce was final. So, that's me, except to say, after several months of depression, I was back in the land of the living. I rarely ever think of him, and despite it all, he did give me two beautiful children who have made my life worth living."

Bill did not reply or speak. I wondered if he was thinking about his own life. The sun was gone, the light was fading, and mosquitos relentlessly attacked us. We returned to the cabin and prepared for bed behind our mutual curtain. I knew Bill was exhausted. I heard him snoring minutes after he was in bed.

CHAPTER 12

I rose before Bill woke. I had my rod ready for fishing and went down to the creek. The creek wandered through tall grass, and I noticed many marshy inlets that could hide some trout. It was cold without the sun, and I was glad to wear my goose-down jacket. I had a Parachute Adams and a copper-colored nymph. The stream was too low for the nymph, so I removed it.

I soon had three small trout for breakfast, and I returned to the cabin. Bill had gone, and the oven was going once again. I made coffee, and I fried small, chopped potatoes and eggs. I noticed Bill's appetite was improving each day. He may have been gaining weight, but he was still thin. He entered the cabin and smiled when he saw the trout frying in the skillet.

"Woman of my dreams."

"Don't let Myrna hear that." He didn't laugh, but I quietly chuckled to myself. I sneezed several times.

"I could eat more trout. Those are so good." Bill was studying me after breakfast. I knew that look. It was the silent exam he would give a horse when deciding the anatomical area as a source of lameness. Bill would stand alongside the owners, interns, and barn crew. His thumbnail would be between his front teeth. He bent and released the nail several times as he clenched his teeth. Eventually, Bill would direct the interns to perform a nerve block or take a radiograph of the area he was considering. I waited, knowing I was about to be nailed to the wall.

"Hayley, do you think about your ex much? I mean, you have good reason to."

I stopped him. "I've been given a gift. I forget and move on. I don't go back, and I don't want a repeat because who loses if I am bitter and can't forget? You, of all people, should understand this. Our lives aren't that different. I have no regrets. It's a wonderful gift. I sleep well, and I hope I haven't let my feelings affect the kids and their relationship with their father." I sneezed again.

"Are you getting sick?" Bill stood up and felt my forehead. "You feel cool."

"Allergies." I used my napkin to wipe my nose. "I think it's the cabin. I am going to woman up and do some dusting. Why don't you go down and catch dinner? I want to do a bit of sweeping and get some of the mold out of here. How about we take the mattresses and drag them out onto the porch? I'm going to take the curtain and wash it. Step aside and let an old woman clean for you."

"No problem with that, but where will we find an old woman?"

"Smart answer, Billy Boy." I sneezed again. We took the mattresses out on the porch, and I beat them with a stick. I could see dust and probably mold spores rising in the sunlight.

"Hey, Bill? On a scale of one to ten, how saddle sore are you? I'm an eight." I was really a nine, but that won't be public knowledge.

"Twelve, but waking up and seeing that old ceiling, sitting on the porch last night, and eating fresh-caught trout for breakfast makes the pain all worth it."

I knew this was Bill's last trip. Would it be mine as well? The sneezing continued, and I became a woman on a mission. I dusted, cleaned, and swept. I decided to take the opportunity to move the bed frames and clean under them. Bill's was easy but very dirty. I opted to take a break. I walked outside and turned the mattresses and could see Bill across the creek, probably stalking a giant fish. He turned and waved, and I returned the gesture. I thought this could be the only day that might be good for fishing. I considered going down and joining him, but this journey was for Bill. I would let him have the day.

I returned to my bed. It was impossible to move it. I eventually gave up. I noticed one large piece of timber under the bed. With great effort, I moved it and ran the broom under the frame. I realized the bedpost was stuck in a hole, and once I lifted it, I could get good access under the bed.

After removing years of dust, I saw the board that had jammed the bedpost was loose. I retrieved a knife and pried it open. I searched for my flashlight and used it to examine a small compartment that held papers and photographs. I reached in a removed what I could. Maybe this was Bill's boyhood treasure-trove of porn. I expected to find another Playboy and perhaps some erotica he'd hidden away.

I found letters and very explicit pictures of a young woman who seemed familiar. She was posed in various positions. It hit me like a hammer. This was Myrna. I kind of laughed. So maybe Bill and she had a secret life after all. I knew I should not be looking at their private life when I noticed an object in one of the photos. It was a crude prosthetic. Myrna held it, and there was no mistaking the photographer.

I jumped up and ran to the front door. I watched Bill still far enough away that he would not return soon. I put the photos back into the hole. I couldn't imagine anything remotely innocent about this. I opened one envelope. It was addressed to Clive. The postmark and date were unreadable.

Myrna appeared to be explaining that she was considering divorcing Bill so they could be together and was asking Clive to please wait for her. They would soon be free to love once again. It went on, but I didn't need to see anything more. I was sick. I could not think of what this revelation might do to Bill. I could see no reason to tell Bill any of this, but I was human and curious. I took the letters and put them in my duffel bag.

My flashlight fell into the compartment when I attempted to close it, and as I reached below the floorboard, I felt a sting. As I withdrew my hand, a black widow spider emerged. I slapped it off my hand and stepped on it, but the damage was done. I'd wait and see if I became ill or if it was simply a painful wasp-like sting. I didn't have time to find out. I closed the compartment, replaced the timber that covered the floor, and moved the bed back into its former position.

I ran down to the creek and put my hand in the icy water. I squeezed the site and left my hand in as long as I could stand it. The pain was intense, and I felt a stinging sensation travel up my forearm. I lay by the creek for several minutes. When my hand got too cold, I would pull it out for a minute and then resubmerge it.

After thirty minutes, I walked back up to the cabin. I took one mattress in and placed it back onto the bed frame. I found an antihistamine and ibuprofen in my duffel bag. I laid my sleeping bag back onto the mattress and lay down inside it. I had chills and mild cramps. I don't know how long I slept. I woke when I heard Bill approaching the cabin singing a Buck Owens song. "All ya gotta do is act natural-ly. Hayley, get your sorry donkey out here and see what I brought you."

The last thing I wanted to do was to get out of bed. I couldn't fake this. I closed my eyes and sat on the edge of the bed. I was dizzy as I attempted to stand, and I fell. I hit my head against a chair which went crashing to the ground. The room was spinning. Bill entered the cabin and stood above me.

"What the hell?"

I pointed to my hand. "Spider bite," I replied, then threw up on the floor. Bill helped me up and took me outside, where I vomited several times. I saw the ibuprofen come out. He retrieved a cloth and washed my face and some hair stained with vomit. He helped me back into bed and put a wet towel on my face and took the bucket of now warm water and went to the creek to get more cold water.

"You done puking?"

I shrugged.

He gave me two acetaminophens and only a sip of water. He sat next to me while I tossed and turned and eventually fell asleep. When I woke, it was dark, and I was disoriented, but I felt much better. I reached for the flashlight I had left on the table next to the bed.

I knocked it to the floor, and Bill jumped out of his bed and came to me. "You okay, kid?"

"I'm going to live. But if I don't get to the outhouse soon, we may regret it."

Bill helped me up and led me to the outhouse. He checked it for spiders, and I went in. I sat, emptied my bowels, and just stayed there.

Bill knocked on the door. "Hayley, is everything all right?"

"I'm doing a little reading. You can go to bed. I'll be back in a minute." Or ten. Finally, I cleaned myself and stood. I came out of the door and realized Bill was waiting for me. "Sorry, Doc."

He put his arm around my waist, led me back to the cabin, and sat me down on the bed.

"Do you think you can keep anything down now?" He handed me a canteen.

"Uh, that's a big no for now. I think I'll sleep. I'm sorry. This trip is supposed to be me helping you. Switching roles has got to stop, Billy Boy."

CHAPTER 13

When I woke, Bill had coffee and some porridge waiting for me. I looked out the open door and realized it must be late. He smiled and thanked me for last night.

I apologized, and he laughed. "Apologized for what? Last night? Are you joking? You were magnificent. I need to check your birth certificate. Yep, I saw you. There is no way you could be your age. You're at least ten years older."

"Bill, you're pretty up-to-date with computers, aren't you?" I stirred the porridge, but it was like eating spackle.

"Yeah?" He was still smiling, but I detected a trace of nervousness. "The delete key, Bill. One key and the whole book could be lost. Just sayin'."

"Then we can start over. Do you think you're up for a hike?"

"No. You go. I'm going to rest this morning." I had no energy.

"We can go later." He reached into his pocket and brought out a small digital recorder. "Do you think we could do a little chatting about the book? I thought of some other cases. I could record them, and you could get them off the recorder."

The urgency to get Bill's stories had diminished. I kind of wanted to hear the stories firsthand. I had other plans. I wanted to read some of the letters. I felt guilty that I was a voyeur into something that would never be part of the book. I knew this information would kill Bill, but I had to know.

I encouraged Bill to go for a hike or to go fishing. I promised Bill that I would join him later. He would not budge. I returned to my bed and fell asleep. Several hours later, I woke to a small tin can with flowers by my bed and corn muffins on the table. My heart melted at this small gesture. I knew it was from one friend to another, without any romantic implications, but still, I was touched.

"Outhouse." I stood and wavered for a second, and Bill took my arm.

"Are you okay?" He gazed at me as my internal gyroscope oriented itself.

"Never better. Thank you. I'm going to live." My arm was swollen and itchy, but it was improving.

When I returned to the cabin, there was trout, cornbread, and beans. Bill surveyed me and asked if I wanted a beer. We kept the beer in the creek to keep it cool.

I declined, and we sat eating without comment. I finally asked. "You didn't see me naked, did you?"

"Sadly, yes. I'm sure I will recover someday, but for now..."

I shook my head. "Sorry, that damn gravity and time have a lot to answer for." When we finished eating, I announced I was ready for a walk.

Bill had fashioned two walking sticks, and we started down the valley. "How about the story you remembered? If you tell me, I'll remember it. Where are we headed, anyway?"

"It's a surprise." He turned and stumbled as he glanced back at me.

"You okay?" I was the one who should be watching over him.

He didn't respond. I knew his ego was on the line. Watching a virile man that I had known at his peak of life, now struggling to maintain his vitality and dignity, was painful. Who was I to talk? I was on the decline and probably wasn't far behind him. At eighty-two, he was still handsome, and today he was walking on forest trails. His physique was still well above the men I knew of a similar age.

After an hour, I was exhausted. I used the excuse of the altitude and the spider bite. We sat down on a rock, and Bill told me about the next installment of his book. "Hayles, did you see many foals with ruptured bladders in your practice?"

"A few. I hated those cases." I always knew they needed immediate surgery and loathed explaining the surgery and cost to the owners.

"Yeah, me too."

I scooted down onto the ground as Bill began to tell me his story.

When I was a surgical resident, I was called to the clinic at night to see a sick foal. The medicine department was overwhelmed with other cases, and I was on call for the surgery department.

A foal was born in the early hours of the day. It showed no abnormalities at daybreak but began to show signs of colic by the afternoon. The colt passed urine and feces, so a ruptured bladder or a meconium impaction was ruled out. The owner was a young mother with two small children. Of course, money was the overriding consideration.

One of her children was a precocious four-year-old boy. He was a charmer, and he loved this foal. He walked up to me and asked me to care for his foal. He was going to the Olympics with it in a few years. The boy had named the colt Champ. I knelt and looked this kid straight in the eye and told him I would do my best—pressure.

The foal's vitals were all over the place. The temperature was below normal. Champs' heart rate was twice the standard rate, and the pain was four out of five. The intestinal motility was reduced, but his respiratory rate was all right. I had the intern take some blood for analysis. He also put an intravenous catheter in, and we began fluid therapy. I waited to hear about the blood and the foal's response to the treatment. My kids had chickenpox, and Myrna was overwhelmed with worry and their care, so I left for home.

In the morning, the foal was no better. Champ wasn't nursing, and the mare's udder was swollen and painful, and in the rare moments when the colt attempted to nurse, the mare would kick at the foal.

Two students reported the foal had urinated, so a ruptured bladder was still off the differential list. The blood report was equivocal. If the bladder was ruptured, I would have expected a rise in the kidney enzymes and potassium. Neither were above the normal range for a foal of this age.

I watched the foal all day, and in the afternoon, the head of surgery came by, read the reports, and examined the foal. He asked if surgery was an option. The pain was increasing. I explained that the owners were unprepared to pay for the surgery.

I asked if we could do a pro bono and use some of our discretionary funds to explore the abdomen. Apparently, we had used the funds for another case. So, we waited and watched the foal deteriorate over the day.

In the late afternoon, I was in the stall when I observed the colt urinate. The urine was coming from the umbilical cord and not the penis. I suspected the foal had a ruptured urachus, and the urine was somehow not accumulating in the abdomen as quickly as a ruptured bladder. The head of surgery was furious that everyone had missed the urine source. He decided that we would do the surgery anyway at our cost.

The foal went into cardiac arrest on the table and died before the surgery began. I had to call the owners and tell them what we found and that their colt had died. A month later, I received a picture the little boy drew with a note thanking me for trying. I admit, I cried when I received that letter. I still have it. Whenever I think about all the cases where I've successfully saved a life, returned a horse to soundness, or discovered a procedure that changed the way many vets practice, I remind myself of that pony and little boy. That's what has kept my ego in check. Bill turned away.

I put my hand on his shoulder and reminded myself about my failures. "I did laundry every Sunday or went fly-fishing. That kept me humble."

Bill stood up and extended his hand to help me rise. He examined my spider bite. "You'll live."

"Not if we don't get to your destination soon, Billy Boy. I'm fading."

"Hayles, you're such a lightweight. Isn't that what you say? Don't expect me to carry you. It's not much farther."

We walked for another thirty minutes and arrived at a waterfall that was deafening. There were two rainbows. Bill leaned against a rock and gazed at a sight he had witnessed many times. "Myrna loved this place. She said she came here every time she stayed at the cabin."

I felt sick thinking of her here. She was most likely there with Bill's brother. I did see her in one of the photos, standing naked next to a waterfall. I'd decided not to tell Bill what I had discovered. He would die never knowing this betrayal. I couldn't do it to him. I felt a profound sympathy toward this lonely man.

"Let me take your picture, Hayles. Turn around and let me photograph you watching the falls." He did have an artistic eye. I obliged, and then I took several of Bill. Bill wanted to do one of us both together. His camera would not work for the phone selfies commonly used, so he set his camera on a rock and set the timer. Bill would hurry over to me and put his arm around my waist. We waited for the snap, and then he would check the image and repeat the process. He finally announced he was satisfied.

I took the camera and checked the last photo. Bill's face was turned to me, and he was smiling as I looked into the camera. I could see his admiration. I blushed.

"That picture goes into the book or else." Bill turned back and took a few of the falls. "These are for you. I want you to take all the pictures and keep what you want."

We returned to the cabin in the late afternoon. My pain meds had worn off, and I sat on the porch and watched Bill catch dinner. The sun was on my face, and in the warmth of that moment, I dozed and awoke several times until Bill returned with dinner.

As we lay in our beds with the curtain separating us, Bill thanked me and mentioned he needed some time alone tomorrow. "I hope you don't mind."

"Not at all. I'm here to serve." I smiled, knowing how important this trip was to him.

"Goes both ways, old girl. Both ways. Pleasant dreams." A minute later, I heard Bill's rhythmic breathing.

Chapter 14

I made pancakes and meatless sausage. Bill didn't know it had no actual pork. No sense in disturbing the peace. Bill wanted to visit some sacred site he and Jasper had encountered several times. I was worried that he would come to harm, but I didn't say anything. I said I would fish. That's what I told Bill anyway. I secretly planned to read some of the letters I'd retrieved from the hidden compartment.

Bill thought he would be back midafternoon, which gave me time to read a few letters and then go fishing. I sat on the porch until Bill was out of sight. I entered the house and reached into my duffel bag where I'd hidden the letters. They were in no particular order. I tried to find the oldest and the newest. The one I had partially read was in a yellow envelope. Was that the last one? Myrna had suggested that she would divorce Bill, but she wanted their daughter to finish high school. It was confusing.

You would be so proud of her, darling. I wish I could tell her about us, but that will have to wait.

Why would Clive be proud of his niece? The letter went on.

I will tell her someday, but for now, we must wait. I miss you terribly. That letter went on and talked about their last time together.

I randomly picked another one from an earlier year. This note was one from Clive to Myrna. He described the sale of cattle and how the first snow had come to the valley. He said he was maintaining the property to begin preparations to sell and move down to Colorado so that he could be nearer to Myrna. The price of land had dropped, and he would wait until spring and see if a sale was financially possible.

I miss you all and can't wait to see our daughter again. It kills me that she only thinks of me as her uncle, but someday she will know.

I was shocked. This revelation would be devastating to Bill and, I assumed, his daughter. I was sick. I didn't finish that one and quickly took one dated in the seventies. The last digit of the date was unreadable.

I wonder how she received these letters without Bill's knowledge and hid them. I suspect she had a secret compartment in their old house. I speculated she had one in the new home as well.

Dearest, your brother is making my life hell. You know what he wants at night. I try to ignore him, we argue, and then he always gives up. He is like a sick little puppy that makes you feel bad, but in the end, he can never be satisfied. One more month, and I will be in your arms.

I did find one that dated in the mid-nineties. I was shocked to my core.

Clive, I am not going to pretend anymore. I have a new love, and he is the man I plan to live with. His name is Mitch Reynolds. He is the builder of my new home up at the lake. I am sorry I have to tell you this, but there is no use pretending I have feelings for you. You will always be Jessica's father, and someday I will tell her, but now we must end it. I expect you to do the right thing and destroy those pictures. I know you are an honorable man. To ensure your honor, I want to remind you that I know you killed that Jasper man when you were on leave. I would not hesitate to inform the authorities about your role in his death. No homicide is justifiable. I don't care if he did father your sister and was still seeing your mother. Killing people is wrong, Clive. Get rid of those the letters and the rest or else.

Jesus, this family is bizarre. How did Bill escape these nutjobs? How can I sit back and not tell Bill it was his own brother who killed his friend? How do I do that and not reveal these incriminating letters which would crush my friend?

I was sick at heart with this revelation. That was enough for now. I did see other letters that were dated later. So, did they get back together after Myrna abandoned him for the builder? I would read the rest of the letters when I was back at the lake house, and Bill was visiting Myrna. In her state of dementia, did she blurt out any of this to Bill? I was sick thinking he might even have a hint of this.

Chapter 15

By midafternoon, I was mildly concerned. By late afternoon, I was genuinely anxious. By sunset, I was sure Bill was lost, injured, or dead. I took my flashlight, went out on the porch, and called for him. The valley was too large to get an echo. I called for thirty minutes, went back into the cabin, and climbed into the loft to search for the mythical rifle.

There was none. I hadn't cleaned up there, and it was dusty. I should have started there first. I did find some old books and magazines. Nothing was remotely risqué, but they were from the 1950s. They were probably valuable. I returned to the first floor and again went out and yelled for Bill.

I sat and waited for another thirty minutes and then took the largest knife in the cabin and headed out on the trail to find Bill. I walked along the creek bed until it veered off toward the path Bill said he used when traveling back and forth from his grandfather's cabin. I was sure my activity would attract a bear or a mountain lion. If that didn't, my calls would undoubtedly bring a creature that would kill me.

I was sure I'd been out for an hour, and I wasn't convinced I knew my way back. I was frightened that I would be the one found dead, and Bill was probably back at the cabin. I turned around, and something moved in the bushes next to the trail. I stopped and used my flashlight to peer into the brush. My heart was racing. It was a standoff. Whatever was there, didn't move. Neither did I.

After what seemed like an hour and was probably less than a minute, I heard it move away. This was stupid and dangerous. I decided to return to the cabin. I was confident I could find my way back, and after several tries, I found an opening out of the woods and onto the open valley. Again, I called for Bill. He didn't answer. It was eleven at night before I found the cabin. Bill was not there. If he were alive, he'd spend the night out in the woods.

I stayed awake all night. Tuck was coming in the morning, and I expected him to arrive after ten. We could use the horses to try to find Bill. When dawn broke, I sat on the porch wrapped in my sleeping bag. I must have dozed for a minute because I didn't hear Bill approach the cabin.

He quietly called my name. There he was, standing off the porch looking like a child caught stealing. I jumped up and ran to him and hugged him. I was both furious and relieved. I wanted to thrash him, and I said so. Without another word, I turned away and walked back into the cabin. I began to stoke the fire in the woodstove and ignored his pleas for forgiveness.

"Just shut up, you idiot. There's no excuse for what you put me through last night. None. I went out to try to find you. I was scared to death. I was sure you were injured or dead. I can't begin to..."

Bill came up behind me and turned me around. He took me in his arms and hugged me. Dammit, I began to cry. Me—the ice queen lost it.

"Hayley, I'm so, so sorry. I got lost. I went up to a place where I wanted to spend some time. I can't explain it. I needed to go alone, and somehow, I just became disoriented near the ridge where I usually came and went from this valley. I'm embarrassed and ashamed, and I know you must be mad. I'm really so sorry."

"I thought you were dead and being consumed by a mountain lion. I could kick your ass from here to Christmas." I realized this was my mother's voice and her words. It made me laugh, and my tears were interrupted by the thought. I pushed him away and went to the outhouse and then down to the creek to wash my face. I was exhausted, emotionally drained, and mad.

I thought about this poor man who knew he would never again see this place that was his haven from such a dysfunctional life and family. As beautiful as his lake home was, I guessed he sensed it was not his making, and it held painful memories of remembering his beloved wife had all but left him for the builder.

I knew Bill would never find the love he desperately sought from this evil woman. But was she evil? Myrna found herself pregnant by a professor who had used his power to have her removed from law school. She found herself with no options so readily available today. She was so wrong to pretend to love Bill. That was evil. If she had told him the truth, I was sure he would have taken her in and given her the marriage and respectability Myrna required.

I could understand that, but then she secretly found love outside of the marriage and carried on for so many years. No, she's evil—evil to the core. I would never tell Bill what I knew. I would destroy the letters, finish his opus, and return to my home. I would replace Miss Bossy Boots and find companionship and love in the characters I conceived for my books.

Bill wouldn't be around much longer, but I would. The thought made me profoundly sad. He'd had a remarkable life, living beyond his age expectancy. Still, he would never receive the love he so willingly gave to that woman. He would die thinking Jessica was his daughter. I would make sure of that.

All the love, and I admit, I did love him, would never make up for his desire. Fifty or more years of a loveless marriage was heartbreaking. I would stay until the end. I would help him pass from this earthly world and comfort him, then attend to my needs and the rest of my life. I splashed water on my face and returned to breakfast and a very embarrassed and humble man.

We were both exhausted. Bill laid down on his bed, and I went to mine. We were polite, but I wasn't ready to let go of my anger at what he had put me through. That would take time. I rose an hour later and began preparing for our return to civilization.

I packed the panniers, put my sleeping bag into the duffel bag, and washed the tin plates we had used. I swept and removed any food scraps which would attract a marauding bear. I thought about the pictures I'd left in the compartment under my bed. Someday, someone would find those. I should have taken them and burned them. The thought nagged at me, but it was too late. Bill would be long gone before they were discovered, and hopefully, their children would never know.

I remembered we promised Tuck some trout, and I went down to the creek to catch a few, hoping he would bring some ice to protect them for our trip back out of the National Forest. I was grateful we'd seen no bears during our time here. I could not imagine how we overlooked the danger and at least brought bear spray. I was premature in my relief of no bear encounters.

I had four nice fish on a line in the water when I cast out into a marshy pool among the reeds. I distinctly heard footsteps, and I cautioned Bill to stay away from my back cast. "Are you feeling better?"

Bill didn't answer, and I recast my line. My line caught something behind me. I was sure it was Bill as I knew the cast was too high to be the grass. "Oops. Sorry." I turned and realized it was a grizzly with a cub. I didn't know what to do. I was so frightened I just stood there. Do I run and make a lot of noise, or do I crouch and play dead? I was paralyzed. We stood facing one another. I knew she could outrun, swim, or climb to kill me. She went up on her hind legs, and I thought she would attack. I was paralyzed with fear.

I saw Bill come out on the porch, and he immediately ran back into the cabin. He reemerged and began clapping two iron skillets together. The bear turned as Bill ran toward us. She went down on all fours, called to her cub, and ran up the creek, leaving me with a year less on my life and Tuck's trout. Four was plenty. I picked up the string of trout and ran to the cabin.

I could see Bill was as frightened as I was. I knew he wanted to hug me, but I handed him the trout and barely made it to the outhouse on time. Get me the hell out of here. I was so unprepared for this. Thankfully, we would be back in town this evening, ending this adventure.

I was wrong. This was a walk in the park compared to what was to come.

CHAPTER 16

Tuck arrived and asked how our time was at the cabin. We were too embarrassed to tell the truth. Bill was the first to answer. "Tuck, it was so good. We may be back next summer."

Uh, I don't think so, buddy. I coughed and mentioned that I had already booked a condo in Hawaii for next summer. Bill turned, stared at me, and cocked his head. He thought I was serious.

"Don't you remember? It's in my contract."

Bill turned and shook his head. "In your dreams, sweetheart. In your dreams. Tuck, let's do the short trip. I think Hayley's seen enough."

I was so tired that when we returned to town, Bill checked us back into the hotel, we went to have an early supper, and returned to our rooms. It was hot, and the air conditioner could barely keep up. I took a long shower and laid down on my bed with only a towel covering me. At some stage, I was cool enough to get under the sheet, and without a stitch on, I fell asleep and only woke when I heard the sound of a car backfiring near the hotel. I retrieved clean clothes from my suitcase and dressed.

I decided to transfer Myrna and Clive's letters into my suitcase. I had a hidden area in the lining. I took the bottom end of the duffel bag and tipped it, spilling the contents onto the carpet. I was going to do laundry today. I laughed, reminding myself that doing laundry was my way of re-maining humble.

As the clothes tumbled out, I was shocked to see this was Bill's duffel bag, and he had mine. What were the chances of him opening the bag and discovering the letters? I had to act quickly. I ran next door and knocked on his door. There was no answer. I quietly called his name—still no response. I raced down to the café and found him sitting at a booth. He smiled as he saw me and motioned for Minnie to bring another cup of coffee. By his manner, I guessed I was safe, and he had not opened my duffel bag.

Minnie took my order and left. Bill was reading the news-paper, and I sensed a change in his mood. I asked him if he'd slept well, and he nodded.

"We mixed up the duffel bags. I'm going to run a load of laundry, so if you can give me mine back, I can add yours too."

He stared at me, and there was no doubt he had discov-ered the letters. I pretended I didn't notice. He took a bite of his pie and stood to leave.

"Hayley." He didn't finish whatever he was going to say.

"Bill?" But Bill turned, went to the register, paid the account, and left.

I was sick. I ate a few bites of my food and returned to the hotel. My duffel bag, minus the letters, was sitting outside my room. I went inside my hotel room and lay face down on the bed. I wanted to cry, but I only clenched my fists and moaned. I finally took the clothes to the hotel laundry room and began a wash. I sat in the room and agonized about the hurt and betrayal Bill must be experiencing. I hated myself for even taking those letters.

By lunch, I had the laundry done and folded. I would wait for Bill to come to me. I stayed in my room all afternoon writing up the stories he'd told me. There was nothing about Myrna in these stories. I waited until dinner, but I had still not heard from Bill. I went down the street, and instead of eating at the diner, I went down to a hamburger shop, ordered a hamburger and fries, and sat down at an outdoor table.

I ached for the man. His whole life and the pretense of everything outside his work had been a lie. He'd been so innocent. His naivety had no boundaries until this morning. Now he knew he had been a hopeless fool. I suspected his anger would be directed more at me than Myrna. It was easier to hate someone you didn't love than someone you did. I would begrudgingly take the blame if it helped him accept the truth of his marriage.

As I ate my hamburger, Tuck drove up in an unfamiliar truck and honked. I thought he was searching for a buddy, but he waved me over.

I approached the driver's side. "Hey, how did the trout taste? Were you a hit on the home front?"

"Yeah, good. Angie loved them. Can you help me with a horse?" Tuck appeared worried.

"I dunno. What's the problem?"

"Colic." Short and sweet.

"Sorry, I no longer practice, and I don't even have a license."

"Doc Hadley and Bill said you would say this. Doc hasn't had a license in the last two years. Besides, you're the only sober person in town who knows what they're doing."

"I don't have any drugs or instruments. Sorry, Tuck."

"I sort of borrowed Doc Hadley's truck. He's in no shape to drive it anyway. Neither is his drinking buddy. Climb in Hayley. Please?"

"Lead the way." I picked up my food and got into the passenger seat. I was surprised, but in a way, pleased Bill was drinking away his sorrows with a friend.

"It's a bit of a hike. It's a new horse I bought this spring. I paid a little more than I should. Chester's been a great horse for both riding and packing, and I would like to save the bastard for my little tyke, who's starting to ride with me on the shorter trips into the mountains. He wasn't right this morning, and I had to pick you guys up. When I got back, he seemed okay, but now he's rolling."

We drove thirty miles to an old ranch with a house, corrals, and a new barn. I could see which horse was colicky when we entered the gate. I jumped out and began opening the various compartments and found everything I wanted. With effort, Tuck made the gelding rise and walk up to a tie rail next to the truck.

The stethoscope was old and hopefully functional. I needed to get a heart rate and auscultate the abdomen for intestinal motility. I could do this by several methods, including using my ear to listen to the horse's flanks for gut sounds.

I approached the horse and patted his shoulder. Even good horses can kick, so I put my left hand in front of his chest, so I would feel if he would lurch forward, and cow kick me as I ascertained his heart rate. Tuck saw what I was doing. "You don't have to worry about him. He's a lamb."

"Yeah, I'm sure." But I had been kicked by a "lamb" early in my career.

The stethoscope transmitted no sounds. I suspected it was blocked with dirt or, even worse, Dr. Hadley's ear wax. I pushed the back of my hand under the left elbow and could easily feel the heart beating.

"His heart rate is sixty-four. It should be in the forties."

I put my ear against his left flank. I heard no gut sounds. I went on the other side, and Chester kicked at me when I put my ear on his right flank. I finally examined the gums under his lip. They appeared to be slightly pale but showed no toxic purple line.

I went to the truck and found pain medication and some drenching solution. Apparently, Dr. Hadley used a funnel and probably lots of mineral oil. That was kind of "old-school." I used electrolytes, lots of water, and some stool softener. I found an old wooden ax-handle twitch that I guessed he used for restraint. Tuck assured me we didn't need one, and he twisted Chester's ear as I quickly passed a long tube up his nose, into the esophagus, and down to his stomach.

I climbed up the corral fence and poured the slurry into the funnel I attached to the nasogastric tube.

He was still painful when I finished treating him, and he still had no gut sounds, so I decided to do a rectal examination. I found obstetrical gloves and lube and had Tuck hold up the front leg while I performed the exam. Chester was compliant as I reached through his anus and rectum to palpate the back half of the abdomen. I was sick. I had only felt a few in my career, but there was no mistaking the enterolith sitting directly next to his left flank.

I explained to Tuck that enteroliths are large stones that form in the intestinal tract over the years. I had a picture of one on my phone. I thought Chester's was the size of a large grapefruit. This would not pass without surgery. I asked where the nearest referral center was and if they were prepared to spend the money on surgery.

"Too far and no. Should we put him down? Are you positive he can't get better without surgery?" Tuck went up to him and put his arms around his neck. "Oh, you poor bastard. I'm so sorry. I wish I were a millionaire."

I wished I could be somewhere else. I hated this, and I didn't regret leaving this aspect of practice. I went back to the truck. There was one option if Dr. Hadley had what I needed. His vehicle was stocked with most of the modern medicine and tools I was used to. Did he have a surgical kit? Did he have modern suture material? Part of me prayed he did, and part of me prayed he didn't.

He did. He had a surgical kit, gloves, and suture material. I watched this horse starting to bloat. The pain was the same, and the horse had no increased intestinal motility—a bad sign. I watched Chester for several minutes. There was no improvement. Doing surgery in a barnyard with no competent help was verging on malpractice. I didn't have a license, and I had no insurance.

I did find what I needed to do a rough job. I had no surgical gown, but I might not need to stick my hand in the abdomen very far. I'd observed other vets do things like this with far less.

"Tuck, when you found Bill and Dr. Hadley, how drunk were they say on a scale of one to ten?"

"Twelve. Do you need help? Are you thinking of doing surgery yourself?"

I hated asking drunk men for anything. If I could get Dr. Hadley to sober up, he could help me with just the enterotomy part. "Tuck, can you go to town and see if Dr. Hadley will come out and help?" I also asked him to bring some sterile saline. "We'll need it to wash the enterotomy incision."

The truck was well equipped, and I found clippers and began clipping the left flank in preparation for a standing flank laparotomy. I took all the drugs and equipment I would need and sent Tuck to town to retrieve a possible surgical assistant.

I stayed with the horse and prayed the vet was sober enough to help with a tiny part of the surgical procedure. Even if he weren't, his presence would be enough to keep me from being sued. The chances of these people suing me were small, but I would sleep better if I didn't have that hanging over my head.

It had been an hour since Tuck had departed. At a distance, I saw headlights heading toward the ranch. Tuck's wife, Angie, had come out of the house and brought some lights to help in the dark surgical setting. I began injecting lidocaine after sedating Chester in preparation for the incision. As I turned to get more lidocaine, I saw Bill exit the pickup truck. Neither man appeared to be anything more than happy.

However, when Dr. Hadley asked about the horse, his words were slurred. Bill showed no signs of intoxication. He asked to do a rectal to confirm the enterolith, and with a gloved arm, he immediately found the stone up next to the left flank wall and stated that there was a "chance."

Dr. Hadley went to the truck and found more suture material and the sterile saline hidden behind the back seat. I did a final scrub of the flank. We had no surgical drapes. I tested the anesthesia and observed no reaction. Chester stood like a champ—better living through chemistry. I made a vertical incision in the flank. I dissected the muscles in a grid that mimicked the direction of the various muscle bands I would need to penetrate. I pushed through the peritoneal wall with my fingers by extending them and forcing them through the tough membrane.

I was in the abdomen. I had only a short distance to grasp the small colon where the stone was stuck. I had to extend the incision to exteriorize the enterolith. Everyone gasped when they saw the enterolith positioned in the stretched intestine as I pulled it through the incision. I could barely grasp it in my outstretched hands. I was nervous about having Bill watch the surgery. He was a master, and he made a suggestion or two to help me. I needed a second surgeon, and Dr. Hadley pointed to Bill.

Bill scrubbed his hands and put on surgical gloves. They were tight, while I practically swam in mine.

I turned my head in Bill's direction. "I can hold, and you can do the enterotomy if you like?" Bill had done hundreds, while I had only done twenty or more in my time. Bill declined, and he held the intestine so that when I made the incision, the stone would drop. Any intestinal contents would not flow back into the incision. The rock hit the ground as I opened the small colon on the thickened antimesenteric band. Tuck knelt and picked it up.

"Jesus, it's like a rock." He handed it to his wife and returned to holding Chester's head. Chester was becoming agitated, so Dr. Hadley administered a small sedation dose.

I quickly sutured the enterotomy incision using a simple continuous pattern and then a Lempert technique designed to bury the suture material and decrease the chance of adhesions. Dr. Hadley poured sterile saline mixed with some antibiotics over the intestinal suture line until Bill was satisfied we had cleaned it as much as possible. I changed gloves and pushed the intestine into the abdomen. I quickly closed the flank incision. Bill cut the sutures for me, saying very little during the procedure.

As I tied the last exterior mattress suture, Dr. Hadley emitted a long low whistle. "Mac, you'd a thunk she might have done one or two of those before."

"Yeah, you might," was Bill's only reply.

"I learned from the best." I always gave credit where it was due.

Dr. Hadley had sobered considerably. "Folks, as fun as this is, I need to get home and sleep. I've got a herd of cows to preg-check in the morning. Can someone drive me home?"

Bill said he was sober, but Tuck had to go to town to get his truck anyway. After we scoured the vet pack for everything we would need until morning, they left with Tuck driving, and I stayed with Angie and Chester. Bill had not spoken a word as he departed. I guessed we would return to Colorado tomorrow. I had everything I needed to return to my home, and I thought I could have Bill drop me off at the airport in Jackson. I guessed he was thinking the same.

Angie made coffee, and she and I prepared to watch Chester through the night. I would typically have the horse on intravenous fluids, but that would have to wait. We sat in deck chairs outside a makeshift stall and wrapped blankets around our shoulders for warmth. I always felt an extreme release of tension after doing one of these heroic surgeries. This time was no different. I sat in the chair and slept for several minutes. Angie went into the house to check on her children. I woke and realized I was alone with Chester. I heard him passing gas. That was an incredible sound. He seemed comfortable, and I was now confident he would survive the night. Dr. Hadley would take over his care and recovery. My return to veterinary medicine would be over in the morning.

Tuck returned and woke me again. He asked if I would like to go to the house. He said Angie had gone to bed and had put sheets on the lounge in the living room. "How can we pay you, Hayley?"

I was ready for that. I stood and watched Chester lift his tail and pass a motion. "I need to go back up to Bill's cabin?"

"Are you kidding? I can leave now. What did you leave there?"

"No, I need to go with you. There's something I need to do."

"Is it safe to leave Chester?" Tuck was cleaning the watery manure he had just passed.

"If we left at dawn, he would be ready for more pain medication, and then how long is it to ride up there and back?"

"We could ride from here, and it would be two hours each way. I'll stay up, and you go sleep. Hayley, I can't thank you enough. Live or die, it was an amazing night. You and Bill are incredible together."

"Yeah, I think so too." Too bad it has come to an end. I knew once I got on the plane, I would never see Bill again. It was not the end of the world. He was so flawed, and despite my rising infatuation, it was just that—a short-term feeling never to be returned.

Tuck woke me up around four in the morning, and we examined Chester, who had passed two more motions and was calling for feed. "Can he have something to eat?"

"Nope. No food until we return and then if you have some green grass, he can have a nibble. We can decide when we come back. In most cases, I deal with getting what we call post-operative ileus. The intestines go into a hibernation-like mode from the trauma and damage. It usually turns around after the first day, so we limit the build-up by only offering a small amount of food many times on the first day or so."

CHAPTER 17

Tuck had two different horses saddled and ready to leave when we left Chester. "I hope you can ride this morning. Your horse is a great ride, but he likes to travel. I thought it would help to have the two fast ones, so we can cover ground and get this little adventure over."

"I'll be fine. I bet Bill will be ropable when he finds out I'm not ready to leave this morning."

"I guess you don't want to tell me what we're doing?" Tuck led the way. It was still dark, and I was following him and praying my horse was safe in the night.

"Sorry, a state secret." To change the subject, I asked Tuck about his life and how he ended up here in the town.

"Hayley, I come from New York. I went to college and had a degree in journalism. I came out here to do a story on the Forestry Service and fell in love with the area, but more importantly, I fell in love with Angie. Do you know she's a distant cousin of Bill? Bill's mom had a sister, and she was married to a rancher near Helena. That's Angie's grandmother."

"Sheesh, you are an incestuous crowd here, aren't you? Does Bill know this?"

"I don't rightly know for sure." Tuck stood up in the saddle and stopped his horse. He dismounted and tightened the girths on both his and my horse. He remounted, and we continued our climb up the mountainside.

I was almost pain-free riding in the saddle. "You don't sound like you're from New York."

"No, I suspect not. If I revert to my old accent, Angie beats it out of me."

We rode without talking for several minutes. Finally, Tuck broke the silence. "How'd you meet Bill anyway? He thinks you hung the moon."

Uh, not right now, that's for sure. "After I graduated from vet school, I came to his clinic and did an internship. I stayed on and worked for him for several more years until I met my husband, then I left."

"So, did you know his wife? I hear she has dementia, and he visits her daily where she lives."

"Yes, he's very devoted to her." I was suspicious about where this conversation was going. I didn't want to be part of anything other than celebrating their long and happy marriage.

"She's a funny woman. She was a good horsewoman and so beautiful, but still strange."

"I didn't know her that well." She hardly ever came to the clinic or any clinic parties when I worked for Bill. I didn't know her at all and neither did Bill, by my reckoning.

"I wasn't around, but she would hire the packers to bring her up to the cabin, and she would stay by herself for weeks or bring the children up. The only person ever to visit her was her brother-in-law. Did you ever meet him?"

"No, I just worked for Bill in Colorado. I knew he had a place in Montana. Still, we only had a professional relationship, and I didn't know much about his family. We were all workaholics, and we spent a lot of time together, but I was one of many vets who worked for him."

We reached the summit. At the top, I could see the valley that had been Bill's family's homesteads. On the other side, I could see the valley and the cabin. We stopped, and Tuck pointed to a small wooden cross that had recently been carved and planted. "That's new. It looks like someone fixed old Clive's grave marker."

"Huh? Is Clive buried up here?" Now I knew what Bill was doing when he was gone all day and night.

"That's what I was told. Clive wanted his ashes up here to see the ranch and the valley. He spent many weeks up here in the summer. Word has it that Clive would come up when Bill's wife was at the cabin, so he could play with the children. He never married, you know. I hear he loved the children like his own."

"Bill never talked about it. I knew he liked to come up as well, but I think you can see what it was like for us when we were in practice." I wanted to steer the conversation away from Myrna.

"Yeah, I don't know how Doc Hadley does it. It's a demanding job for sure."

"I'm glad it worked out last night, but to be honest, you got lucky. I was trained by a great vet who was a pioneer in his field and was willing to teach his interns and colleagues how to do what many would think was impossible."

"I sure do thank you. Hayley, what are his chances now?"

"Never say never, but I'd say they're pretty good. He'll need some time off, of course."

We descended into the valley, and by sunrise, we arrived at the cabin. "Tuck, I need to do a few things by myself. Do you mind going for a ride? It will only be twenty minutes."

"Anything for you. You said there was a bear there on your last day? I might go and see if I can chase her away. Some people are coming up next week, and I would like for them to have a safe and boring visit."

Tuck took my horse and rode away to water the horses and search for the bear. I quickly entered the cabin and moved my bed and the large timber covering the hidey-hole. I made sure there were no unauthorized critters before I retrieved the photographs. It made me sick to see these. I immediately put them into the woodstove. Using the matches left in the cabin, I began to burn the photographs.

I made sure there was nothing visible left once the flame was out. I scooped the ashes into a tin can, took them to the outhouse, and dumped them. Seeing those images would kill Bill and his children. If I never see Bill and his family again, I know I have saved them a great deal of pain. When I was finished, I went out to wait for Tuck. I didn't wait long.

Tuck smiled and didn't mince words. "Did you destroy all the evidence?"

I searched his face for a clue. "Yes?"

"I saw the smoke. It must have been very incriminating or salacious." He grinned.

"A bit of both. Ready to ride?"

My mount was still fresh, and crow hopped as we rode from the cabin toward the valley's end and the beginning of our journey over the mountain pass. I knew he would tire soon as we began our ascent over the pass leading to the ranch. The chill of the morning was finally receding, and I was becoming tired from my night caring for Chester.

Now that I had completed my duty. The events of the last few days began to weigh me down. I planned to sleep as Bill drove me to the Jackson Airport. I explained the treatment regime for Chester's return to work and suggested dietary changes that might prevent further enteroliths from forming. After two hours, we returned to Tuck's ranch. As we walked through the gate, I asked him how long he'd owned the property.

"I don't. I lease it from the Harrogate Cattle Company. This once was Bill's grandparents' property."

"Oh, I see. I guess it gets fairly cold up here in the winter?"

"Sure does. Hey, I think I see your ride." Tuck pointed to the corral where Bill's truck sat next to the barn. "Hayley, I don't know what was so important, but your secret is safe with me. I owe you one."

"Thanks, Tuck. I appreciate you going back to get my necklace. It was my grandmother's, and I can't believe I forgot it."

Tuck nodded. "I'd sure love to take you back there sometime."

"You never know." But I did. This would be my only time in these mountains and at that cabin. I hoped I was wrong.

CHAPTER 18

Bill leaned against his truck as we rode up and dismounted. He didn't smile or acknowledge me. He gave Tuck the antibiotics that Dr. Hadley had dispensed with the instructions for administration. Bill mentioned Dr. Hadley would be by this afternoon to ensure Tuck's horse was progressing. He gave Tuck his card and told him he was available to talk if Tuck had any questions.

Bill got into the driver's seat while I climbed into the backseat and announced I was going to sleep. I asked Bill to let me know when we were close to the Jackson Hole Airport. He didn't comment, and I knew we were of a similar mind.

I slept for several hours until Bill announced we were just north of Yellowstone, and he was refueling. I was in a daze. I was still beyond sleep-deprived and was unhappy to be wakened.

"Hayley, I didn't sleep last night either. You can drive for a while. I'm using the bathroom, and then I'm going to take a turn at sleeping."

I stayed with the truck as Bill filled the tank. When he returned, I went to the restroom and said I was getting something to eat and drink and asked Bill if he wanted anything. He didn't respond. He got into the passenger seat and pushed the chair down as far as it would go.

An old car was getting fuel across at the other bay, and then a black sports model car with a single driver pulled up to the store and pay station. I walked behind him, as did a mother and daughter from the other vehicle. The little girl was excited and spoke to her mother in Spanish, asking how long it would be before they would be at Old Faithful. I knew enough Spanish to respond and tell her it was worth the wait.

I went to the bathroom and returned to the counter. The attendant had a frozen gaze, and he didn't respond when I placed my drink and chips on the counter. I heard the mother plead with the man not to take her daughter in Spanish. I spun around and realized the man had a gun and planned to take the child as a hostage. The poor child had wet her pants and was frozen in fear as she clung to her mother.

So, this would be the moment I had to be a hero. I knew it would not end well. Would I be remembered for my sacrifice and service to the greater good? I knew in an hour or so that I would be dead.

"Sir, take me instead. I can drive your car, and this little girl will only hold you back. I promise to do anything you wish, but please spare her and take me instead." I tried to stand between the family and the man.

I saw a gun trained on the mother, and I stepped in between the two. I could see his hesitation. "Please sir, I know all the roads, and I can get you away from anyone chasing you. Tell me where you want to go, and I can take you. Please." For an instant, I thought he would ignore my plea. He stared at me and then pointed the gun at me.

We went to his car, and I was told to go to the driver's side. I tried to talk to him about his plan, but he told me to "Shut up and drive, or I'll blow your head off."

Ignoring that command, I told him I could help him, and I knew how to get to the border undetected. He hit me with the gun and again said, "Shut up." This time I didn't reply and did exactly what he commanded. I noticed several tattoos and many piercings on his face and ears. My hands shook as I drove north.

We drove for several hours when I remembered my phone was off. By now, I knew that Bill would have realized that I had been abducted. I didn't know if my phone could be tracked if it was off. Part of me knew it wouldn't, but a small piece of me prayed I was wrong.

The fuel was getting low, and it was getting dark. I didn't know this cretin's name. He had not spoken to me since he hit me with the gun barrel. He began rocking back and forth. Was he coming off some drug? Was he just worried? I was glad I had emptied my bladder before we took off. He finally asked me to stop. He told me to turn off the engine and hand him the keys. He walked a short way from the vehicle, turned partially away, and relieved himself. He returned to the car and gave me the keys. "Drive and don't talk."

I complied, but we were going to run out of gasoline. I pointed to the gas gauge. He then directed the gun at my head, and I restarted the engine. We drove into a small town, and I was instructed to pull up to a gas station. He told me to get out and put premium into the car. I searched for video surveillance and could not detect any, but perhaps there were hidden cameras.

Another car pulled into the station. The driver exited her vehicle and began pumping fuel as she stared at us. I tried to make eye contact, but she only smiled and complained about the fuel price. I knew I could not speak, so I smiled and nodded. A small boy got out of the car and stood with his mother while she stood beside her car, pumping her fuel. My captor pointed the gun at the boy from inside our vehicle. I was instructed to pay the attendant inside the store and return. I was cautioned not to speak to the woman inside the store. He handed me the cash and told me to get Coke and sandwiches.

When I went to the counter, I stared straight at the man hoping my face might have been shown on television. I received no indication that the attendant recognized me. I returned to the car, and we left the station and town. I was directed to take a narrow dirt road once we left the township. We finally came to a dead-end where I was sure I would be shot or raped.

"Turn off the engine and get out of the car." This was it. I was going to die. I had no options. We were in a forest and miles from civilization. I faced my abductor and decided to lay it on the line. "My name is Hayley Alexander. I'm no threat to you. I'll do whatever you say, and so far, that's what I have done. If we drive north, we should be at the border by midnight, and we can quickly cross the border undetected. I've done it many times." A small lie. I wanted to survive, and my mind raced with possibilities of how this could end with my survival. I would not consider the alternative. I'll survive, then get the hell out of here and return to my home in Georgia. I'll go to Europe or wherever for a chance to see my grandchildren and be a memory in their lives. No wonder there are so many books written about Montana. These people are all crazy. I'll take quiet and boring in my cabin along the creek.

The man ate his food and didn't share any. I wasn't hungry, but I was becoming exhausted. I'd driven for over eight hours. With my lack of sleep from the previous night and my anxiety, I could not continue much longer. He wouldn't talk, but he went to the car trunk and opened it with a key. He brought out zip ties and began to secure my hands behind my back. I begged him to let me pee before tying my other hand. He pointed the gun and indicated I could.

He watched as I pulled down my pants and knelt to urinate in the secluded woods. He showed no interest in my nakedness, and once my pants were up and I was dressed, he finished zip-tying my hands together and shoved me to the ground.

I lay on the cold ground while he sat with his back against a tree. I saw his head nod. He was falling asleep. I knew there was no chance of escape, but so far, he had done no serious physical harm to me. I guessed he valued me as a hostage. I prayed that would continue. I slept and woke periodically. I finally realized dawn was near. My captor woke with a start and grabbed the gun, which had fallen to the ground.

I had not moved. My strategy was to do whatever it took to stay alive. If he wanted me to drive, I would drive. If he wanted to do other things, I would do them. I would oblige his every wish. I had to pretend I was his co-conspirator. I was on his side.

When he went to undo the zip ties, he discovered my phone. He spoke for the first time since my abduction. His accent was southern. Since I also lived in the South, I hoped to engage him in conversation. He took my phone and smashed it against a rock. It flickered on for a moment and then went dead. Was there any chance the moment the phone was on it would be traceable? We were in a remote area, and I doubted there was any cell coverage, anyway.

I wondered if my family knew of my abduction and what they thought. I knew Bill would be agonizing. Despite his disappointment in me for hiding and probably even finding Myrna and Clive's letters, at some point, he would have to acknowledge that I didn't write the letters. I never intended to show the notes to anyone. There was no point.

If I could only reason with this man. I needed to get a small amount of control. My chances of survival were so small that I was emboldened to take some risks.

"Start driving." The man handed me the keys and shoved me to the driver's side. I tripped and fell.

I stood and turned. "I won't go with you unless you tell me your name. All I want is your name. I don't care what you've done, nor do I care where you want to go. I'll drive you all over the States, but I want your name." Small steps might lead me to find a weak spot.

The man's unshaven face showed a life that had been hard. He was thin, and I guessed he was a drug addict. He'd taken nothing in my presence. Was he going through withdrawal, or had he ever taken drugs? Was he ill? If I could only talk to him, I might persuade him to let me go. I had nothing to lose.

"My name is Paul, but my friends call me Pauly."

"You have friends?" A wedge in the door. "That's all I need to know now, but I'm here to help you. I've done everything you've asked. If you tell me more, maybe I can do something to help you get where you're going."

The car's engine would not engage. I was sick. I tried again, and this time it fired up. I knew we would get back on the main road where the police might spot us.

I thought I would press the point and try to make him think I was helping him. "Pauly, we need to be careful. I'm sure the police are looking for this car. Maybe we should stick to the back roads."

He hit me with the gun barrel again. This time it cut my temple, and I bled. "I make the decisions. You just drive." He pointed the gun toward the road.

I didn't respond and attempted to stop the blood trickling down my cheek. I drove for an hour, and we got to a highway where Pauly directed me to head east. I was disoriented and realized I was on one of the few roads to cross into North Dakota. As I drove, I saw two Sheriffs' four-by-fours move in the opposite direction. Pauly ducked as they passed, and I thought I saw a sheriff slow his car and glance back.

"We need to get off the main road. This is suicide." I tried to sound like I was now his ally. Oh, please ignore me.

"Shut up and drive." Then he told me to turn around. I did—happily.

Several hours later, I found myself back in the mountains. This crazy bastard was literally driving in circles. He became more agitated and kept looking at his phone, showing him that he was approaching a dead-end road. It was now late in the day. Our gas was getting low, and we had found a radio station that occasionally sent out updates on a kidnapping.

The reporter was announcing, "Paul Tainter, of East Kentucky, has taken an unnamed grandmother and was believed to be heading east on Highway 200. He is armed and dangerous. He's wanted for the murder of three women in Colorado. Do not approach the car, a black Nissan Altima, Colorado license..."

I drove without glancing at Pauly. Pauly turned toward me. "What's one more?" I think he meant one more dead woman.

"We need gas, Pauly. I think I see a station ahead."

He pointed the gun toward the station, and I drove up to the outside pump. He handed me a credit card. I was dubious, but it allowed me to fill the tank. Was it stolen, and were they using it to track his presence? Now I was starving and thirsty. He told me to drive over to the main building, and he handed me a ten-dollar bill. "Get a bottle of Coke and a sandwich." A teenager was standing by the door. He nodded to her and then to me. I understood the implication. If I did anything to attract attention, the innocent girl would be killed. I nodded and asked if I could get something, and he said I wouldn't need anything and then said, "A drink. No funny business, or she gets it."

I was back in the car in less than five minutes, and we were on the road and heading to the mountains. I was going to die for sure. I had saved at least three young lives. I'd lived a life that had no limits. I'd raised two beautiful children and now was a grandmother. I laughed inwardly that the news outlets described me as a grandmother. I was so much more than that.

We drove to a secluded logging road. I thought this was a nice place to die, but I would go down fighting. I would die trying to take this bastard with me. Or would I? If I ran, he might not have the stamina to follow me. The revolver might not be as accurate as a rifle. If I could duck to the side, Pauly might not be able to shoot me. It was my only hope. We came to the end of the road. All around was a steep embankment. Running for my life was futile. There was no way but down.

Pauly told me to stop the car and get out. I thought this was the end of my life. My instinct was to run, but somehow, the Buck Owens tune kept running through my head—act naturally. I don't know why but I didn't beg, cry, or run. I stood on the edge of the embankment and explained I needed to live as I was writing a book, and I wanted to finish the book. It was so ridiculous, but I knew if I begged, he would have shot me sooner. If I could buy even a minute, I would take that minute to breathe and survive. Please, Lord, just one minute.

Pauly shook his head. "Hayley, you've been real good to me, and you done everything I ast of you. I wish I could just leave you here, but it ain't in my nature. If I were ever gonna let one go, it'd be you. But in the end, youse still just one of them."

The gun was in his left hand. As he reached to change hands, I took a step backward and fell off the cliff edge. I knew there was no hope if I stayed and little chance if I fell, but that slight possibility was my only one. I immediately began to tumble backward.

I heard two shots from the gun and another crash. Still, I continued down until I felt an overwhelming discomfort in my left forearm. Then I felt consuming peace. Blessed peace.

CHAPTER 19

The euphoria didn't last. I became aware of overwhelming pain, then the cold. It was dark, and I was confused. Was I alive? I didn't know where I was, but my consuming need was to get back to the cabin and destroy the letters and pictures. Buck Owens was helping me, but he was dead. Was I dead as well? I must be dreaming. I tried to wake up. This nightmare was the worst dream I could remember in years. If I could only get warm, then I would be all right.

It was so dark, and I wasn't sure why I felt so much pain. I decided the best thing was to go back to sleep until morning, and then I would be back in my bed at Bill's house. I'll get up early, have coffee, and type that last story he told me. What was the final chapter? I fell asleep, trying to remember.

A few minutes later, I saw a man several yards away from me with his eyes open and covered in blood. He wasn't talking. I asked him what was happening, but he didn't respond. I couldn't move, and I was so cold. However, the sun was rising, and soon I would be up and ready for the day. My arm hurt terribly, and I wondered if I would have enough strength to take the kayak out and go fishing.

I knew something wasn't right. I wanted coffee and some of Bill's fruit cocktail this morning. I wondered if Bill was still mad at me. I knew my arm hurt, and my clothes were dirty. I would have to change, or Bill wouldn't let me get in the truck. I thought if I slept for another few minutes, the sun would be up enough to warm me. I shouted to Pauly to stay where he was, and I would get help after I had a short nap.

I heard voices. I didn't understand what they were saying, but I attempted to tell them that Pauly needed help first. I tried to see from where the voice originated. I looked up the side of the mountain, and then I was sure it was Buck Owens coming for me. "Hi, Buck. I think I'll be famous. All I have to do is act naturally, but my arm hurts so bad that I might not be able to."

Then I saw it wasn't Buck. It was someone with a helmet on, and then there were two. "Can I have some coffee? No milk, please." The man peered into my eyes and lifted my eyelids when I tried to close them. "I really need some coffee. There's a gas station not far from here. Can we stop there so I can get a cup?"

The man smiled and told me I could have a cup as soon as he got me up the side of the mountain. That sounded all right with me. I asked him to see how Pauly was, but the man said the other man wasn't going anywhere and asked me just to rest. "I can do that. It comes naturally." I laughed, and then I felt two men lift me onto a long tray and tie me in. "You know, I may be shot in my arm, so be careful."

The next thing I remember was the sensation of motion. I stared up, and I was in the back of a vehicle. I asked if it was an ambulance. The man had a bright orange uniform. He said it was an ambulance and asked me how much pain I had. I wondered how much pain I had to be in to get to suck on the pain pipe. I'd seen those pain pipes when I watched an ambulance television program.

I heard a siren and knew I was going to the hospital. I asked them to turn off the siren and if there was a light to turn that off too. The man asked why. I wanted to sleep, and I remember as a child, I'd been told it was more expensive if they turned on the light and siren.

I slept for a long time. When I woke up, I asked for the little pipe again. I now had an intravenous catheter, and observing the fluids going into my vein, I asked the man to slow it down unless they wanted to stop so I could pee. My other arm was strapped to a board and was killing me. I was still worried about Pauly and asked if he was also coming. "Please don't kill him, but don't let him loose. I can't drive the car anymore, and he might kill me."

The ambulance stopped, and the back doors opened. I saw many people in bright uniforms as I was wheeled into a building. I thought I saw Bill in the background. I knew he would still be mad at me, and I tried to ignore him. He stood over me and told me he was sorry. Then I remembered the colicky horse, and I asked if the horse was okay, and he said yes. Then I wondered why he was sorry, but I didn't hear what he said because they took me into a room, put me in a tube, and told me to be still. I said I would if they let me suck on the pain pipe.

I woke up in a different room. It was dark, but there were so many machines and flickering lights that I reached over to turn them off. Someone restrained my hand, and I thought it might be Bill.

"I'm trying to sleep. Turn off the lights." The door to the room opened, and a woman entered. She told me to be still. She was so bossy, but I did what she said. I thought Bill was sitting next to my bed, so I turned to him and asked him to get me out of here. He smiled and said that wasn't possible. He said I was in a hospital, and I had a broken arm.

"No, I've been shot." I was exasperated that these idiots couldn't even see what was wrong. The bossy lady attached a syringe to my catheter, and I asked if it was coffee because I was promised coffee. So far, no one had given me any.

I don't know when I woke up later, but the room was light, and two people in white coats stood over me. Bill was gone, thankfully. I didn't need that complication in my life right now. I had to find out if Pauly was in the same hospital, and I needed to tell him that I wouldn't be able to drive the car.

That was when the woman in the white coat told me that Pauly was dead and that I was in the county hospital. I had a broken arm from falling off the cliff. I had a concussion and internal injuries. She said her name, but I was so shocked I forgot it. Was she sure Pauly was dead? I asked her to make sure this was true. It was a relief. That was one less of a worry. I asked if she knew how the horse was, and she said she didn't.

The doctor said I would have surgery for my broken arm, and I asked her to look for a bullet wound. She assured me there was no bullet. My humerus was fractured. I wondered what a humerus was, and she pointed to her arm above her elbow. "Your upper arm has a spiral fracture, and I will pin and plate it tomorrow if your vitals stabilize."

I was coming out of a fog. "What isn't stable? If I could get some coffee, I'm sure I could get better."

The doctor turned to a man in a uniform and asked if he would bring me some coffee. Sheesh, finally.

"I'd like to sleep, and if you could turn off the flashing lights and the beeping machines, I know I will be okay for surgery. Also, I need to leave after the surgery, so could you get me a taxi to the airport? I'm going home."

I thought I saw the doctor laugh. If my condition was laughable, I was sure I would survive. I was irritated as the hospital staff did not take my wishes to heart. The damn beeping and lights continued. When I received the coffee, it was only a sip, and it was cold. Bill held the cup. Bill ignored my need for privacy, so I could sleep and fart. Bill sat beside my bed and dismissed my suggestion that he should drive home without me.

I became uncomfortable and constipated by the medication. I would have to stop them soon. When I did sleep, I was haunted by dreams of Pauly shooting the children and ignoring my desire to protect them.

My surgery was delayed by a day due to a change in surgeons, further annoying me. My mind was clearing as the pain medicine decreased. Bill was ever-present. It was heartbreaking watching him sit there, knowing he probably wanted to be with Myrna. I was sure the revelations that she was never faithful to him would not stop his love and care for her.

On the morning of the surgery, I finally said what I thought we both must be thinking. "Bill, go home. I'm sure you would rather be at home, and I would rather be alone. I have taken care of myself for over twenty years. I don't need a babysitter, and I know where your duty lies, so do us both a favor and leave. I'm going home after this anyway. It won't be long before the water is cool enough to begin fishing, and I need to prepare for the Southern fishing season."

Bill ignored me and just laughed. I was furious. An hour before I went to surgery, two men asked to talk to me. They were investigating the abduction and eventual death of my captor. Bill was still sitting in his chair next to the bed. He asked if they needed him to leave. They said no. They had a couple of questions. I still didn't know how I survived and how Pauly died. I was worried that they would think I killed him.

"Dr. Alexander, I'm detective Ramon, and this is detective O'Connor from the FBI. We have video surveillance of the actual abduction near Yellowstone. There was some misunderstanding about how you became involved. The mother of the little girl who was the object of the kidnapping came to the Sheriff's department and told us that you asked Tainter to take you and not the little girl. Is that correct?"

"Yes, but what difference does it make? She was so young and so scared. I knew Paul Tainter would kill her."

Bill sat up and watched us, while the agent continued his interrogation. "When you were getting fuel later in the day, why didn't you say something? We could see you on the camera in the store. You didn't say anything then either."

"Are you thinking I was involved in this?"

"No, but sometimes in periods of stress—" Detective Ramon appeared sympathetic, but the other was writing and shaking his head in disbelief.

I interrupted him. "Did you think after a day I had Stockholm Syndrome—after only a day? I don't believe it. Pauly waited until a person getting gas was present, and he would show me his gun. He knew I would not do anything because he gave me every indication that he would kill them. It was always a child. Do you know how badly I wanted to run or tell the attendant I was a prisoner? I knew Pauly would kill someone if I didn't do what he asked. They were kids. I would have been just as guilty."

"Dr. Alexander, we're sorry to bother you, and this is what we thought. Now, on the last night, can you tell us what happened when you got to the end of the road?"

"Pauly and I heard a radio report that they were closing in. He decided to go up into the woods for the night. I was so tired, and my driving was getting bad. When we realized it was the end of the road, I think he planned to kill himself. His erratic behavior and desperate choices over the last hour made me think he was going to kill me as well. I thought I would try the chance to survive by jumping off the side. I stepped back as he changed the gun from one hand to the other. I know I heard the gunfire twice, and my arm hurt. I thought he'd hit my arm. I don't remember much else."

"That's all we need. Thank you."

"So, did Pauly kill himself?" I still could not comprehend the final moments of the abduction.

"It appears he shot at you, then slipped and accidentally shot himself as he fell. His head hit a tree, and he died of a broken neck. As far as we can see, you're innocent. In reality, you're a hero in all aspects. We'd like to interview you more in a few days."

"I'm leaving here after my surgery. You can call me. I don't have a phone anymore, but when I do, you can call me then." They reached the door, and I remembered what bothered me. "Sir, I would appreciate it if you would keep my identity quiet. If they need to refer to me, find something to say about me other than I am a grandmother. I'm more than that."

"Yes, ma'am. You certainly are."

A nurse entered my room and told me the surgery would be in thirty minutes and asked if I needed anything. "I need to use the bathroom. I want to use a real bathroom."

Both she and Bill helped me sit and stand as they guided me to the small room next to mine. Bill had heard the men, and now he knew what I had done to save the little girl and the other boy. Bill peered at me and shook his head. He reminded me that I didn't need to be a hero. "Heroes don't last long as horse doctors, Hayles," was drilled into the interns. I could see he was thinking just that when the two nurses entered my room.

"It's time to meet your surgeon. Somebody's sure lookin' after you."

"Pardon?"

"You got the top dog doin' your arm today. Somebody knows somebody." The nurse turned to Bill. "Dad, you can come as far as the double doors, then you'll have to say goodbye."

I laughed, which was the first time I had laughed in days. "Come on, Daddy."

Bill smiled, but I think he was embarrassed. "To see you smile is almost worth it—almost."

I was left in my bed and rolled down the hall. Several people turned and gave me a thumbs up or a thank you. I was confused. I was also becoming drowsy. I saw Bill talking to a gray-haired man. They seemed to know each other. Bill brought him over to my bed. "Hayley, this is Dr. Greg Bennet, who flew up from Denver to do your surgery. He and his wife are longtime friends of Myrna and me. They have a cabin on the other side of the lake."

The man smiled warmly and told me not to worry. "No more hero stuff, young lady. You need to finish writing a book, I hear."

I knew it would be impolite to tell him I was leaving for home when discharged from the hospital. I thanked him for coming all this way, and Dr. Bennet replied, "Don't thank me, thank Bill. He saved my daughter's horse many years ago. I'm just happy to return the favor. We'll see you in a few hours, and I'll talk to you again."

Bill held my hand briefly, and I was wheeled through the double doors. I tried to say, "Bye, Dad," but I don't think anyone understood my joke.

CHAPTER 20

A very obnoxious nurse was asking me to cough. I didn't have the energy or the will. I tried to ignore her, but she told me I couldn't leave unless I did what she said. Did they call a cab? Was I finally getting out of here? If a cough got me away from this hellhole, I would cough. But, oh no, I had to cough several times.

"Can you call me a cab?"

"No, but you are getting a ride for sure. You're a celebrity, you know."

Finally, some respect. "I need to get to the airport."

The nurse rolled her eyes and said I had a first-class ticket back to my room. "Don't push your celebrity status. You aren't going anywhere today."

Like hell. "Thank you for what you have done, but I'm pretty sure you may have the wrong information."

Two male nurses entered the room where I was recovering from anesthesia and took my gurney back to my room. This time the people in the corridors clapped as I went past them. I could not understand why. I re-entered my room which now had two vases with flowers. Bill and the surgeon were sitting chatting and drinking coffee. I was not happy, but I was raised to be polite no matter what. The problem was that I had lost my filter.

"I want to thank you for fixing my arm, sir, but what I desperately want is some effing coffee."

Bill got up and left the room. The surgeon said my fracture repair went well, and I should have full use of my arm in a few weeks. He said I had to spend at least two days in the hospital, and then I would be transferred back to Colorado, and he would see me at Bill's.

I don't think so. It occurred to me that I had to pay the hospital, and then the worst news was I didn't know where my credit card was. How would I pay for all this? I panicked. Now I was going to be the one asking for help.

"Sir, I may have a small problem." I can grovel with the best of them when I know I'm wrong, but I wasn't sure if I was wrong or not. Maybe Bill had my credit card. He re-entered the room.

He brought me a cup of coffee—finally. I whispered in his ear, "Do you have my credit card?"

Bill smiled and nodded. "Sadly, it's of no use here."

I was confused. I sipped the coffee and promptly threw it up. Bill cleaned up the vomit and called a nurse who helped change the bed linen while the surgeon helped me sit up.

I couldn't remember the surgeon's name, but I think he understood my confusion and asked to speak to me privately. When even Bill left the room, the doctor sat on the bed. "Hayley, I don't know what happened to you and Bill, but he feels horrible, and he is trying to make it up to you. Bill told me about his diagnosis and how you were helping him, and something went wrong. It's not the story that he wants from you. Bill needs you. He chose you to help him.

"Bill's not just an old man who's dying. He isn't just an icon in his profession or his community. He's so much more than that, but I'll let him tell you. That story is not for me to tell. I can see you're cut from the same cloth. What you did to save those children is remarkable, and Bill knew you would understand his intentions. I know you'll write about him without damaging anyone in the process.

"So, I'm asking you to cut him some slack. You're coming from a concussion, and I know you're a bit confused. Let Bill help and guide you for a few days, and then if you both decide to part, well, so be it. By the way, I think you have me by several years. My name is Greg, and I'll see you in a few days. I need to get to the airport. Do we have an understanding?"

Nope. "Yes, sir." Smile and nod and let him think he is in control.

Then Greg kissed me and walked to the door.

"Greg, thanks for what you did. I'm sorry I am being such a pain. I guess I don't do the patient thing well."

"A bit of an understatement." He did not smile.

Chapter 21

I spent two more days in the hospital. Bill was there every morning and stayed until late. He decided it was an excellent time to introduce me to more of the classics. Bill read parts of Homer's Iliad, Chaucer's The Canterbury Tales, and the more modern Ayn Rand's Atlas Shrugged from an iPad. He read excerpts and pointed out what he thought was important about their place in history and the evolution of society and literature.

He asked me questions and never corrected me or disagreed. I knew my answers didn't always make sense. At some point, instead of answering by referencing Buck Owens, I switched to Dolly Parton.

"Well, that's a step," was his only comment. We both regained our sense of humor. Of course, I was much funnier, and I made him laugh, which was a change since his discovery of the letters in my duffel bag. He never commented about them while we were at the hospital.

The FBI agents came back and asked if I wanted to go public with my name and role in the abduction and days that followed. I declined, but they had a letter from the local department saying I was a hero, and my deeds would not be forgotten. I was credited with saving the lives of the children and possibly more.

I thanked them and explained that I was not given a choice. I was unlucky enough to be in the wrong place at the right time. The men and women who risk their lives daily and choose to do so are my heroes. Blah, blah, blah, but it was true. This was a small adventure in my dull and regular life that I was happy never to leave again—ever.

I knew I was departing from the hospital, and it was time to pay the piper. I was now up and walking, so I ambled downstairs to the billing office. I told the man sitting at the desk my name and asked for the final account. I steeled myself and prepared to take a vow of poverty while he stared at his computer screen and then excused himself, stood, and left the room.

He returned with a check for sixty-two dollars and handed it to me. I was confused. Obviously, something was wrong. I gazed at the check and then at him. He knew my thoughts. "Your bill has been paid. You're free to go. There was an overpayment of sixty-one dollars and ninety-nine cents. That penny will haunt me, but the hospital director said to make it an even sixty-two."

"Can you tell me how much the original bill is?"

He went back to his screen. "Including the ambulance ride, it came to a little over fifty-eight thousand. The surgeon waived his fee, so I don't know how much that was."

"Did I get the lights and siren fee removed as well?" I remembered little of the ambulance ride, but I remembered asking them to turn those off.

The man behind the desk shook his head. "There's no extra fee for the lights and siren in our service. I saw you when you arrived, and you got all the bells and whistles, so don't try to make this any cheaper. Now get out of here before I find reasons to charge you more. You have many friends in this community. I know who you are and what you did. Scram."

I returned to my room, where Bill sat with clothes from my suitcase. "Can I help you dress, or do you want a nurse?" He smiled at me as he asked.

"I think I'll take one more day of dignity. You'll get your chance when I leave the hospital. Save your eyes while you can. It will be an ugly scene soon enough."

Why hospitals make exiting patients ride in wheelchairs is beyond me. If they cared about their patients, they would ensure they were competent to walk before leaving the building. As I entered the corridor, I was cheered and high-fived by several people. At the entrance stood the mother and daughter I defended and prevented from abduction by Paul Tainter. That is when both Bill and I had a moment. All four of us were in tears. We exchanged contact details. They presented me with a new phone, and our pictures were taken by the hospital and law enforcement authorities.

I knew this would happen, so I practiced my Spanish and asked the little girl if she had seen Old Faithful. She hadn't, but they were leaving today, and they promised me they would send a picture of them at the geyser. She hugged me, and her mother thanked me for saving her daughter's life. I asked her to ensure her daughter didn't squander that life and for them both to find joy in the small things.

I stood up from the wheelchair, turned, and told the nurses how sorry I was for my initial rude behavior. They laughed, and then I was presented with a travel mug full of coffee.

Bill had to help me into the truck. He reached across and buckled my seatbelt. Then he turned to me and said, "Prepare yourself."

"For what?" I was worried.

"To be cared for and to accept help. You're not going home. You'll be with me until you are well and the book's written—one month or a year. I'm holding you to our agreement. We may argue, and we may even yell at one another, but we will see this out. Am I clear?"

I said nothing. I was in no position to argue. I knew I could not function three days after major surgery. I would not be able to type, but I could use my dictation app on my computer, and I could edit with one hand.

"Bill, can I ask if you arranged the payment for my hospital bill?"

"It was a community effort. Many people helped. It wasn't only me. You know you're a hero. What you did was exceptional—very foolish, but extraordinary and totally stupid. Still, if I could have, I would have done it myself. Are you comfortable? I can change the seat angle."

"No, I'm fine. Thank you. Bill, I'm sorry for everything. I didn't mean for you ever to see those letters. I'm sorry for whatever I said at the hospital too. I wasn't thinking very well. Thank you for Greg too. He was a great help. I'll help you all I can until you are happy. I won't leave unless you ask me to leave."

"Hey, I know. I do understand. I guess I had my suspicions, but I didn't know it was my brother. I thought it was one of the men from Harrogate's. My brother?" Bill shook his head.

"I never asked, but how did your brother die?"

"Yeah, how did he die? It was shortly after Myrna went up there. I think she went to get anything incriminating. It said suicide on the death certificate. I guess he couldn't live without her. Funny that. Then to find out that my brother killed the one man who was kind to me and taught me more than anyone." Bill leaned forward and put his forehead on the steering wheel. I reached across, and with my free hand, I patted his shoulder.

I would have given anything not to let Bill see those letters. I didn't tell him about the pictures. Myrna was beautiful, and she was one of the rare women who could pull off those artistic nude shots, but unless there were negatives, I hoped Bill never would know.

The one subject he didn't mention was his daughter's true parentage. It would never be part of the book, so it was not something I would ever discuss. I would wait and see if Bill addressed the topic. Life has not been kind to my friend. Our lives were so similar in many ways. While we dedicated our lives to our profession, our personal lives were less than perfect. Would I change this? I knew my answer, but I wondered about Bill.

CHAPTER 22

B ill asked if I minded pushing through. Sitting up for hours killed me. However, I knew he wanted to get home and see about Myrna. I felt so sorry for this man. I could not imagine loving and caring for someone who hated me. Then I thought about my kids when they were teenagers and quietly laughed.

"What?" Bill glanced over as we drove into his driveway around midnight.

"Nothing." Not going there tonight.

"It must have been something. You were almost asleep, and you smiled."

"I was thinking about my kids and something they said. It was nothing. More to the point, Billy Boy, if I don't get to the bathroom in two minutes, it might get ugly."

Bill quickly helped me out of the car and into the house. I looked down, and we realized I couldn't unbutton my jeans. He reached down, unbuttoned, unzipped them, spun me around, and pointed me to the bathroom. "The rest is up to you. I have my limits."

"Actually, I don't think you do." Now there was some truth.

As politely as he could, and ever the gentleman, Bill helped me into a nightgown. We were both exhausted. He put water by my bed, asked if I needed anything, kissed me on my forehead, and headed to bed.

If I thought I could go through a trauma like I had experienced and then just get on with my life, I was mistaken. I had not adequately slept since before my abduction. I was experiencing flashbacks and nightmares. I had heard of the term "post-traumatic stress syndrome." It became a popular term to describe how men and women who returned from war reacted to their experiences.

I was fine during the day when I could rationally process my memories and thoughts. Still, when I slept, my dreams were vivid variations of what I had seen and done. Pauly was my constant companion. He had a gun, made me rob banks, and drive off cliffs to get away, or he would kill children.

At the hospital, the nurses would wake me up and help me orient and get back to sleep. I had sleeping medication, but my lack of REM or dream slumber made me crave sleep. I was rather vocal, and I was glad I slept away from Bill, so he didn't hear it and would get his needed rest.

Bill told me he had an appointment to see his regular doctor in the morning. He should have gone last week. I was sure Bill would also include a visit with Myrna, and I wondered if he would ever attempt to confront her.

Bill's weight and color had improved since I first came to Colorado, when I was reunited with my old boss. We both knew as welcoming as it was, it was only temporary. He was receiving vitamin injections and an iron infusion.

Sometime during the night, Bill knocked on my door. "You okay, Hayles?"

"Yes, thanks. Go back to bed."

"Your light's on. Can I get you anything?"

"No, I'm fine." I was not. I'd just woken with possibly my second or third night-terror. I decided to stay awake and turned on the lamp on the bedside table.

"Do you mind if I come in?" Bill was persistent.

"No, you can come in, but I'm fine." I was slightly embarrassed.

"I'm not." He entered the room hesitantly. "Do you mind if I lay down next to you?"

"I guess. Are you okay? Are you sick?" I was alarmed. This was strange.

"I'm having trouble sleeping, and I thought if I maybe had someone nearby, it might help. I liked sleeping next to you at the cabin. I won't do anything. I just enjoyed hearing you breathe."

"Sure. That might be nice. I'm kind of having problems too."

Bill lay down on my blanket and pulled the quilt over himself. I reached up and turned off the light, and when I woke, Bill was gone. It was nine in the morning. There was a note with instructions for heating the breakfast. He said he was also going to the grocery store and should be back by eleven. If I needed anything, please call him.

I was able to dress in shorts, a short-sleeved shirt, and no bra. It was ugly, but that would be my life for a few more days. I would see the surgeon in two days. I opened my laptop and downloaded a backup from my old phone onto my new one. I would have to go to town to get a new sim card with my old number.

I saw emails from my kids asking how the surgery went. They offered to care for me if I would come to their places in Texas. I wrote back and thanked them. I told them I would have phone contact sometime today or tomorrow and gave them Bill's home number if they needed to contact me urgently. "Don't worry. I'm fine and safe." I lied. Who would tell their kids they had PTSD? Not me.

Bill returned with sweatpants, food, and a dressing on his inner elbow. I tried to help bring in the bags of food but was told to sit on the porch and behave. When he finished with the groceries, he brought lemonade and a sandwich. We both sat on Adirondack chairs and ate our lunch. We were still tired from the last few days, but Bill wanted to read to me. A thunderstorm was brewing, and we returned to the living room and watched the darkening sky. Bill read some Dickens, and I promptly fell asleep. I woke an hour later with a blanket over me. I searched for Bill, but he was gone. He returned later and said we would have a guest for dinner. Bill's friend, Martin Goodman, was coming for dinner. He and Bill were going fishing if the storm blew over, and we would have trout. Otherwise, it would be lamb.

"Either sounds good to me. Are you two capable of getting out onto the lake safely?" I got the look for that comment.

"Hayley, don't test my limits." He brought out some wine to chill in the refrigerator. "Did you have wine before we left? I seem to be missing a bottle."

I remembered the wine Martin and I consumed the night Bill was off telling his kids about his diagnosis and why I was with him. When I moved in, Bill told me to have whatever was in the house.

"Uh, that would be me and Martin."

Bill replied, "Martin and me."

"Yeah, whatever. Nice drop."

Around four in the afternoon, Martin arrived and said the storm was gone, and he wanted to go fishing. He had a new outboard motor, and he wanted to try it out. The men left, and I decided to check any news on my computer. The hot news flash was about the death of the serial killer Paul Tainter. There was new evidence he had killed another woman shortly before he abducted me. I was still not named, but there was a picture of me leaving the hospital.

The men returned from fishing an hour or so later. Martin was so happy with his new engine, and both men caught three trout each. I attempted to help, but I was forced to sit and watch as they cooked and drank wine. Bill's mood had lifted. Bill told Martin about my ordeal. Martin didn't watch the news often and was unaware of the drama. I sensed Bill and Martin had discussed more than just the kidnapping, and when dinner was over, we sat on the couch and stuffed chairs in the living room.

Martin put his hands together between his knees and leaned in my direction. "Hayley, Bill told me about what happened. He mentioned you're having trouble sleeping. I don't want to interfere, but this was one of the things I dealt with in my job. I would like to suggest that you both get some counseling. Bill, I know you think it's just Hayley's problem, but you've also been through it. I can't imagine the guilt you must feel about the abduction."

Bill and I glanced at each other, and I could see Bill was surprised at the remarks. He probably thought I was the one with the problem, and he was just the guy picking up the pieces. From my perspective, Bill has had several great shocks and revelations over the last week. When he came into my room last night, I thought it was that he genuinely wanted the comfort of another person. Now, I wasn't sure if it wasn't to comfort me and help me get through the night.

I wouldn't respond in front of Martin, but it did remind me. Bill had received news that his wife was unfaithful again, and his daughter was not his child. Then his friend was abducted while he was sleeping in the truck. I sensed Bill and Martin might want to continue the conversation alone. My arm was sore, and I was weaning myself off the last pain meds. I thanked Martin for his observation and told him I would try to get some help and bid everyone goodnight.

My demons returned during the night. I knew there was no hope in sleeping. I didn't want to wake Bill, so I took the flashlight, went down to the shoreline, and sat on the bench. I don't know how long I was there when Bill came out and brought his jacket. He wrapped it around me and sat down next to me. I leaned into him, and we sat for some time in silence.

Bill finally spoke. "Hayley, Martin gave me the counselor's name if you're interested."

"Yeah, that might be good. And you?"

"I probably should, but considering my prognosis, I don't see the point."

I started to protest, but then I realized it was true. I might live for another twenty years. Bill maybe had a year's extension, but nothing would change for him. He would never abandon Myrna. Bill would never tell his kids they weren't biologically related. Possibly one or the other of Bill's children would get tested if a heritable link to Alzheimer's was ever established. Still, both Myrna and Bill would be dead.

"I'd like to get back to the book tomorrow if you don't mind." Bill's voice had a sense of urgency.

"Sure. We can talk, and I can record what you tell me." I could begin collecting the stories and writing them up later when I could use my arm. I wondered why such a humble man would want to write a book about himself and his work life. He led a double life, and he was so flawed. His personal life and his professional life were at odds. He controlled and directed his clinic and helped both employees and clients. At the same time, he appeared to be the pawn of his wife and children. The surgeon hinted there was more, but would I get to the truth of Bill O'Neal?

We returned to the house, and Bill asked if he could continue the sleeping arrangement. He was so polite, and he was pleasant company. There was nothing in it except the comfort of a human body next to one another. For a second night, I slept for more than a few hours without nightmares.

CHAPTER 23

Bill asked me if I would be all right if he went to town for a few hours. I knew he would visit Myrna, and of course, I said I would be fine. I no longer questioned this absurd devotion Bill had for his wife. They were both flawed. I asked him if I could look at some of his photograph albums. He brought some out and left for town. Standing at the door, Bill asked me if I was worried about being here alone.

"Bill, compared to my dreams, being awake and alone in a house is a cakewalk. I'll take the offer of the counselor, though. I must wait for my credit card, but that should be here soon."

I got a look of exasperation. "On the house. After all, you were working for me when it occurred. Hey, Angie and Tuck called. Your surgical case is doing well. I never said anything, but you did a bang-up job. I was impressed."

"You can thank the guy who taught me." I smiled. It was good to be talking again.

There was one album from his work. The one photograph that struck me was of Bill, standing in front of the office with his three partners, taken before I arrived as an intern. They looked so happy and innocent. All three were younger, and all had passed. Both Dr. Richards and Hamilton had children who had become vets, and now they owned and ran the veterinary practice. Bill was the last to retire. He mentioned he still attended the annual board of directors' meetings and went to the company social events. They occasionally asked him to consult on cases. I thought that the early days of his practice life would be an excellent place to begin.

As I progressed through that album, I found pictures of the initial years of the practice. Bill and two nurses grooming a horse in a cast, and one with Bill standing next to a boy I did not recognize. The boy seemed to have Down's syndrome. There were pictures of the social events and family members. I even found a few of me attending to horses.

In the second album, there was a picture of Bill sitting alone and reading a book. He was outside of a stall, and I was reminded of how he would watch horses that were on intravenous fluids, so we interns could get dinner or simply get away for a few hours. The other vets in the practice would admonish Bill for letting the interns off, but Bill said he needed to finish a book, which was the only way he would get some time alone.

There were several pictures of Bill holding a baby. Some included his children standing next to him, so I knew it wasn't his child. Who was this baby?

I heard a knock at the front of the house. "Hello? Hayley?"

I went to the screen door and saw a fifty-ish athletic woman with blond hair dressed in a tennis outfit. I had no idea who this woman was.

"Hi. I'm Greg's wife—your surgeon. I'm Cathy. I wanted to come over and introduce myself. Is now a good time? I can come back, but I brought some morning tea."

I detected an accent. "Hi, no, please come in. Morning tea? Are you from the UK or Australia?"

"New Zealand. It's so lovely to meet you. I know you wanted to remain anonymous, but Greg told me about you and what you're doing for Bill, and I wanted you to know we're so happy you're here helping him. We think the world of that man. Oh my, I do tend to rabbit on. Let me help you." She went to the kitchen and began making tea and coffee while heating some sweet rolls she'd brought. "Greg told me about your arm and how you broke it. I knew you had to be someone special to have Bill invite you, and despite what the neighbors are saying, I want you to know that Greg and I admire you, and we're here to help you."

So, what are the neighbors saying? I could barely respond before Cathy began again.

"You know we've been coming up here for the last fifteen or more years. Our kids were so young, and Bill and his children would take them water skiing and fishing and give us time to be alone. He was so good with our kids when they were little. Now, who would have them? Thankfully, the oldest, Tiff, is off to college, and her brother and sister, the twins, will be gone soon. I can't wait to be an empty nester. I don't know what my friends say, but I say good riddance. Do you have children?"

I nodded. That was all I was allowed to interject. "Of course you do. Greg talked to them after the surgery."

This was news to me. "Cathy, would you like some milk in your tea?"

"Oh yes, but let me get it. I know Bill has some for when I come. Isn't he just the nicest man? It is so sad that his wife—did you know Myrna when she was, I mean before—well, I think you know what I mean."

"You mean before she lost her…" I was going to say marbles. "I mean, was diagnosed with Alzheimer's."

"Marbles? Yes, that was what she said when she told us. She flat out told us at dinner one night, and it was apparent that Bill didn't know. The look on that poor man's face. I tell you. Greg and I wanted to slip under the table and crawl away, but I guess that wasn't the worst. She began to tell us that her kids weren't Bill's, that she never loved him anyway, and Bill was poisoning her. We felt so sorry for him. Of course, none of it was true, but we felt horrible. We knew this was not how most people act when they"—she paused—"lose their marbles, but we think she was mad at him for some reason.

"It wasn't but two months later that she attacked Bill and stabbed him. Bill wanted to keep her in the home, and he planned to hire someone, but his kids would not hear of it. They feared for their mother! Can you believe it? They said their father was a thorn in their mother's side and had driven her to madness. Who knows what goes on inside a person's mind? Can I cut that for you?" Cathy didn't wait for an answer, took my Danish, and cut it in half.

"Was Myrna—" but again, she interrupted me.

"A little different? Oh, yeah. She was way different. She would leave for a week at a time and then come back and rant at Bill. The kids were trained to take her side. When they left for college, she would leave and be gone for most of the summer. We weren't here in the winter. We only came in the summer. She would be here alone all day. The first few years were good. She was building the house, but when that was over, she lost her purpose in life. Bill would be at work, and we think that might have been part of the problem. I don't know, but being a vet or a doctor's wife is like being a widow. The bad news is that you can't move on. You're kind of stuck. That's why I have so much going on."

Hang a medal on both Bill and Greg Bennet. Sheesh, this woman never stopped talking. Which was worse? The nonstop chatter or the threat of a stabbing.

Finally, Cathy looked up and realized she had not let me finish a sentence. "Where are my manners? How are you doing? It must have been horrific riding around with that murderer. I can't tell you how upset Bill was when he called Greg and told him that your arm was fractured, you had a concussion, and how worried he was that you might have permanent brain damage. Still, I can see you have," she paused and then laughed, "all your marbles."

There was another knock at the door. A familiar woman stood at the door. "Hi, I'm Lorna Westover. I live down the way. I'm Myrna's friend." She stared at Cathy, and the two women gave each other a knowing glance. "Am I interrupting something?" Lorna walked in without waiting for an invitation.

Cathy was quick to respond. "Hayley was just telling us about her horrific kidnapping. I know you want to hear the gory details as much as me. Go on, Hayley."

I could hear Bill correcting her grammar, "As much as I."

"Actually, I can't talk about it. There are some details that the FBI has asked me not to discuss. I'm so sorry."

Lorna grimaced and replied, "Or are you doing a deal with a news station? Your story would be worth some money, and that's for damn sure."

"Lorna, I wish. I could probably make a killing, but why do that when I can write my own story?" I pointed to my arm. "Stand by, and you can read the book."

I needed a break. Both women realized they would not get any gory details this morning. I finally got them to the door. I laughed as I remembered Bill warning me there were worse things outside the house than bears. Cathy was on my side, but Lorna would not abandon Myrna for Bill's new girlfriend. I admire loyalty, and as they left, I said, "Thanks for coming and for your loyalty to Myrna. She needs all the help she can get. I'm sure Bill appreciates it. We should all get together more often. I need time to recuperate, and then I'll have you back." I think they realized that visiting would be by invitation next time.

CHAPTER 24

B ill went to the kitchen and saw the dishes cleaned and stacked. "Did you have someone in when I left?"

"My two new besties, Cathy and Lorna." I waited for a response.

Bill leaned against the kitchen counter. "Your ears are still there, and I don't see any strips of hide missing. That must have been interesting."

"You were right about worse things out there than bears. I'm hoping that when I said I would invite them over as soon as I felt better, they got the message. What are my chances?" I tried to look innocent, but I had to suppress a laugh.

"No hope. How does soup sound for lunch?"

"I'm not really hungry. Cathy bribed her way into the house with a sweet roll."

"Hayley, Dr. Hendrix is the man that Martin suggested. I made an appointment with him for tomorrow after your checkup with Greg. It's in the city, so we need to leave early.

Will you be up to it? We can postpone the therapist but not Greg."

"No, I'll do both. I can't rely on you to sleep with me forever."

"No, I definitely have a short expiration date on me." Bill cocked his head and smiled.

I went over to Bill and hugged him with my free arm. "Bill, I didn't mean it like that. I know you are doing it as a sense of duty."

He didn't say no. He just hugged me and said he owed me. Despite everything, that hurt. I didn't want to be an obligation. I turned and said I would rest, and then I'd like to go over the photo album with him. I made it to my bedroom before the tears came. The concussion and the recent drama made me more sensitive.

I took a quick nap, washed my face, and returned to the living room. Bill was sitting on the couch and looking through the albums. He was smiling as he looked at pictures of his past. He patted the seat next to where he sat. This allowed me to rest my arm on the end of the couch. I asked him to talk about the album I had perused when he had gone to town.

I pointed to the picture of him holding the baby. "When was this? Whose baby is that? It seems you have a lot of pictures of this baby."

He stared at the first picture and said nothing. Was this his love child? This baby was something to him. I quietly reached into my pocket and turned on my recorder.

"I'll tell you everything, but I know you will figure out what can go in the book and what can't. That would have been after you left our practice. So, you remember Tammy Chandler?" Bill smiled and fingered the picture.

I did remember her, but where was her photograph? "Was she the lady you hired to ride with the interns and was a whiz at handling horses?"

"Yes. Tammy worked for us for about five years. I remember the first day she began work. She was a miracle. The partners were reluctant to hire anyone for nursing duties. After all, our interns were cheap labor in those days." Bill ran his finger over the edge of the picture of him holding the baby.

Tammy was married to an idiot. He knocked her around quite a bit. This was after you left. I think she was single when you knew her. Anyway, by then, the partners all fought over who would have her ride with them for the day. Mainly we sent her with the new interns to keep them from making fools of themselves. She educated them, and I remember Mr. Himes said he was not happy to get an intern when he called for an appointment, but he would accept them if Tammy came. We had several "Tammy clients" on our roster.

Tammy was as respected as much as the partners. She was something else, and she saved everyone's bacon at one time or another. I remember castrating a colt once, and when I finished and was packing up, Tammy quietly came over holding both testicles and suggested that one of the testes was the epididymis and not the testicle. It was huge, and I completely missed the real testicle. We opened the mass, and she was correct. We returned to the still sleeping colt and gave him more anesthesia. I reopened the incision and found the testicle at the end of a very long piece of the epididymis. The client was none the wiser. I remember telling her she could name her price. I owed her. She laughed and said a raise would be nice.

She got the raise and several more after that. The whole clinic went to her wedding, and that was when we knew Tammy wasn't the goddess that we all thought she was. It took two seconds for us to realize she was marrying a controlling jerk. He had returned from the armed forces, and he wore his uniform to the ceremony. We initially thought what a great match they would be. When she danced with anyone other than him, he went ballistic.

She returned to work a week after her honeymoon and had a black eye. I took her on a call and tried to talk to her, but she wouldn't discuss the situation. She told me to mind my own business—end of discussion. By that time, we were equals. I was her boss, but she was treated like a partner. She even attended many of the partner meetings. She essentially had four fathers who loved and cared for her, and we all saw the train wreck and tried to help her, but you know love does crazy things.

I shook my head, thinking of my marriage and then Bill's. "Don't I know that." Bill shook his head.

Anyway, several months later, Tammy made the long-awaited and dreaded announcement that she was pregnant. I remember the chorus of groans from the partners when she told us. She said she would work until a few weeks before the due date and return a week or two after the birth. We had no maternity leave policy as the number of female employees was almost nil.

The partners decided to allow her a month off, and we would give her half-pay during that time. She declined.

She quietly told me that her husband had lost his latest of several jobs, and they needed her income. The marriage was disintegrating by the week. He saw other women when he wasn't working or knocking her around at night.

We tried to get her to leave for the child's sake, but again, Tammy told us to leave her alone. She was handling it. She and her husband saw a marriage counselor, and things were much better. She said Jake was now employed at a lumber yard, and he was painting a room in preparation for the baby.

Tammy was young and only had the basics of obstetrical care during the pregnancy. There was no need. She did everything she should do and stopped drinking and ate well. We had a huge office party when she began her maternity leave. The partners bought her a stroller and a car seat. Even our wives helped with selecting baby items and attended the sendoff.

Tammy was so pleased that she even had tears. She quietly asked me to be the godfather of the baby. Tammy had opted to have the sex be a surprise. I was pleased that she had invited Myrna and me to be involved. That was an awkward moment. Tammy had picked our office manager, Dot Webster, as the godmother. I knew Myrna wouldn't care. We were building our new house, and it was almost done. She was busy and only reluctantly attended the clinic baby shower.

A week later, Tammy gave birth to a beautiful baby boy with Down's syndrome. Daniel William Jensen was a loving, happy child. He was adored by us all at the clinic. It was a different scene at home. Tammy stopped by the clinic and took me aside. She asked me to honor my pledge to care for Daniel if anything happened to her.

We begged her to leave. Myrna and I were moving into our new house, and I offered our former home to her until we sold it. She declined and was still trying to save the marriage. Tammy returned to work and had daycare arranged with an older couple who loved the baby. I begged her to consider the baby's safety, but she ignored our pleas.

Several months later, she didn't show up for work. She had called in sick once or twice, but she never failed to call when she could not work. There was no call. Dot drove over to her house and found several sheriffs, a fire truck, and two ambulance vehicles surrounding the house. Dot called the clinic immediately, and I came over.

Tammy was still alive, she even talked, but she was severely wounded. Dot was allowed to see her as Tammy entered the ambulance. Tammy was hysterical, and when she saw Dot, she asked her to take Daniel. She died of a ruptured liver and spleen before entering the hospital.

I arrived as they were taking Tammy's husband into custody. The baby was bruised and crying. He was taken to the hospital in another ambulance along with Dot. Dot was in her sixties. Her husband had been diagnosed with cancer. She was in no position to care for the baby. Daniel was examined and found to have a broken arm. That's when I met Greg Bennet, your surgeon. I explained the situation and said I would be responsible for the child's care until relatives could be located.

Tammy's parents felt they were not in a position to care for an intellectually disabled child and declined to meet Daniel. Her husband was in jail, awaiting a trial. He would not tell authorities where his parents lived, so I was awarded temporary custody of Daniel. What was one more mouth to feed? It would be short-lived.

I stopped at the clinic and called Myrna to tell her about the baby and Tammy's passing. She was shocked and concerned until I mentioned bringing the baby home. That was when I learned about her lover and her pending departure.

I was dumbfounded. This had to be the worst day of Bill's life. "Bill, I had no idea. I'm so sorry. I can't imagine. What about the baby's arm?" Now I knew what Greg was getting at.

"Not one of my better days, that's for sure. You know some of it is embargoed." He went back to his story.

Well, I had a baby with a broken arm, a dead co-worker, and my wife said she was leaving me. I kept gazing at this poor, innocent baby. The fracture was several days old, and Greg said he thought it would heal well enough that it didn't need anything but support. He would re-evaluate the fracture in a few days. Dot's husband was in the throes of chemo, and I didn't want to burden her.

I remembered the Hastings out on Cedarcrest Road. They were foster parents, and I knew they currently had no children. I called them, explained the situation, and asked them to take the baby overnight, so I could go home and try to save my marriage. Dot ran to the store and got formula and diapers. I went back to Tammy's house. I explained to the sheriffs, who were still processing the murder scene that I needed the baby's clothes, car seat, and anything else that Daniel required in the short term. I had to wait outside, but the sheriff handling the forensics returned and gave me everything I needed for the next few days. I took Daniel to the Hastings' property and left him for the night.

I went home and pleaded my case to Myrna. The kids only had a few years to go before leaving for college, and I said I would do whatever it took to stop her from leaving. I promised Myrna that I would find a home for the baby. I would be home at six every night and every weekend. I would quit work, I would move away, and we could go to Europe or wherever she wanted if she would stay. She said she would consider it. I suggested we get counseling, and she declined.

She told me, "No amount of counseling would make me love you. I have never loved you."

You would think I would have fallen apart and gone and killed myself. The truth was that I always knew. I knew when our son was born that she used me. I knew my daughter wasn't mine. I didn't realize until last week it was my brother's child, but I knew the dates didn't match up. Our marriage was a sham, and yet, I still tried and prayed she might see something in me that would make her love me.

The harder I tried, the less she respected and loved me. So, for the kids' sake, she stayed. She began to take short vacations without the children. At least, that was what I thought she was doing.

He paused for a moment. "Hayley, I know you think I'm a fool, but I knew who I was married to, and I knew there was no place for me in her heart. I knew the kids were not mine, but just like I loved those kids, I loved Daniel."

I nodded and he continued.

So, I went back to work. The Hastings agreed to keep Daniel, and I paid them to care for him. I went to visit him every day I could. I maybe missed one day a week. I took care of all his needs. Daniel did have surgery to correct the fracture a few weeks later, and he also had heart surgery for a septal defect. I took him to baseball games and got him into special education programs.

Finally, the Hastings were too old to care for him. I placed him in an apartment with a boy with similar issues. He stayed there for a few years, but Daniel had numerous health issues, so I eventually moved him into the same facility where Myrna is now. I visit Daniel every day I am able, and at the same time, I check in on Myrna. Daniel is my focus. If it was only Myrna, I could walk away and never come back. I watched my parents as they negotiated their marriage. I knew my mother was unfaithful to my father, and I have sworn I would not be like them. I have never considered breaking my vows. I think I told you that.

I'm not embarrassed to say that you test my resolve. If I was younger and wasn't so ill, I don't think we would be having this conversation. You can, and I hope you find someone who will love you. I suggest that you open your heart and see what you have to give and get on with your life. I wish it were me, but...

"Well, that's not going into the book. My arm is killing me. I need to change positions."

Bill stood and suggested I lay flat on the couch while he fixed dinner. As he turned to the kitchen, I asked if I could meet Daniel.

"I'll think about it."

My demons returned that night. This time it was Daniel that I had to protect. I know I must have talked in my sleep. I tried to resume my sleep, but it was even worse.

Pauly wanted me to run over Bill and Daniel, and then he wanted me to drive up a steep bridge which I was sure was missing a large section of road. The sun was in my eyes, and I panicked. I would drive off the side of the bridge. Pauly was going to shoot me, and then he saw Bill walking up the walkway, and he pointed the pistol toward him. I cried out and tried to get the gun out of his hand, but I was restrained.

I woke up and realized Bill was holding my hand and trying to talk to me. I was somewhere between frightened and relieved. I stopped fighting his restraint and smiled. "Whoa, that was a doozy. You just saved me from driving off a bridge." I took several deep breaths and then calmly said, "Thanks, you can go now."

Bill shook his head. "Not a chance, sweet pea. I get more sleep when you aren't ranting. Scoot over."

Gladly. "Bill, I don't want to impose, but can we make this sleeping arrangement a regular thing until I get my brain sorted out?"

"With pleasure, old girl." He took my hand and squeezed it. We didn't let go.

CHAPTER 25

"Dr. Bennet will see you now." A plump woman with a birthmark on her forehead escorted me into Greg's office. I had a radiograph done several minutes ago. The resulting image was on his computer. He was pleased and felt that the fracture was healing nicely. He asked how I was doing otherwise and mentioned his wife had been to see me. "Cathy sure likes to talk."

"Yes, she does. Bill and I would like to have you over for dinner when I'm a little more useful." I thought about how that sounded.

"Oh, so you settled your differences?"

I laughed and nodded. "Oh, yes. Once Bill realized he was a mere mortal man and I was a woman, he fell right into line. Or something like that."

Greg nodded thoughtfully. "Hayley, I know you're joking, but I know Bill well enough to know he could use a little TLC in his next few years. I don't know how long you'll be around, but Bill deserves to be loved, treated with respect, and generally placed on a pedestal. He's never discussed anything with me other than..." Greg paused and searched my face for recognition of a common problem.

"Do you mean Daniel? He told me yesterday. I was going through albums, and he explained what happened."

"Oh, good. So, you're aware of Daniel's father harassing Bill and all the trouble he's caused." Greg saw my face. "Or not. Damn, Bill's going to kill me. Please don't pay any attention to me. I'm sure it's been sorted. The bastard is probably in jail again anyway. Please don't leave, Hayley. I can see Bill loves you, and a particular episode aside, you appear to have made him so happy. He was beside himself when you were abducted."

"I'm guessing you're referring to my appalling behavior in the hospital? Thanks, I'm here for the long haul, and I'll only leave when Bill wants me to go. I promise."

"Are you getting any counseling? I know a guy who deals with traumatic events."

"I think Bill has me going there right now. I'm a pretty tough nut, but this has been rough."

"Okay, I'll see you back in three weeks, and Mrs. Childers has a handout on the exercises you can start next week. If Cathy has her way, we'll see you before then at the lake. Is Bill out in the waiting room?"

"Yes, unless he's done a granny dump." I laughed.

"Oh, I think you tested those limits at the hospital."

I blushed. "I am still embarrassed for what I said and wanted to say and didn't."

Greg walked out and greeted Bill. "Oh, good. You're still here. Hayley thought you might have run for the hills."

"Nope, still here. With all I have invested in her, she better stop sitting around feeling sorry for herself and get on with the project she has to complete. Thanks, Greg. Once again, I'm in your debt."

"I need to balance the books on that one. I'll get back to you." Greg shook Bill's hand.

"You've been saying that for ten years." Bill put his hand on my good arm and guided me out of the office.

We had a quick lunch, drove to another medical complex, and found the office of Dr. Morgan. His secretary immediately took us to a separate room where we waited. I guessed it was to hide from the stigma of mental health disorders.

I was escorted into a small room with two chairs. I laughed to myself, thinking that it was a couch shy of a proper psychologist's office. Dr. Morgan was an ancient, thin, bearded man dressed in a suit and bow tie. He had a twinkle and could have passed for a nineteenth-century psychiatrist.

I didn't waste time. I recounted what I had been through and described my nightmares and inability to get a good night's sleep. I told him that when Bill slept in the same bed—I ensured he understood it was non-sexual—I slept without the night terrors that I had when I was alone.

"So, why do you need me?" He laughed and could hardly speak without laughing after that.

I was surprised and slightly annoyed that I was seeing a therapist who could not control his mirth. "I want to stop dreaming of the cretin who's still controlling me in my dreams."

Dr. Morgan then had me detail my experience and repeat the two days of my abduction. He then prescribed a sleeping pill and suggested I consider joining a group of people who meet regularly. "If you talk about it, this will often free your mind of hidden thoughts. Dr. Alexander, I'm happy to help, but if you're not experiencing any fears during the day, I suggest you try this first. If you are still having issues, you come back and see me. I heard about what you did, and this visit is on the house."

I thanked him but thought it was essentially a waste of time.

"Oh, one more thing. Many of my clients have benefitted from equine therapy. It seems contact with horses helps, although I don't know why."

I smiled. I do.

Bill and I left for home. As we drove through his town, he slowed and turned into the facility where Myrna was living. "Want to meet my other son?"

"Yes. Will we see Myrna?"

"No. Myrna's in a different section of the facility. I told Daniel about you before we went to Montana, and he wants to meet you as well."

We entered the main building. It was clean and seemed cheerful. Everyone greeted Bill and said Danny was in the games room. "He's playing checkers and taking the other residents' money. The new heart medication appears to be helping. He's walking out in the yard and doesn't seem as tired this week."

I was surprised to see a middle-aged obese man with an oxygen line attached to a nasal apparatus. He smiled and waved to Bill as we entered. He stood up and left the woman he was playing with and strode over to Bill, pulling the small oxygen cylinder in a cart.

"Hi, Dad. Did you bring your girlfriend? Is this her?"

I could see Bill was embarrassed. "Daniel, this is Dr. Alexander. She's not my girlfriend. She is an old colleague I worked with before you were born."

"Why isn't she your girlfriend?" He seemed disappointed.

I reached for his hand and shook it. "Hi, Daniel. I'm Hayley, and I am your father's girlfriend. I'm a girl, and I am definitely his friend."

"Do you sleep in the same bed and do you—" but Bill cut him off.

"Daniel, that isn't a question you ask in polite company." Bill's face reddened.

I laughed, knowing Daniel was hoping for a simple answer. "Daniel, we aren't that kind of friends. I hear you're a good checkers player. Can I have a game with you sometime?"

"Can you come and watch me?" He turned to the woman sitting at the table, waiting for Daniel's return.

I whispered, "Is she your girlfriend?"

Daniel turned to me and quietly replied, "Yes, but don't tell her, or she'll run away."

We watched Daniel play two games, and Bill saw I was tired. We said our goodbyes and returned to the foyer. Bill left me for a minute, went down another corridor, and poked his head in the door. I heard a woman scream, and he quickly retreated. I saw the nurse shake her head.

We left the building, and I stayed in the truck while Bill entered the grocery store and returned with steaks and asparagus. We were silent, and I knew Bill was worried. Both his adoptive son and wife were in decline. He knew once he was dead, his son would have nobody to look after his needs. Again, it was a race to the end.

I decided to ask Bill about the long-term arrangements for Daniel's care later. Then there was this issue about Daniel's biological father. I didn't want to betray Greg's slip by mentioning a potential threat.

"Hayley, would you like to have a nap before dinner?"

"No, I think I slept enough on the way back. I'd like to look at another album if that's all right. Do you have one of the veterinary clinic and your partners? Bill, can we go to the clinic sometime? Do you ever go there?"

"All the time. I stop by every week or so. I still have a desk and occasionally consult with the current practice owners. I own a small piece of the practice, and I own the facilities. They extract their pound of flesh from me once in a while. I attend monthly board member meetings four times a year, and I try to attend their social events when I can." Bill found an album that contained a pictorial history of the veterinary clinic.

"Whoa. Can we go there tomorrow? I want to write about that as well."

"Sure, if you're up to it."

Bill cut my meat when we sat down to eat. He stared at me, and then when he finished eating, he cleared his throat. "I'm guessing you have some questions?"

"Of course. How did you do the meat? It was delicious."

"Hayley, Daniel's heart is deteriorating, and he's not a candidate for anything heroic. He might live for another year, and he might die tonight. Every day is a blessing. He is a kind, loving man, and his needs are minimal. I was sure he would outlive me. He's financially secure. If I go first, he will be the one person who will genuinely mourn my passing. Thank you for being so kind to him today. It means a lot to me."

I took a long time to swallow the last of the steak. I wiped my mouth. Bill took a new napkin and wiped my chin. "Thanks. He won't be the only one. I'm glad you have set this up, and I am surprised at what you have done to help your son over the years. I do have questions. Like, what happened to his biological father?"

"Yeah, I guess I should talk to you about that. Let me finish the dishes, and then we can do some couch time. Can I get you anything more?"

"No, but I can help with the cleanup."

Bill pointed to the living room. I was dismissed. He finished cleaning and poured himself a glass of wine. I declined any alcohol tonight and opted for pain meds. It had been a long day. Bill sat down, and there was a long pause before he began to recount the aftermath of Tammy's murder.

Jake Jensen was tried for Tammy's murder. He had a public defender. Jake had his armed services record and his former commander's letter of support. Jake didn't deny that he killed her, but he claimed it was self-defense, and it started with an argument over Daniel's parentage. Jake claimed that I was Daniel's father. That was never explored as genetic testing wasn't commonly done then.

Jake was given a fifteen-year sentence and was eligible for parole in ten years. I went every year, gave evidence, and attempted to block his early release. So, when he was paroled, he began to make my life hell. He discovered where we lived, and he began to stalk Myrna. Daniel was still living with the Hastings, and he then began to harass the couple as well. He insisted on seeing Daniel. He had no interest in the boy, but child support was taken out of his welfare check, and we thought he might try to kill the boy.

I decided to stop the child support by adopting Daniel with the hope of Jake going away. It almost worked. He did stop trying to see Daniel, but he continued to harass my family. I had a restraining order which was worthless. He was arrested several times but spent no jail time for breaches of the order.

When Myrna was placed in the care facility, and I was the only one left in the house, he began to leave threatening messages in the form of dead animals and excrement on my porch. I installed security cameras and then put a picture of him on my porch last year. He stopped any contact, and I received no messages.

I began to receive phone calls in the middle of the night. After the first one, I was able to record him threatening me. I went to the police, who then called him and told him they would be prosecuting him if the calls continued. I had his number blocked, but he used other people's phones to send messages. In short, it's been hell.

Bill took a sip of the wine and took the photo album I had been holding.

Why hadn't Bill warned me? "I'm guessing that was the reference to things more dangerous than bears lurking outside your house?"

"I know I should have warned you, but I was afraid you would leave. It's not just your writing skills, Hayley. I like your company."

I considered this twist in my time with Bill. "Do you have a picture of him in case I meet him? Shall we do some target practicing? For that matter, do you have a gun in the house?"

I had a shotgun in my house in vet school when some unwanted men came and harassed me. They were sure my kindness to them at school, where they worked as barn crew, indicated my desires. The gun was only used once when a rattler came into the yard, and in a ridiculously lucky shot, I blew its head off. Rumor spread, and my paramours ceased to explore my intentions. I have not used a weapon since.

"Hayley, I'm sorry. I have several rifles locked in my closet. My hunting days are over. I'm happy to teach you how to use them."

"Billy Boy, perhaps you never heard the story of my prowess with a firearm. Let me enlighten you." I described my experience with my snake and shotgun. Bill shook his head.

"Or maybe you could teach me. God, I pray we don't have to test our skills. At least Jake hasn't attempted to see Daniel. That would be the end of Jake for me. I'd kill the bastard if he tried to harm my son."

"Better get me a pistol. I don't think I will be any good with a rifle right now."

Bill feigned fright. "You aren't going within ten feet of me at night with a gun by the bed."

CHAPTER 26

I rose early and went to the office. I read the last story I had entered on my computer. I had several emails, and I typed replies with my free hand. I liked what I had discovered about Bill. He was a remarkable man. I knew I needed more insight into his work at the clinic. I hoped he would take me there today or tomorrow. I was anxious to see how the hospital had changed since I left almost thirty years ago.

After breakfast, I suggested we do one more story and head to the clinic. Bill agreed.

"Tell me about your last interesting case before you officially stopped doing regular practice." I turned on my phone recorder while Bill thought about which case he would recount.

"I guess it was Smokey." Bill chuckled, remembering the case. "Smokey belonged to Art Saunders. Do you remember him?"

I shook my head. "No, I don't."

He was an ornery cuss, and he was never pleased with our work. He made life tough for the interns. Smokey was a rope horse at the end of his athletic career. He was maybe fifteen hands and was a sorrel quarter horse. He was a great horse to work on if you stayed away from his mouth.

Art found him drooling one morning, and Smokey didn't touch his breakfast. So, Art called the clinic and said he would drop him off on his way to work. We had many quality interns, and we even had a surgical resident from Purdue. He's still with us. I don't think you ever met Tom McCann. Great surgeon.

The interns were warned about Smokey's reluctance to an oral exam. They drugged him and attempted to open his mouth to look for the usual grass awns. Smokey went up and over backward and hit his head. Luckily, it was on the rubber matting, and he appeared to be none the worse.

Tom McCann walked by, saw the drama, and offered his services. They took Smokey out on the lawn and tried again with the same result. That is when I returned from a call and observed the drama. I remember watching the spectacle from my car where I was writing up the bill on the horse I had attended that morning.

I remember shouting, "Better living through chemistry," to the group of vets and nurses. I could see they were struggling, and McCann said, "He's cleaned out the pharmacy, and this is the best response we have."

I let them work on him for an hour, then they decided to watch him for a while and see if there was a grass seed that dislodged. By the afternoon, it was evident that he was no better. So, we anesthetized him, and I took over as Tom was in surgery. Boy, did that horse need a dental? His teeth were razor sharp. So, we did that and searched for grass seeds and found none.

We sent him home, thinking his razor-sharp teeth had caused the problem. How many horses suddenly stop eating and drool from sharp teeth?

I shook my head.

Yep, rare as hens' teeth. But I fell for it. Two days later, I got a call from Art saying Smokey was no better. You can imagine how I felt. I'd lectured the interns many times about teeth and not to be fooled about sharp teeth causing weight loss or excessive salivation.

Smokey was brought back to the clinic, and I ordered radiographs of his head. We saw nothing on the radiographs, so we decided to scope him. This young intern felt under his jaw, and while there was no swelling or smell, there was a wet spot. I thought it might be an incidental finding. I prepared for Smokey's reaction to the endoscope, but, surprisingly, as long as we didn't try to open his mouth, he was fine.

We found nothing in his pharynx or esophagus. So, we decided to re-examine Smokey's mouth and tongue. Yep, another anesthetic. Still, we found no swelling or puncture marks, and the tongue was soft and supple. There had to be something. I went over the radiographs with the interns, and I still couldn't find a reason for this drooling.

We discussed all the possibilities, including botulism and other neurologic conditions. Finally, the newest intern, Shelby Cotter, walked up to the computer screen where the radiographs were displayed and flipped the images back and forth. She sat back down without saying anything. She was timid and never spoke up when we had more than two vets together. I was sure she was in the wrong field of veterinary medicine.

I left and went out on a call and took Shelby with me. She sat in the truck and didn't say a word. I had to ask her questions, and only then would she speak. It was torture. Finally, when we returned, she asked me to allow her to point out something on Smokey's rads.

"Dr. O'Neal, are you sure this isn't something?"

I remember how shy and soft-spoken she was in her first year with us. She pointed to a very fine sliver sitting in front of the throatlatch. It had to be metallic, and she outlined it on two other views.

You can imagine how I felt. That was it. It had a wavy appearance that caused it to blend into the complicated head radiographs. I allowed her to scrub in with me, and after two hours of probing and further radiographs, she found it. It was one side of a fine hairpin.

I took her under my wing until I stopped seeing regular clients. She stayed, and now she's a partner. Amazing what a little mentoring will do for a person. You'll meet her today.

I was pleased to hear we were going to my old stomping grounds. "Great. I'll try to decontaminate myself this morning, so give me some time. Gregg said I was allowed to shower now."

"Yeah, I better help you with that."

"Nice try, Billy Boy. Save your eyes and remember my age."

"I could close my eyes." He smirked.

"I'm going to let you do the buttons and zipper. If you're lucky, you can do up my bra."

"I'll be standing by, Hayles. I'm here to serve. I take my obligations very seriously."

"Yeah, right." It was nice that we were joking again. Hang the equine therapy. A good night's sleep with Bill by my side was all I needed.

CHAPTER 27

We arrived at the clinic just before lunch. Bill was warmly greeted by the staff, including the newest receptionist, Mary Lois. I was introduced and then ushered into the staff room. Some team members were preparing lasagna for a communal meal.

I noticed that a few staff members were intellectually challenged. They all came up to Bill, hugged him, and asked how Daniel was. One man, who was not visibly different from the mainstream employees, walked up to me and shook my hand vigorously. My whole body shook, and Bill had to intervene when he saw me grimace in pain. "Lenny, slow down, son. You're hurting Dr. Alexander. Lenny forgets how strong he is sometimes. Lenny's our gardener, and he keeps the property neat and tidy. Lenny rides the lawnmower."

"I took over for Daniel. Mary Lois says I'm as good as Daniel was. I was abused as a child and hurt my head in a car crash. Doc says I lack bounties. I've been looking for them, but they're gone for good." Lenny helped himself to lasagna.

I guessed bounties meant boundaries. "You know Lenny, I lost mine too. Bounties are overrated. They keep you from telling people what you really think. For instance, I really like you, but if I had bounties, I might just think it and not say it. Wouldn't that be a shame?"

"I'm not married. I can get married if you really like me, and we could sleep in the same bed." Lenny smiled as he looked at me and then laughed. "I'm fooling you. I have a girlfriend, but her parents won't let us sleep together."

I watched Bill observing this conversation while trying not to laugh.

"Um, Lenny, maybe some bounties are good. I still like you, but I'm too old for a good-looking, young man like you."

Bill intervened. "Lenny, she's taken." No explanation and no taken by who—just taken.

How did I miss this? I looked up at Bill with a smile. He nodded. "Our first employee was Daniel until he was too sick to work. He was still living with the Hastings, and another boy lived with him. We weren't saints. We employed them and gave them a wage, and the government gave us a subsidy for hiring them."

I was amazed. "Still holding back? Anything else I need to know for the book? Obviously, I need to go to the source. And who would that be?"

"Mary Lois knows where the skeletons are buried if that's what you mean."

The veterinarians started to trickle in for the staff lunch. Bill introduced me to three older vets and two younger ones. I met Dr. Cotter of the bobby pin escapade and others. There were no others that had been around when I was employed.

They'd heard on the grapevine I was staying out at Bill's and had been the woman abducted by the serial killer. They all thought I killed Paul Tainter and congratulated me. Tim Fergusson leaned across the table and asked Bill if he locked his bedroom door at night, knowing my capabilities.

Bill was amused, but I could see the tension in his voice when he told Tim, "You don't know the half of it. Don't ever mess with her."

Dr. Cotter asked to speak to Bill in private. He and she left the room. I noticed two male doctors glance at each other in a knowing way. Maybe they knew something I didn't know. Mary Lois entered the staff room, and everyone began to give her catcalls and wolf whistles.

The two male doctors asked me about my time at the clinic. They were both partners, as was Dr. Cotter. They knew I was one of the early interns, and I had stayed for over ten years, but they didn't know why I'd left.

"Worst possible reason ever, gentleman."

"Love?" answered the bald, chubby vet.

"Hand that man a prize. Yep, guilty as charged."

"Regrets?" asked the thin man with hair in a ponytail.

"Nope. The love thing didn't last, but the rest and the professional part were tremendous. I have two beautiful children and grandchildren. I'm happy. Say, while I have you here, any good gossip on Doc?"

"What you see is what you get. Doc's a good vet, good family man, good scholar, humanitarian, workaholic, poet…" The balding vet turned to the other and asked, "Did I leave anything out?"

"No, that about sums him up. Lonely, and maybe he feels he has never reached his potential. I wish I could be half the man he is." The thin vet looked up as Bill reentered the room. "Oops, speak of God."

"Interesting. I'll have to find his poetry. He must have that in a secret compartment."

Bill sat down next to me and asked how I was doing. "Hayley's a lightweight when it comes to pain." He knew both men were single, and he turned to them and said, "Find yourself someone like this woman. You may starve, but life will be interesting."

I was embarrassed and pleased. My face reddened. "Oh, you say that about all the women in your life."

"Nope, just the ones who will leave my stamp on the world when I'm gone." He went to the dessert table and brought us a slice of cake. Mary Lois slid over and told Bill he would get fat with that stuff.

Bill asked her how she was and how were the grandkids. He knew their names and their interests. If Mary Lois had any information that would put Bill in a bad light, I knew that would die with her, but she might be a source of events or deeds he was too humble to mention.

"Mary Lois, what is your favorite memory of Bill?"

"Hmm, that's hard to say. I think it was when that Shetland pony had colic, and you sat down in the stall while the fluids dripped in, and the little girl sat in your lap and sang to her pony."

I clutched my hand to my chest as I pictured that scene. I quietly whispered in Bill's ear, "That is what I want to know about, Billy Boy. Stories like that will keep you in the memories of people years past your endpoint."

He squeezed my hand under the table. "Sadly, my aim was for the little girl's buxom mother."

Mary Lois gave him an eye roll. "She would have Doc. Many women would have if you'd let them." She turned to me. "Don't you think he looks like Gary Cooper?"

I turned to him and stared from the side. "Yeah, kind of. Sheesh, Mary Lois, I have to live with the guy for a few more months. Don't make it any harder. So did the pony live?"

Bill cocked his head. "I don't remember. Probably not."

Mary Lois reached across the table and slapped his hand. "Don't be modest. Yes, she did, and it bit Doc when he removed the catheter."

"Safe to say my lap-sitting days are over, so the point is moot."

I turned to Mary Lois. "If you think of any other stories, will you let me know?"

Mary Lois nodded and smiled. "So many stories, so little time."

CHAPTER 28

"Is there anything else you care to share about your life? Sheesh, Billy Boy. This is like unraveling an enterolith—one solid rock built up over time from a single piece of shale. I guess it started with Daniel?"

He gave a nod.

When Daniel was about thirteen, I began taking him on calls. He was never allowed to come to the house, so it was easier to have him go with me on the weekends and sometimes after his special school. He was a robust, healthy boy then and loved attending the calls. It gave the Hastings respite from caring for him. He was so eager to help and please everyone. The clients all knew the circumstances and were kind to him. Even the other partners took him on occasion.

It dawned on my partners that having him work for us would be a great way to get him into a paying job. None of us thought we would outlive him when he was young. The heart condition was diagnosed when he was five, but the deterioration was slow. He finished school and then began to work for us full-time.

Some of his wages went to his board with the Hastings until they felt they could no longer care for anyone but themselves. We were all surprised by how well Daniel accepted the transition to an apartment I bought for him. We found Lenny, who you can see also had challenges, and the two became friends. Our practice was growing, so we decided to add Lenny to the work roster. We've added other people with intellectual challenges over the years. The state subsidizes part of their wages, but that's secondary to the feeling we as partners received.

Our clinic received a lot of attention for our efforts. It's totally undeserved. These men and women pay their way and are valuable employees. I wish Daniel could have continued, but his heart deteriorated faster than anyone expected. He was inconsolable when I finally had to take him off the roster and move him to the special-needs facility.

In hindsight, maybe that's when I should have moved out and lived with Danny. He's the one person who truly loves me. The kids were gone and starting their own families. They were always Myrna's kids. God, I hope they never find out I'm not their father, at least not until I'm long gone. I expect everyone deserves to know the truth.

We went to Greenbriar, and we both went to see Daniel. He was having a bad day, so Bill decided to take me home and come back to sit with him for a while. I said I didn't mind waiting, but Bill insisted. As we drove home, Bill hit his forehead with his palm. "Hayles, I plum forgot. Have you got a dress?"

"Don't be ridiculous. Why would I need a dress?"

"Shelby Cotter has asked me to walk her down the aisle. She's getting married in two weeks. What do you call it when you go shopping?" Bill glanced over at me.

"I believe it's called a waste of time." I laughed but braced for the reply.

"No, it's called therapy or something like that."

"Retail therapy?" I pointed to my arm. "I can stay home. You'll have a better time without me."

"No. And no, I wouldn't go without you. Woman up and let an old man spoil you. I told her I would be honored. I need a date."

"I'll think about it. If you can give me some samples of your poetry, I'll consider your invitation."

Bill's neighbor, Lorna, was just walking off the porch when we drove up. She smiled and hugged Bill as he walked toward the house. Surprisingly, she didn't acknowledge me. "Bill, I was just at Greenbriar, and Myrna asked for you. I know you're busy these days." Lorna glanced at me. "But it's one of her better days."

"Lorna, we were just there, and I'm heading back anyway. Daniel's not well today. I'll stop in and spend some time with Myrna as well."

I excused myself and went inside. I saw Bill standing with his hand on his hip, listening to an earful from Lorna. I wondered if Bill ever considered moving. As lovely as this place was, privacy was lacking. I knew Bill would be gone for hours, and I was beyond tired. When he finally entered the house after dismissing Lorna, he was smiling.

"Something funny?" I stood waiting for a reply.

"I'll tell you later. That's if I survive. When Myrna is having a good day, I am usually the target. I hope I return in one piece. I'll get the anthology of poems I've written. I thought you knew I dabbled in verse. They aren't perfect, and I'm probably not going to allow them into the book, but you can look."

I found several that I thought captured the spirit of Bill's life's work. It captured mine.

<u>Walking a Colicky Horse at Night</u>
It's just you and me, my friend.
We walk in circles, hoping that
When we round the bend,
your pain lessens,
will you care enough to call out to the curious nearby hors-
es?
You lift your head and announce;
I am here, and I will be here in the morning.
Someday we will not,
Will the night shadows we created remember
Our time together?

<u>Please be in Foal</u>
This is the year you test me,
Not much has gone to plan.
My averages have slipped,
As have many mares.
The savable are not saved
The crops withered and died.
You are my last chance, Aphrodite.
I need some wins.
Please be in foal.
Go figure. It's twins.

<u>I Love my Job</u>
I save the unsavable.
I make new lives.
I heal wounds.
I make the lame sound again.
I'm given the credit
And all along, I know somehow
Nature should take the bow.

I chuckled while reading some, but one made me cringe. It was my story. The poem was only partially written. It was about the conflict between the needs of family and the needs of his clients. It appears he was searching for words to express the torment most vets with families deal with daily. I could write that story, but to put it in rhyme? Nope.

About the third time, my head pitched forward, I decided to head to bed. Bill had not returned, but I was sure he would be back soon. I was worried about my nightmares, and when I found myself running from Pauly and the feeling that I was paralyzed with fear and could not outrun him, I must have screamed. My voice woke me up, and I realized I was still alone. I checked my phone. It was two-thirty in the morning. Was Bill all right?

I decided to text him. The chances of him responding were small. I sent the message and heard his phone chime. He'd forgotten to take the phone which was in the kitchen. I saw three text messages, and despite my curiosity, I didn't open them. I stayed awake until four in the morning and read more of his poems. I was so relieved when he pulled in. He came straight to my room, stripped down to his jocks, and climbed into bed. He disregarded the sheet barrier, took me into his arms, and cried.

My arm was pinned against his chest, and my bad one could barely move, but I attempted to comfort him. It was several minutes before he told me that Myrna had escaped her lockdown area and had gone out and down the road looking for him. "They found her sitting on the side of the road, and the police called the facility. When they returned her, she ran to me and then bit me."

I attempted to pull myself away to examine the bite mark, but Bill held me tighter and said the bite didn't break the skin. "Daniel was almost in full-blown heart failure, and the medicine was not managing his weakening heart muscles. I talked to the cardiologist, and he doesn't think Daniel will last much longer. He didn't say how long, but he said the deterioration was rapid."

I turned, held him with my good arm, and tried to comfort him until he fell asleep. I eventually joined him in slumber. I woke an hour later at dawn. I quietly extricated myself and went to watch the morning hatch.

A man I didn't recognize walked up and sat beside me. He was in his fifties and rather good-looking. He grinned and said I appeared to be new to the area. He pointed down the shoreline and stated he and his wife lived down the way, and he often went on hikes in the early morning. He asked my name, and I told him. He stuck out his hand and said he was Craig Reardon. He asked me to come down during the day and join his wife and him for coffee. He said he lived in Denver and only came up once in a while.

The fish exploded, disturbing the glassy lake surface, making me wonder if I was capable of casting and reeling in the line. As the fish settled, I said goodbye to the man and told him I would visit in the next day or two. He mentioned it was the fifth house from here.

"How did you break your arm?"

"I fell. It's hell getting old." I didn't want him to know who I was in the remote chance he didn't know about my near brush with certain death.

"Beats the alternative, though. Hope to see you soon." Craig stood to go. He turned back and suggested I take precautions when sitting out here alone. "You can never be sure who you're talking to."

Bill was in the shower when I returned to the house. I knocked on the bathroom door, and he said, "Come in."

"Uh, no thanks. I just wanted to see if you'd like pancakes."

He opened the bathroom door to show he was dressed. "I'll make them if you want to change. Do you mind if we go to Denver? They're going to transfer Daniel to the cardiac unit. I think they're considering steroids. He isn't a candidate for a transplant. It's a shame."

"Bill, I want to go and help where I can, but if you want to go alone, I'll be fine. I've been invited down the way for coffee by one of your neighbors."

Bill appeared alarmed. "Who invited you?"

"A guy came by early this morning when I sat on your bench watching the hatch. He was good-looking and must be in his fifties and said his name was Craig."

"Hmm, I don't think I know a Craig. Hayley, do you mind not going outside alone this next week? I have a bad feeling right now."

"Yeah, sure. Do you have a picture of Daniel's father? I mean, his biological father?"

"Right, but it's from the security camera." Bill opened his phone, scrolled through the photos, and brought his phone over to me. "It's a bit grainy, but I think you'll get an idea if he ever comes around."

I took the phone and realized it was the same man. "Uh, Bill?"

Bill spun me in my chair. "Oh my God. No?"

"Yes. No doubt." I began to shake. It was a real-life narrow escape. "No, I'm going with you."

I was afraid to even go into the bedroom by myself. I knew Bill could see the effect this had on me. He went with me, walked through my room and bathroom, and then stood outside the door as I prepared to get ready for town.

I watched out of the truck window for any signs of the man but saw no one. I felt all my progress in addressing my PTSD was lost. Last time I thought I was on my own, but this time, I had Bill to lean on. As old and ill as he was, I felt safe in his presence.

CHAPTER 29

Bill stopped into Greenbriar to check on Myrna. I waited in the car with the windows rolled up and the doors locked. It was another warm day, and I was sweating. Thankfully, Bill was only gone for a minute. He apologized and said he should have left the car running with the air conditioner.

We drove to Denver. We were both exhausted and anxious from the activities last night. I was sure I could drive if Bill needed to sleep, but he would not entertain the idea.

"No thanks, I don't have a death wish. I wanted to thank you for last night. I was close to my limit, and I needed to vent. I'm sorry if I overstepped the bounties. I won't cross them again."

I laughed, knowing Bill was referring to the clinic gardener, Lenny, and his mistake in calling boundaries bounties. "You can cross that bounty anytime, Billy Boy."

"Thanks. Nice to know. That's the first time I've..." Bill paused and gripped the steering wheel. "Well, you know, in years. I'm guessing you'll see more."

"Bill, I'm here to help. I'll do what I can, and for sure, I owe you one." I reached across with my good hand and took his for a moment. We squeezed each other's hands, and then I sat back and closed my eyes for a second. I felt sad for this proud man whose life was spiraling out of control. He thought he would be the first to die and be spared the grief of losing his wife and son. While he knew his wife didn't care or really couldn't care, he had not yet begun to prepare this poor, innocent adopted son about his father's impending death, and now he knew most likely he didn't have to. Daniel would never know how ill his father was.

We got lost trying to negotiate the parking lot and then Daniel's room in the cardiac wing of the hospital. When Daniel saw his father, my heart melted. Daniel cried and asked Bill to hold his hand. Daniel was feeling better since he was receiving steroids. We stayed all morning, and he asked us to get him some McDonald's. The nurse said that they would look the other way. They were reconciled to palliative care. He wasn't eating much at the time.

Bill would not let me drive the car one-handed, so we quickly went over and got him a meal. As we waited in line at the drive-through, I saw Bill's tears. I handed him a tissue and patted his shoulder. He was losing his manly reserve at a rapid rate. I saw this with my father when he died. While my mother was a crier from the start, my father, like most men of his generation, didn't display his emotions until he reached an age when he was comfortable showing his true feelings. It was only in the last year that I saw my father's emotions, including openly crying, emerge.

"Bill, do you want some time alone? I can leave you two and go for a walk."

"No, I want you with me. Do you mind?" He patted my arm. "Jesus, I'm losing my grip."

"You shouldn't be so hard on yourself. Your son is dying. You're holding up far better than me if it was my child."

We stayed until four when they suggested Daniel needed some sleep. He hugged and kissed Bill and then asked him to leave the room. Daniel wanted to ask me something. When we were alone, he took my hand. "My daddy loves you, so will you marry him?"

How do I respond? I was not going to marry Bill. Bill was married, and anyway, he was dying. Yes, he had a reprieve, but he could go into a decline tomorrow. "How about this? If he asks me, I will marry him." I felt that was a safe response.

Danny then asked if he could kiss me goodbye and when I would see him again. "Tomorrow, for sure."

"Can you ask my dad to come in again?" He smiled and waved goodbye.

I stepped out into the hall and pointed to the door. "You're being summoned."

Bill was gone for several minutes. He emerged and smiled. I suspected Daniel had passed on my admission that if he asked me to marry him, I would say, "Yes."

He took my hand and casually spoke. "Isn't it interesting what we promise our sick children?"

"Yes, it is. Don't worry. I'm not holding you to anything, and neither should you. I only want to make Daniel happy." I knew it was a tricky topic.

Bill replied, "Yeah, me too."

When we returned to Bill's house, he asked me to stay in the car while he searched the property and garage. He had turned on a security system when we left, so I was not worried about the house. We entered and found everything in order. I opened my computer and checked my emails. There was a message from Craig Reardon saying it was nice to meet me, and he was disappointed I hadn't come down to visit today. "My wife even made cookies, so please come tomorrow." I showed Bill. It arrived on my author's email site. I asked Bill if I should block him, and Bill suggested we keep it open, so we know what he's doing, but Bill asked me not to respond.

I showed Bill what poems I had chosen. "So, you walked colics at night too? I thought I was the only one."

Bill gazed up at a framed picture. It was a thank you note penned by a small child. It showed a tall stick man, a pony, and flowers. He replied, "In the early days, I did. I remember thinking how the whole world was sleeping, and some poor horse or pony and I were the only souls awake fighting for the horse's survival. I hated to euthanize them at night. I always tried to keep them alive until morning. I felt guilty euthanizing one in the middle of the night. I never wanted anyone to think I was doing it, so I could go to bed and get sleep."

Is that where I acquired my sense of duty to animals? "I felt the same. I think it was either you or one of the partners who said that once. I carried it through my practice life. I probably made a few poor horses wait until morning and should have pulled the trigger sooner."

Bill laughed. "Pun intended? That reminds me."

I remember one case. It was a gray horse that had colic. He'd been untouched for several years. The owner was an odd man. He collected horses and had them to amuse a bevy of ever-rotating buxom, young women who all fancied themselves as horse lovers. I don't think any of them knew how to halter a horse.

I had been out to treat the colicky gelding and could not catch him by myself. The partners never minded going there. I knew it was the eye candy, but they were smart enough to take help. It was rainy and muddy. It was the tail end of a snowstorm, and the ground had a light dusting. The horse would let me get close and walk away as I touched his neck or shoulder. I called for reinforcements, and Dot told me to come back to the clinic, and she would send out the barn crew to get the horse. As soon as he would be far enough away to feel safe, he would drop and roll. He was a mud ball.

Once he was caught, he was fine. He wasn't dangerous, but he was wary, and we had a long rope attached to his halter. He was so painful, but he allowed us to treat him. I had to go to the clinic to check him and up his pain meds around one or two in the morning. He was pawing and sweating. I knew what I needed to do. I realized the long rope we used to catch him had broken, and I could not approach him despite his pain level.

I would have to call in a second person, and in those days, it would be a partner. We couldn't afford to pay wages at night. I stared at that horse, and I swear he stared back and stopped any movement. There was some communication coming from his eye. I only felt this once in my life, but it was so real. We had a connection. He told me to leave, and he would either die or be better in the morning.

I went home, and I returned around five when I knew one of the early barn crew would arrive for his day's work. You know, I believe it was Tammy, Daniel's mom, come to think of it. Anyway, that horse was alive and passing feces. He stood in the back of the stall, and we had another talk. I am pretty sure he said, "I told you so."

"So, if you're honest with yourself, Hayley, I'm guessing you probably decided to euthanize too soon once or twice, for whatever reason. I'll bet money you have agonized and thought about that decision ever since. I sure have made that mistake. We aren't perfect, and we aren't God."

I thought about Taco. If I wanted to torture myself, I would think about my hasty decision to give up on that horse. I asked to do an autopsy on Taco following euthanasia. When I opened his abdomen, I knew what he had was fixable. "Yes, but it was only one," I lied.

"Yeah, I only had one as well," replied Bill.

We both laughed, knowing it was far more than one each. We each knew we weren't perfect, but we did the best we could.

"Bill, I've lost three classmates to suicide. Have you ever?" I didn't finish that question. Bill knew what I was asking.

"No. I had two kids and a mortgage. I taught myself coping mechanisms. I learned to forgive myself. They sure don't teach you that in school, do they? Did you ever?"

"No, and no, they don't. I know they try to these days, but the instructors are rarely vets, and I don't think they know all the pressures the young graduates face."

Bill nodded. "I'm glad I'm not starting over again. Do you know how hard it would be if, with everything else, I had Myrna telling me I had no balance in my life?"

I shifted in my seat. "My ex did nag me about the balance issue. I ignored it. I was perfectly happy with my balance. Sadly, he poisoned the kids and told them I was neglecting them, so I could go out and be a hero with the clients. I still never ever remotely considered doing the deed."

We got into bed, and once again, the barrier was forgotten. We assumed our separate positions but still held hands. As I was about to tip over the edge into oblivion, I heard Bill say, "Glad you never considered." He didn't finish the sentence.

"You too, my friend."

Bill shifted. "Gizmo, his name was Gizmo. When I drove past where he lived, I searched the field to ensure he was there. A time or two, I stopped and went to his fence. He would be out with his herd of mares and a cow or two. He would stop grazing, lift his head and stare at me. About fifteen years later, he was gone. I miss that horse almost as much as the owner's rotating collection of ever-younger girlfriends."

I kicked him, but I silently laughed. Although I didn't let him know I found it so amusing. He was so different from most men with his dedication to his one-sided marriage. Still, he was a man.

CHAPTER 30

I awoke early and went to my laptop. It was time to begin exercising my arm, and I wanted to attempt to start typing the stories and memories that I felt were important in Bill's life. I sat at my desk. It was still dark outside. I watched the lakeshore for any signs of Daniel's father, Jake Jensen, or as he introduced himself, Craig Rearden. Thankfully, I saw none. It was awkward to type, but it was not impossible. I could only sustain typing for a short time, then my arm ached, and I had to rest.

I was glad that we could easily discuss complex topics. Bill had a difficult time ahead. He was going to lose his son soon. I could see he loved him as much as he loved his children. I knew there was no lost love between the rest of Bill's family and Daniel. I was glad I was here to support Bill in his time of grief.

It made me wonder, who were Bill's close friends? He hadn't talked to many people since I had arrived. There was no question that Myrna had a loyal following, and the psychologist, Martin, was Bill's friend, but there must be more. I wanted to interview them. Of course, I would have to do this without them knowing my actual intent.

It was another warm day. I knew Bill would spend the day with Daniel back at Greenbriar. Daniel would be transferred back this morning, and Bill would be with him. I was still shaken and wary about Daniel's father. My interaction with him was pleasant, and I would never have suspected he was trying to harm me.

Maybe I could stay at Bill's vet clinic and work on the book while Bill spent the day at Greenbriar. There was Bill's desk for me to use in the back office. If I could hang out, I might get more stories. Mary Lois might enlighten me about cases that Bill had forgotten.

I typed the story about Gizmo. I also encountered a horse that connected with me on another level. I was glad that Bill and I recognized those connections and remembered them. Bill's stories reminded me of my own. I enjoyed thinking about almost forgotten moments of triumph and failures, but this was Bill's story. My life was taking a back seat.

I wanted to go out and watch the sunrise, but I understood the danger. There was no way I would risk my life again. While I would have preferred to stay at the house and work on the book today, I couldn't be alone. I wondered if Daniel's father knew of his son's impending death. How would this affect the man? Would he intensify the revenge or maybe go away? He'd spent years torturing Bill and his family. I couldn't imagine he would go away so quickly after Daniel passed.

Bill entered the office and said he was going to shower. He asked if I needed any help dressing. "Uh, no thank you.

I only need help with my bra, and you know the drill." I would put on all my clothes, and Bill's only role was to hook the back together. I knew few men would not take advantage of that, but Bill announced his eyes were closed. I doubted it, but we were... What were we? I hated the term "old." Maybe the word "seasoned" was a better way to think of it.

Bill wanted me to come to the facility to see Daniel. Still, he understood that it was important to Daniel that he spends time alone with his father. I was left at the vet clinic. Bill would pick me up at lunch, and then I would stay at Greenbriar until Bill was ready to return home. I brought my laptop and sat at Bill's desk. The clinic was busy, and I thought no one would bother me—wrong.

I had barely begun to continue the story about Gizmo when a nurse entered the room. "I heard you're writing some stories about Bill for a magazine. I have one that I think you'll enjoy."

"Well, they have to be clean, and they can't harm anyone. That aside, what's your story?"

She smiled. "Hmm, maybe not."

Of course, I was intrigued. "Just because I can't use it, doesn't mean I don't want to hear it. Are you on duty? I don't want to get you in trouble."

"On a break. We all have stories, and so we are staggering our breaks. It won't take long."

I went with Doc on a call to castrate a colt one day. It was a remote property and inside the pen was a large pile of firewood. It was huge. The colt was a year old, and he was big for his breed and size. Doc commented how nice he was. The owner was an older woman, and she thanked

Doc for the compliment. She was especially pleased as he was well-bred, and she reminded him he was an orphan.

I remember Doc was leaning over his tray where he had his instruments. Doc asked the woman to hand the colt to me, so he could begin the castration. She refused. She would hold the colt. Doc gave me the look, and I knew I would have to be ready to step in.

Doc remarked that he was surprised the owner wanted to castrate him. We knew he was from a well-bred cutting line. He asked her if he gave her any trouble and mentioned that some orphans get confused and become sexually oriented and aroused by humans. The owner was adamant that wasn't the case. Doc realized he had forgotten a scalpel blade and sent me to the truck to fetch one.

As I returned, Doc was bent over his surgical tray which lay on the ground, and I saw the colt had a full-blown erection and was beginning to rear. It happened in a second, and I screamed to Doc to watch out. Doc turned his head and jumped forward over his instrument tray to escape the colt.

The little bastard was now on his hind legs and began running after Doc around the firewood. I entered the paddock and began to chase the colt galloping around the wood with a full-blown erection and mostly on his hind legs. I was trying to catch him, but at the same time, I was laughing so hard I could hardly move. The pair went around the firewood pile two or three times, and finally, I grabbed the lead rope and pulled the colt to a halt. Doc calmly went to the tray and returned with a syringe for the sedation. The surgery was completed, and we returned to the truck.

As we left, the woman apologized profusely. She turned to Doc and said, "I'm so sorry. He does that a lot to me, and I thought that was normal."

Bill said no harm done and good luck with him. The surgery might not be curative. He rolled up his window, turned to me, and said, "With any luck."

Doc began to laugh and admitted he was so shocked and surprised that he could hardly run from the colt. I said the same thing. He then told me if I ever said anything about this, he would fire me.

"I think your name is Sandy?"

She nodded. "But don't tell Bill that I told you the story."

"He can't fire you, and I want you to know that you would have to kill me to keep me from using that story. So, we will both get fired. Do you remember the name of the colt?"

"Lucifer," Sandy smirked as she left the room. "So much trouble."

"Perfect." When I had the story typed, Bill arrived to take me to lunch and see Daniel. I saw no sense in mentioning that story to Bill at present. I needed him to ward off the night terrors. Then again…

"Hayles, let's stop at the mall and see if we can find you a dress." Bill opened the door to the truck and helped me in. His hand seemed to be landing lower on my backside each time—men.

"I don't think I can negotiate a dress in the sling. How about next week?" He didn't respond initially. "Bill, are you okay?" I then saw he'd been crying.

"I think things will be kind of busy next week. Will you do this for me now?"

I was certain Daniel was deteriorating by the look on Bill's face. I reached over with my good arm and patted his. "Yeah," was all I replied.

My heart sank, knowing how he must feel. "Do you want to wait in the truck while I look at dresses?" He said no and recommended we eat at the mall's restaurant. As we walked into the department store, Bill suggested I might want to get some other clothes for a more formal occasion. I knew he meant for Daniel's funeral.

I found shoes and a perfect wedding dress to cover my arm. I found a suit that would be for the funeral. Bill smiled and went over to the register to pay for them. I tried to stop him, and he almost appeared to be insulted.

"Okay, have it your way. I can be bought, but it isn't clothes. Now the food is another matter." I pointed to a restaurant that had a range of lunch food.

Bill laughed, bent over, and kissed my cheek. As he did, Lorna and her husband exited the restaurant and saw us. "Oh, man. Now I'm going to pay for that," he whispered as he waved to them.

They walked over, and Lorna shot me daggers while her husband introduced himself. "Hi, I'm Trent, and you must be the devil in disguise."

Bill laughed out loud. "Hey, Trent. This is Hayley Alexander or Satan, whichever's easier." Bill purposely put his arm over my shoulder.

"Well, I've heard it either way. Hi, Hayley." He stared at the top of my head. "You are a master at hiding your horns." He glanced over at Lorna, whose face was reddening by the minute. "I'll be on the couch tonight, for sure, but I want you to know we still love you, Bill. We know you're going through hell right now. I saw that Danny had a trip to the cardiac unit in Denver. All the best, old man. If you need anything, let me know." I watched Lorna's pursed lips, and I tried to stay neutral.

As we entered the restaurant and were escorted to a table, I asked what Trent does.

"He's a radiologist. Trent's a good man. I think he spends quite a bit of time on the couch."

"Yeah, that's a given. Still, you have to give Lorna credit. She sure is loyal to Myrna."

"Myrna wasn't all bad." Bill was close to tears. We ate, and Bill reached for the account. I put my hand over his to stop him. "Let a young lady spoil you."

He leaned forward. "Okay, do you see one?"

I kicked him under the table.

CHAPTER 31

Daniel crooked his finger to summon me as we entered his room. I approached him, and he indicated he wanted to ask me something. He whispered, "So did he ask you?"

"Not yet." I smiled and held his hand as he drifted in and out of consciousness. He was bloated, and I felt an increased pulse on his wrist. He was catheterized, and a urine-filled bag sat below his bed.

He suddenly looked around, saw his father, and then relaxed. I stepped away and allowed Bill to sit by his son. As Bill sat there holding Daniel's hand, he talked to Daniel, reassuring him they would soon be together in heaven.

"Danny, you'll be back with your mother too. Oh, son, she is the most beautiful woman, and she loved you so much."

It was heartbreaking. I sat in a chair and watched the two reassure each other. Daniel would rouse and squeeze his father's hand, and Bill would attempt to get Daniel to drink water or rub ice cubes on his lips. Daniel would bat his father's hand away.

We stayed until midnight when Daniel told his father to go home and come back in the morning. "Daddy, I need to sleep." This made Bill laugh, so we left the facility and returned to the lake house.

We climbed into bed, and Bill cried again as I held him. This time I cried as well. I had a nightmare and realized I was alone in bed. Bill rushed back and helped me orient myself. "Sorry, old men stuff." He often had to pee. When he returned to the bed, this time, Bill spooned me. I lay awake for several minutes, trying to calm myself down.

"I don't suppose you want to get married? I promised Daniel I would ask."

"Hmm, let me think about it." I smiled to myself. "I'm flattered that you asked, and in normal circumstances, I would accept. Just so you know, it's me not you. So no, I'm sorry. I am such a stickler for details and societal norms. I just have this aversion to polygamy. I hope you understand. Again, it's me and not you."

I was about to go on when he put his hand over my mouth and told me to shut up. "I need sleep, and now when Daniel asks me, I can say I did as I was instructed."

"Yes, you did." I smiled, thinking about the faux proposal.

"You know, I'll need a ring if you plan to make Daniel think you did propose."

The following morning, I woke early, dressed, and entered the kitchen. I turned around and lifted the back of my shirt, allowing Bill to fasten the bra clasps. Bill was dressed and had prepared breakfast. When I sat down, I saw the small box holding the ring Bill had purchased in Jackson Hole.

"Will that do?" He turned and scooped eggs onto my plate.

"Will that do? How romantic—not. I need more than 'will that do' if you expect me to lie to a dying boy. Billy boy, I'm starting to side with Myrna. Can you please pass the jam?"

Bill chuckled. "I was going to give it to you all along. Myrna can't wear jewelry anymore. I didn't want to overdo it back then. I was testing the waters."

"Waters tested and ring accepted. Thank you, and no obligations are required."

We arrived at the facility, and Bill was taken aside by one of the staff. Daniel was much better, but Myrna had a stroke early this morning. The staff were waiting for the doctor who monitored the patients, and her children were notified and were on their way. The nurse said she had tried to call Bill several times. Bill glanced at his phone and realized his phone was on silent and saw the messages. He'd left it on all night if Daniel passed or needed him, but when he rose and left me to sleep, he had turned off the ringer.

Bill stared at me, and I knew my presence was awkward. "I'll see Daniel, and you can do what you need to, Bill. I'm here to help." I excused myself. I was shocked and sad for Bill. His whole life was imploding. Perhaps Myrna would recover, but I knew she and Bill had "do not resuscitate" orders. I expected she would not be given medication to decrease the possible clot in her brain.

I entered Daniel's room and found him sitting up and eating some yogurt. "Wow, Daniel. You look great." I flashed the ring. I had it on the wrong hand, but he didn't know the difference.

He smiled and asked if he could kiss me.

"Of course, I would be honored. Say, your dad is with Myrna. She isn't feeling too good. He'll be over in a while. Can I get you anything?"

Daniel wiped his face. "She came to see me last night. She was really nice. She told me she was sorry I hadn't come to live with her and Dad, but it was against the law."

"Oh, how nice. That must have been lovely. Did she stay long?"

"No, the nurse came when my alarm went off. My oxygen line got accidentally tied in a knot, so they had to take her away to fix it. She was really, really mad, and then she hit the nurse and fell. I said she could stay, but then lots of people came into the room and took her away on a stretcher."

Oh my God, I wondered if Bill was aware. I turned to Daniel, who asked to see the ring up close. "Did Daddy kiss you?"

I'm going to hell for this for sure. "Yes, he did."

"Did you sleep together?" He was holding my hand, and I blushed.

Nope, not going to hell for this one. "No, Daniel. You only do that when you're married." Okay, maybe I would go to hell.

"When I lived with Lenny, he said he had slept with his girlfriend, and they even got under the covers. He wasn't allowed to touch her, though."

"Good thing you had Lenny to learn about the facts of life." I wonder what else Lenny told Daniel. I could imagine this conversation between the two challenged boys.

Daniel was raising and lowering the bed. He'd mentioned it was fun to push the button. "Lenny was my best friend. He comes here now and then and sees me."

"Oh, that's nice. Sounds like Lenny is a good friend." How much had Lenny "educated" Daniel over the years?

"Lenny let me smoke a cigarette once too." I could see Daniel knew that wasn't good.

"That's a bit naughty." I wagged my finger at Daniel.

"Is Daddy coming?"

"I'm sure he will be here in a minute." I stood, walked to the door, and opened it. No one was in the hallway. "Daniel, can I get you anything? You look great today. I think you're going to outlive us all." I returned to the chair next to the bed.

"No, I'm not, but that's okay. I'm going to see my mother soon. I can't wait. She's so pretty. Have you seen a picture of her?"

"Yes, I think I did. Did your mother have long red hair?"

"I have a picture in the top drawer. It got broken last night by accident." I guessed Myrna broke it, but I didn't care to find out.

I waited another thirty minutes, and finally, Bill walked in and went straight over to Daniel and gave him a big hug. "I heard you had a big night, Danny. Are you okay?" He searched Daniel and saw the returned facial color. Bill picked up the empty yogurt container, turned, and pointed to the container.

"Don't blame me. I didn't do it." I smiled and pointed to Daniel, who wanted to whisper something in Bill's ear.

Bill leaned over and nodded his head, and I suspected Bill had confirmed the engagement. I could see the strain on Bill's face as he asked Daniel to excuse us. Daniel was becoming sleepy and said he would be fine. He wanted to sleep for a while. He smiled, gave me the thumbs-up, and pressed the button to lower the bed while Bill leaned over and kissed his head.

There was a patio at the end of the hall where the patients could smoke or sit in the sun. Bill took me out to a bench and sat down. The tears began to flow. When he regained his composure, Bill took my hand. "I hate to ask."

"Not a problem. I've already decided to go up and see our surgical colic horse. The sutures are due to come out." But Bill stopped me.

"No, can you stay? I need you to be here for Daniel. I don't think Myrna will survive, but it won't be today. She's paralyzed on the left side of her body, and she can't speak or eat. She won't be getting a feeding tube, so basically, she will starve to death. The kids will arrive after lunch, and the house will be packed with family. I hate doing this, but there's a clean and safe motel at the end of the town. We can get my other car, and I think you'll be able to drive it. My big worry is you sleeping alone. Hayles, if there were any options..."

I patted Bill's arm. I began to laugh and couldn't stop. I couldn't even tell Bill what was so funny at such a time, but I remembered what the therapist said. I would begin, and then I would laugh. I finally got control, the laughter turned to tears, and it all stopped. "The therapist suggested I go find a horse to pat. He said equine-assisted therapy was helping many of his clients." I knew this was true, and I had been the vet for two clients that ran programs. "I'll go pat horses, and I'll be fine."

Bill stared at me like I was nuts. "Hayley, I'm going to leave my phone on, and if there are any problems, you can always call me. When the kids arrive, I know they won't come down to Daniel's wing. So, if you don't mind staying with him, and I'll come back and forth. Is that okay? I hate doing this to you."

"Bill, this is why I'm here. We both know the book isn't the only reason you asked me down. I'm glad I can help. I think Daniel is wiser than you think. He's ready to meet his mother, and at this stage, he's torn between both worlds. It's a privilege to see this young man on his journey. We could both learn a lesson from him."

Bill got up from his chair. He seemed older today. It will be a trying time for him, and I didn't need to be an impediment. He stood for a moment and then bent toward me and briefly kissed me on the lips.

We stopped in and peered inside Daniel's room. He was sleeping. Bill went in, and I watched him straighten the sheet that covered Daniel. We left the facility and drove back to the house. I collected all my belongings, remade my bed, and tidied the room while Bill set out towels in the bathroom. Bill turned to me and said he hated doing this and would miss sleeping with me.

"You can always sneak out and visit me at the motel. I'll bet Lorna would like to know."

Bill rolled his eyes. "Are you sure you can drive? Once you get to the motel, the distance to the hospital is only half a mile. There are many restaurants in the neighborhood." Bill reached into his pocket and brought out several twenty-dollar bills. He tried to hand them to me, but my pride would never allow me to take them.

I pushed his hand away. "Buy Daniel something, Bill. Maybe he'll be around for a while. How about some comic books or flowers? You would know what he likes."

Bill laughed. "A Playboy magazine would be his favorite, but I think we'll have to settle for the comics."

As Bill closed the door on the car, he reached in and kissed me again. Lorna walked up and observed me leaving, smiled, and waved. I expected she was unaware of Myrna's stroke, and she and Bill would probably have more words.

Thank God and Greyhound. Lorna was Bill's problem, not mine. I struggled with the turn signal and only one arm, but I arrived at the motel and went to secure a room. I went to the registration and found Bill had already registered me and paid for it. The young clerk helped me into a nice room and brought my bags. "This is our best room, ma'am. Your boyfriend asked us to make sure you had what you needed. We have a room off the reception where breakfast is served from six until nine. Is there anything else?"

"I don't suppose you have a horse I can pet?" I laughed, thinking about my uncontrolled laughter at the suggestion of equine therapy for PTSD. I'd probably spend the day diagnosing skin conditions or lameness. Still, the smell of a horse did make me happy.

The young man stared at me, then smiled. "Well, Dr. O'Neal asked me to get whatever you need. Are you sure it couldn't be a cat?"

"No, you've been great. Thanks." I closed the door, lay down on the bed for a few minutes, then left my room and prepared to walk to the facility. As I turned onto the pathway, a car pulled up, and Daniel's biological father opened his window. "Hi Hayley, we're still waiting for a visit from you. Where are you heading? I would love to give you a ride."

"Hey, Craig. Thanks for the offer. I'm fine. I need to burn a few calories." Did he know I was now staying at the motel?

"Are you sure? It might rain."

I peered up at the accumulating clouds and realized I should have driven. I quickened my pace determined to reach the facility before the rain began. Craig—or Jake—kept pace with me in his car. In my hurry and concern for my precarious situation, I tripped and fell. Craig immediately stopped the car and came out to help me. I shook my head and felt my broken arm. My arm was not hurt and I only skinned my knee.

The man would not take no for an answer. "No, I insist." He took my good arm and, with a tight grip, helped me up and directed me to his car.

I was sick. I knew I was in trouble. With Bill's problems, even if I survived this, I knew he would be—what would he be?—enraged, worried, heartbroken, probably all three.

"Where are you going?" Daniel's father turned to me and waited for a reply.

"I'm going to Briarwood, and I'm guessing you know why."

"I have my sources. How is the little bastard?"

I hoped Daniel's condition might lessen the man's fury. "He's dying. He has heart failure. I'm staying with him during the day, so he has company. He's an innocent, kind soul. Would you like to see him, Jake?"

"No. Don't worry. I have nothing against you. Honestly, I won't harm you. Those days are over. I guess it's time for me to move on. God, I've wasted so much of my life, and I know I only have myself to blame. Prison was hell. You would think I would have learned my lesson." He pulled away from the curb, and in a minute, he turned into the Briarwood parking lot.

The rain was coming down heavily. I quickly got out, thanked him for the lift, and ran to the entrance. My heart was racing. When I opened the door, Bill's family stood at the counter. I walked past them and down the corridor to Daniel's room. I think Bill's daughter might have recognized me. I entered Daniel's room. He was finishing a milkshake and watching a television program.

"Hey, Daniel. How are things?" I smiled, came up to the bed, and kissed him on his cheek.

He blushed and asked me to hold his hand. "Still kicken', Mom. I'll call you my mom until I meet my real mom. Is that okay, Hayley?"

"I'm honored, my beautiful son. What can I do for you?" I loved this gesture.

"I'd like to die." I could tell he was sincere.

"Uh, no, Danny Boy, since I'm going to be your mom, I want to make it last."

"I want to go to heaven and see my real mom." He seemed disappointed.

"Yeah, I know. But you have a wonderful father that loves you, and now you have me." I took a washcloth and wiped his face. "We can't let you go to heaven with a dirty face."

"Do you think my mother will recognize me? I'm a lot older."

"I reckon she has been watching you grow up and knows everything about you. I'm sure she's so proud of you and will be happy to see you. Can I get you anything?"

"No, just hold my hand."

I held it as he drifted off again. I searched my phone for messages. I slept for a minute as well. I woke when Bill came in and peered into Daniel's face. He had tears, and I knew they were for Myrna.

"The kids are with her now. The doctors think it will be a few days, but she could go at any time. They don't think she'll rally."

I whispered, "I'm sorry. We do have someone ready to meet his maker. He seems quite aware of what's going on. He's at peace with his life for sure."

"I can't." Bill paused. He was so conflicted.

"No, I know you can't be here all the time, and I know you're going through hell. If you stop in once in a while, that's all this poor soul needs. I've got the rest covered. How are the kids holding up?"

"Not well. You know Myrna treated them like gold. We should have been so lucky." I suspected Bill remembered his mother and her lack of maternal affection.

I had a good mother. We weren't close as I got older, but she was all I needed when I was young. "My mom was good. I feel for you though. Let me know if I can help in any way. I think your daughter may have recognized me when I walked into the main lobby."

"Where's the car? I didn't see it." Bill saw Daniel stir and thought he might be waking up.

"I walked." I didn't want to disclose my interaction with Daniel's birth father.

"In the rain?" He felt my jacket hanging on the chair. "You must have been lucky and missed the downpour. If it's raining later, I'll take you to the motel."

I wasn't about to add to his dramas and tell him about Daniel's biological father. Still, I remembered leaving the lake house as Lorna approached. I looked him over and quietly asked if he had any skin left after Lorna parted.

Bill almost laughed. "I told her the truth. I have two dying family members, the kids were coming, and you're staying in the motel to help with Daniel. She was surprisingly reasonable about it."

"Phew, I guess she didn't see you kissing me."

"Oh, she saw it, but since you are doing my family such a big favor, she must be giving us a pass on that. Lorna's coming in at six, and I'm taking the family to dinner. I wish you could come as well. I really do."

"Bill, take care of yourself and your family. I am simply happy to help. I don't need to be a part of anything." To be honest, I would have loved to come, but I would never disclose that to him. He didn't need any more guilt.

"Oh good, so can I cancel the Shetland pony I have coming tonight to stay with you?"

"Uh, no. I'll need the pony and the good-looking cowboy leading him."

Bill's laugh woke Daniel, and he smiled as he saw his father. They hugged, and Daniel had a short cry. I said I needed to use the bathroom and left them alone. I went out to the patio and waited for Bill to emerge. As he left Daniel's room, he saw me, waved, and headed back to be with Myrna.

I returned to Daniel's room. Daniel asked me to turn on the television. He flicked through the channels and then turned it off. I could see he was disappointed with not having his father staying by his bedside. I tried to think of something to cheer him up.

"Danny, what is something you're proud of? Like what did you do or achieve that makes you proud?"

He thought for a minute and then began to tell me about catching a fish with his father. "Dad took me out in a boat, and we went fishing every year. Sometimes my brother would come too, but he got too old and didn't come anymore. One time, I was the only one who caught one. That was when Richard got mad and didn't come with us again. He always sends me a birthday card though."

"Really? How nice. Are there some in your drawers?"

"No, I don't have them anymore. The lady came in last year and took them."

"Which lady was that, Danny?"

"The one who came last night. She used to come into my room at night. You know?" He appeared to be almost frightened.

"She won't be coming anymore, so you don't have to worry." This place was not very secure. I wonder if Bill knew about Myrna and her night ramblings.

Daniel signaled for me to come closer. He whispered, "Richard told me a secret. I can tell you if you want to know. You just can't tell my daddy, so you have to promise."

"I'm not sure you should tell me. You know, sometimes brothers have secrets. That's part of being brothers."

"I'd like to tell you. Is that okay?" He stared at me, and I could see he needed to talk.

"Okay, and I won't tell anyone." I was unprepared for the secret

"Richard said my daddy is my real dad, and his real father is somebody else. His mommy told him that. You won't tell my dad, will you?"

I had to consider this. I wondered how long Richard knew Bill was not his father. The second part was a shocker. All this time, Bill was Daniel's father. Was the man who drove me to the facility this afternoon telling the truth, or was this one of Myrna's lies? Was she so vicious that she would use her indiscretions to hurt not just Bill but her children?

"No, I won't tell your father. It can stay between us. I'm so sorry this has happened to you, Danny."

Daniel continued with his story, not realizing how dramatic his admission was to me. "You know that I am special."

"Danny, all children are special. We all have unique qualities. So, what is your talent?"

"I was the first worker with Down's at my father's vet clinic. I did such a good job that they hired more like me. The people who brought their horses to the clinic always asked me to help them, and they always gave me a quarter or sometimes even a dollar. I would hold the horse or get a bucket of water. I had a shirt that said I worked at the clinic. My shirt had my name. Daniel O'Neal, and it was blue, like my father's. I have a picture of my dad and me standing by the clinic sign. It was in the newspaper."

"I'd love to see it." Another photo for the book.

"I think someone took it. Maybe she still has it."

I knew the "she" was Myrna. Man, this place has a lot to answer for.

Around seven, I saw no one else. Lorna must be sitting with Myrna by now. Daniel was ready for bed and had eaten a small portion of his dinner. I excused myself and walked to the café that seemed to be popular. The sun was still up, and I had plenty of time to get back to the motel before it was dark.

I was seated at a small booth. As I read the menu, a policewoman walked up and asked to sit with me for a minute. "I want to discuss something with you."

CHAPTER 32

The woman didn't wait for me to reply. I guessed this was official business.

"Have a seat." I was exhausted and emotionally drained.

"It's about Bill. And a bit about you too. We know who you are, and we want to make sure you're protected. Your picture appeared on a 'be on the lookout,' when you traded places with that child near Jackson."

"Yeah, not one of my better days. Is there a problem?" I began to relax. Maybe she was on my side.

"We think there may be one brewing. Poor Doc has been through the wringer these last few years. We know about the kid's father. You were observed getting into his car this afternoon." The policewoman stopped and watched me.

"Again, not one of my better moves. He seems okay, though, and Jake told me he knows he screwed up. He claimed he was moving on. Can I believe him?"

"Maybe, but probably not. I guess we're wondering what you're doing here. We want to protect Doc. He was our vet when I was growing up. Did he tell you about the Hannigans?"

"I used to work here about thirty years ago, and I knew some people named Hannigan out on Timber Cove. Are they the ones you're referring to?" It was a multigenerational family that bought and sold horses. I hated going to their place. It was run down, the horses were starving, and the Hannigans were less than trustworthy.

"Did you know what Doc did for us? Do you have a minute?"

The waitress took my order, and the policewoman ordered a coffee. I was tired and wanted to go to the motel and sleep. Still, I needed to know what was going on to be prepared in case something happened. If listening to this story would keep the woman happy, it was a small price to pay.

"Go on." I quietly reached into my pocket and pulled out my phone. I hit the record button. I knew I was too tired to remember the fine details.

I'm Malcolm Hannigan's daughter. We had a colicky pony that was a terrorist when he was healthy but a lamb when he was ill. Porky belonged to my sister. He'd had colic for a day or two. I think Dr. Mitchell had been out twice. He had given him pain meds and water up through his nose. He wasn't any better. It was Dr. P's night off, so Doc came, but he was sick. Doc had a cold or the "man-flu," and Mom could see he was struggling. Doc was supposed to give more medication, and then if Porky wasn't any better—well, you know my dad.

I nodded. More than one trip by a vet for a horse at their place was unusual.

Doc went out to the paddock with my mom and my sister to help. Porky belonged to Darleen. She was Dad's favorite. The rain was becoming slushy, and it was coming down pretty hard. Porky wasn't letting Doc catch him. According to my mother, he was being a right bastard. Finally, when they almost had him trapped in a corner, Doc yelled for Darleen to run up to block his exit. He swore when she failed to keep Porky from escaping. Doc didn't know Darleen had cerebral palsy. When he turned and watched her trying to run, my mother said he covered his mouth and never said another word.

The following day, Doc was still sick, but he showed up with the redhead nurse driving a truck and trailer. They took Porky to the clinic, did colic surgery, returned him two weeks later, and said the account had been settled. Dad would have spent a lot of money to save that pony for Darleen.

"What happened to your sister?"

"She got married and had a son. She named him Bill. She lives in California. Porky lived until he was twenty-seven. Doc came out every year to vaccinate Porky and brought his son to help."

"Thanks. You know I don't even know your name." I had another great story and now had a new friend. I thanked her for the story. I tried to hide my tears with my napkin, but I didn't fool her.

"Celia, but the guys all call me CeeCee. I'd like to return the favor. My brother owns the motel. That was my nephew who helped you move in. What time do you want to go to Greenbriar tomorrow? It turns out that several men on the force go that way every few minutes, and they would love to meet a hero, so we want to ensure that your stay here is a pleasant one. Actually, you don't have a say in this."

CeeCee handed me a card with a phone number and asked me to call it if anyone was bothering me or when I needed transportation. Her final words were, "Any other mode of transportation is not negotiable. We all owe Doc one way or another."

I gave her my phone number, and CeeCee took the bill and said it was on the house. The receptionist nodded and pointed to the door.

We entered the police car. "Do I get the lights and siren?"

"Don't push it, Hayley." For a microsecond, she turned them on.

CeeCee took me across the street and down a block to the motel. She thanked me for my time and asked if she could join me for dinner tomorrow night. She waited until I entered the motel room and stuck my head out to say I was safe.

"I'll call you unless things aren't going well." I waved.

Chapter 33

The nightmare was horrific. My old kidnapper was in Daniel's bed when I arrived. He had a nurse, and she was bleeding from a wound inflicted by Pauly's knife. Daniel was on the ground holding his pee bag. I tried to return to sleep, but the dream returned. I was sweating and gasping. I decided to remain awake. I had two more hours until I would be allowed to enter Briarwood.

I found my fractured arm was not nearly as painful, and I could prop it on a pillow and type for more extended periods. I entered all the stories. I felt the whole of Bill's remarkable life was taking shape and was worthy of publication, even without the addition of his marital dramas.

When the breakfast bar was open, I walked down to grab something to eat. Bill was sitting and chatting with a man who might be the owner. Bill stood and introduced me to CeeCee's brother, Merle Hannigan. Bill pulled a chair out for me and kissed me on the cheek. He appeared tired, and I guessed he had remained at Briarwood all night.

I gazed at him and cocked my head. He pursed his lips and shook his head. Merle excused himself when more people entered the dining room.

"So?" I bit my upper lip waiting for his response.

He knew I wanted an update. "No. There's been no change. I stayed with Myrna and checked in on Daniel all night. They have comfortable recliners, and I did get some sleep. I guess that this won't end soon. The kids went out to the lake. The grandkids are old enough to be on their own. They'll stay out there today. Richard and Jessica will go back and forth.

"They know Daniel's in the same facility. While they understand I have two obligations, they want nothing to do with their adopted brother and suggested that my loyalty should remain with Myrna."

I couldn't tell Bill what Daniel had confided in me. Daniel's parentage would remain a taboo topic, at least until Daniel passed. "How was Daniel this morning when you left? Was he awake?"

"I spoke with him briefly. His oxygen levels were good, and he was alert, but he didn't want to eat, and his urine production was down."

That's because it was all over the floor when he was kicked out of the bed by Pauly. Well, that was my explanation from my dream last night.

"I'll keep a watch on it today. I'll text you if anything looks imminent."

Bill knew what I meant. "I'm going home to sleep, and the kids will be with their mother." He stood and asked if I was going his way.

"You may not know, but I have new options." As I said that, CeeCee walked into the breakfast room. I mentioned she had treated me to dinner, and she and her colleagues would give me a ride to and from Briarwood.

CeeCee walked up to Bill and hugged him. "I had some minor resistance, Doc, but I think she sees who is calling the shots now. Don't worry. We have it covered."

Bill hugged her again and asked how her sister was doing. He then turned to me and, with a self-satisfying grin, informed me that it helps to have friends in high places in the town. CeeCee and Bill high-fived each other.

"Well, the pony and cowboy didn't show up, so not everyone is on board." I tried not to smile and failed.

Bill stared at me. He got the inference. "Come on, Princess. Your chariot awaits."

Bill helped me into the truck, and when he was seated, he turned to me and told me he missed sleeping with me.

"I missed you too. How are you holding up?"

"I've had better times. I feel pulled in three different directions. I want to be with Myrna, and I know it's crazy. Then poor Daniel, well, I hate that this is happening now. The kids are acting so strangely. The truth be told, I miss you. You and I have limited time, and there is so much I want to tell you."

I took my arm out of the sling and took his hand. It seemed to be shrunken and withered. "I miss you too." In the back of my mind, I could not get Daniel's secret out of my mind. I knew Daniel didn't understand the inferences, but somehow, he knew not to tell his father. I had a difficult time believing this, but these days genetic testing is available.

Bill pulled into the parking lot and saw his children enter the building. He waited and then kissed me once again. "Tell Daniel I love him."

"Bill, he knows. He tells me how much he loves you too. We discussed his favorite times, and he said one was when you, Richard, and he went fishing, and Daniel was the only one who caught a fish. It's the small things that are important. If you have any pictures of you and Daniel, can you bring them when you come back and, for God's sakes, take a shower."

Bill smirked and gazed skyward. "Myrna lives."

I entered the lobby, and both of Bill's children were there waiting for me. I smiled and attempted to walk past them, but they stopped me.

Richard put up his hand. "We know who you are."

I waited for an explanation, but they simply stood and blocked my way to Daniel's wing.

Jessica put her hand on her hip and said, "We want to thank you. We know you're only doing what our father has asked of you, and we know he's torn between the love for his real son and our mother. That's all. We ask that you respect our wishes for privacy at this time. Our mother wasn't perfect, but she put up with so much from our father that she felt for her sanity that she had to reach out to others. We know our real fathers, and once our mother is gone and properly celebrated, we'll leave you two to do whatever you're doing."

I couldn't help myself. "I won't bother you, and I am sorry for your pending loss, but you might consider there is another side to this story. Again, I'm genuinely sorry."

They let me pass. I entered Daniel's room and noticed a significant decline in his overall stability and vitals. An attendant was sitting with him and holding his hand. She smiled and pointed to his eyes, indicating he was sleeping. We exchanged places, and she whispered that he had been asking for me.

I nodded and looked at the urine output, which was low according to the marks on the urine collection bag. I could feel his pulse was thready and weak, convincing me his time was near. He woke, looked at me, and smiled. He crooked his finger, indicating he wanted to talk. The attendant left. I leaned over to hear him.

"Dad came in and stayed with me and told me how much he loves me and will miss me. He said he would be glad to share me with my mom."

"We all will, Daniel. You are a very special man."

"We had a man-to-man talk. I'm supposed to take care of my mother in heaven."

"Hey, how about if you take care of each other?" I had another question. "Do you know where your mother's buried?"

Daniel faintly smiled. "Yeah, Daddy takes me to her grave once a year. I'm going to be next to her when I die. There's a spot already for me."

I nodded. "Danny, what do you want on your headstone?"

He was confused. "My name?"

"Yeah, but would you like something else on it like a saying or a poem or some words that you like?"

"Can I choose that?" He appeared to consider this option.

"Well, it can't be too long but yes."

He didn't say anything and closed his eyes. I wiped his face. There were now swabs to moisten his lips. An hour later, he woke and smiled when he saw me sitting with him. He bent his finger again, and I moved my ear near his lips. His chest was becoming rattly, and he occasionally coughed. "Say, I did my best."

"Perfect Danny. No one could ask for more." I swallowed hard. "I might do the same."

He slept most of the day. The doctor came and said it would not be long for him now. I waited to let Bill get another hour of sleep, but he showed up and gave me a box of pictures. I told him what the doctor said, and he sat next to Daniel. Bill squeezed Daniel's hand, and Danny's eyes flickered. He saw his father and whispered, "I love you."

Bill smiled and nodded.

Bill stayed for an hour, then leaned over, kissed me, and left. I couldn't imagine the agony Bill was experiencing. I suspected he was not as welcome in with Myrna. I wondered if the children had let him know they were aware of their biological parentage. It was none of my business, and I could only hope they would be kind to the man who had raised them.

As Daniel slept, I noted his breathing had slowed. I took the time to thumb through the box of pictures. There were pictures of Daniel as a baby with Bill and more as he grew. There was one with Bill, Richard, and Daniel. Both boys held fish. Richard must be ten years older than Daniel.

In the box was a poem. It must have been written by Bill many years ago.

To Daniel,

> Your innocence knows no bounds,
> Your loving nature confounds.
> You are the joy in my heart,
> I vow never to part.
> When you are laid to rest,
> Know in your heart
> You did your best.

Daniel must have remembered this poem. I did my best.

He woke and saw the picture I'd placed on his side table. He reached over, took the picture, and kissed it. "Danny, I'm going to step out for a minute." I didn't want him to see me in tears. I went out and sat on the patio bench for a moment. When I composed myself, I returned to Daniel's room. I peeked into the room through the door window and saw Richard sitting with him.

I walked back to the patio. I could see the hallway and waited until Richard left the room. I entered, and Daniel sat up a little higher in his bed. He told me his brother stopped by and gave him a card. The card said, Get Well Soon. "Richard said he would look me up when he gets to heaven. He even remembered the poem my father wrote with me."

"Oh, so you and your father wrote this together?"

"I like to rhyme. Daddy would speak a line and let me find a word to rhyme with the last word. Hayley, I mean, Mom, do you know what rhymes with Daniel?"

"No, what words rhyme with Daniel?" I knew he wanted to answer it.

Daniel was wheezing. He said, "Spaniel," but then he began to cough. He didn't have the energy to cough efficiently. He gave up, closed his eyes, and lay still—too still.

"Daniel?" I waited and felt his pulse. I palpated a very thready, weak pulse, but he breathed intermittently. I remembered watching my father die, and this was the beginning. With Dad, it went on for a day.

"Daniel?" I asked again.

He didn't respond. I sent Bill a text, but I received no reply. I waited a few minutes and then went out to find a nurse. She said she would go down and see if Bill was free to come to Daniel's room.

It was an agonizing hour before he arrived. I saw tears on his drawn face. Had Myrna passed? I stood and gave him the chair. He took Daniel's hand, put his face down on the bed, and wept. I didn't talk and allowed him to cry. I rubbed his back and stood beside the bed.

His convulsive sobs finally ceased. He reached back and took my hand. He raised his head and announced Myrna was the same. I was confused. I handed him a tissue. He finally sat quietly.

He sighed and appeared to want to talk, but then he lowered his head and would give a small sob. Finally, he turned to me and said, "I had a vasectomy two years after Jessica was born. It was something I will regret to the day I die. I hoped it would make Myrna stop sleeping around. She knew if she became pregnant that her game would be up, and maybe she would come to love me and forsake the others. I know Myrna had one abortion after my surgery. I wasn't supposed to know, but she had a bleeding complication, and when I took her to the ER, it came out. My poor kids think I am Jessie's real father. I don't know if I will set them straight or not."

I agonized over whether I would tell him what Richard told Daniel. I would wait. Believing he was Bill's real son would not be the worst thing for Daniel as he faced death.

Bill and I spelled each other during the night. At one point, Bill reported that Daniel seemed to revive and look around. As I took over, the intervals between breaths became longer and longer, and finally, he ceased to breathe. Bill was with Myrna. I sent him a message. The staff were already making arrangements and would wait for Bill to come.

After forty minutes without a word from Bill, I was exhausted and decided to return to the motel. I suspected that Myrna was in her final stages. I asked the attendant to leave Daniel until Bill could view the body and that I was going to the motel. I called for my ride. Fortunately, CeeCee was still on duty and was at the door within a few minutes.

"Sorry, we missed dinner. Can I have a raincheck, CeeCee?"

"Maybe tonight. I'm guessing you aren't needed?" CeeCee pulled out of Briarwood and onto the main drag.

"No. It's over. It was a good death." I did my duty, and now my next would be Bill. I hoped this would not be soon.

"Do you know the plans for a celebration or whatever?" CeeCee asked as she pulled into the motel's parking lot.

"I don't, and to be honest, I don't know if there will even be one with the family issues and Bill's wife. Well, you know." I shrugged. I would be the last to know, and I wouldn't be invited to Myrna's funeral.

CeeCee ran into the same diner and got me some pancakes and coffee to go while I waited in the car. It was five in the morning, and the motel's continental breakfast wouldn't be open for an hour. I thanked her and tried to pay.

"Get that stinkin' money out of here. I thought we bonded. I'm totally insulted."

"Sheesh, sorry. Is that an arrestable offense? Can we meet for dinner tonight, or are you on a late shift? We could meet before you go on duty if that works?"

"That would be great. Mind if I invite a friend or two? We all want to hear more about your adventure if you want to talk about it."

"It's a little raw, but talking about it might help. I have to admit it's been a challenge to sleep at night."

"PTSD?" CeeCee pulled up to my motel room.

"I guess. I saw a shrink, and he suggested I go pet a pony. Frankly, I would rather pet the cowboy leading the pony."

"Well, I'm married, so the pony sounds good. Shall we say six tonight, and I'll pick you up."

"Thanks. If you have any other Bill stories, I'd love to hear them."

"Oh, so you have more than a passing interest in Doc?" She raised her eyebrows several times, clicked her teeth together, and chuckled.

"My original role was to write a book about his life. Things have changed slightly with the pending death of his wife and now Daniel's death."

"Got it. I'll try to remember some."

I entered my room and gave CeeCee the all-clear. I quickly showered and went to bed. I had no trouble sleeping. It was daytime, and a few hours later, I heard Bill knocking and calling for me. I was in a deep sleep. It took a few moments to wake up and orient myself. I opened the door and let him in. I waited for him to speak. He hugged me and pulled me onto the edge of the bed. He didn't cry; he simply sat holding me.

My sling was off, and I could use both arms to hold him. He sat for several minutes and then stood and asked to stay with me for a while. He went into the bathroom and returned.

"I used your deodorant, so I don't want any complaints." He lay down on the bed, and I threw the bedspread over him and joined him under the cover. He spooned me and was asleep in merely seconds. I lay awake for only a few minutes myself.

It was midafternoon when I felt him leaving the bed. He smiled and said sorry. "I have the wrong room. I thought this was Bo Derek's room."

"I can see how you would be confused. I'm often mistaken for Bo. But really, any updates?"

Bill sat down on the bed and squeezed my foot under the covers. "Daniel's at the mortuary, and he'll be cremated. His ashes will go next to his mother. I've collected his personal effects and placed them in the truck. The kids are with Myrna. She's beginning to show a decline. We now have a rotating eight-hour schedule so that it won't be too hard. My time is from five to midnight. Prepare for a visitor later tonight. I said I would stay close. I'm going home to shower and get my phone charger."

"What can I do? If it's to be several days, I might go up and see our surgical colic case, or I could even fly home. I could get some clothes for autumn and winter unless you think we'll finish the book before then. I could even fly down and see my kids. I should call them anyway."

"Hayley, please don't leave now. Please. I need you. I can barely walk into Myrna's room anymore. Telling the kids that I was Daniel's father while knowing I'd had the vasectomy was the ultimate betrayal. I don't care when or how she dies. I won't say anything unless it becomes an ugly scene. I have my limits. I love Richard and Jessica. I love the grandkids, but I will not put up with them passing off lies and half-truths to anyone."

"Bill, give them time. They're upset and grieving as well. Deep down, Richard and Jessica know what you did for them over the years. I saw Richard visiting with Daniel a few hours before he passed."

"Really? Interesting. I can't thank you enough."

I remembered the poem. "I almost forgot. Daniel wants you to put 'I did my best' on his headstone. It's from your poem."

"All right then. I'll be sending the account to Jake on that one." Bill stood, walked around the bed to where I rested, and kissed my forehead. "See you about midnight unless I find Bo's room first."

"Good luck on that. Did you count the silverware before your kids arrived?"

"They can have it all as far as I'm concerned. God knows how long I'll need it anyway."

Bill did appear thinner, but despite all his worries, he retained a small amount of his sense of humor.

"Oh, CeeCee and the boys are taking me to dinner at six. I'm hoping it goes well. Maybe stop at the front desk to get a key if I'm not back."

Bill shook his head. "A girl can dream—be careful. I'm not too worried. They're all younger than your kids. I know they aren't your type anyway."

"Oh, what's my type?" I sat up, hugged my legs, and rested my head on my knees.

He pointed to himself. "Crotchety old geezers."

"That's only a recent interest, and there's a twelve-step program to cure that affliction."

CHAPTER 34

At six in the evening, CeeCee called. She was not going to be available. Canceling dinner was not the worst thing. I was still tired and overwhelmed at having witnessed Daniel's death. "An old client of Doc's is going to pick you up. He wants to talk to you."

I groaned. I didn't want to meet anyone new tonight. "CeeCee, can we wait until tomorrow? I'm done in from last night."

"No. My guess is he's probably standing outside your door. He knows you and remembers you. It's Ronny Hughes."

"Ron? The most important man in my life at the time, Ron? Okay, no prob. Gee, I wish I had a dress."

CeeCee laughed. "I'm pretty sure Ron will take you as you are."

I heard a knock at the door. "Gotta go. It's date night."

"Be easy on him, Hayley. He's had a rough life."

I opened the door, and we immediately enveloped one another, and we both cried. "How are you, Hayley? How many years? I've thought about all those times. My, didn't we have some laughs? I'm so glad you let me have dinner with you." It went on.

"Ronnie, in a million years—the most important man in my life when I worked here." I hugged him again.

"You know when you told the partners what you called me, they made a plaque and gave it to me when I retired. It said, 'To the Most Important Man in Our Practice.' I'd show it to you, but you know I could never work those damn phones."

"Let's head over to the diner. I thought I wasn't very hungry, but now I am." We walked over to his old beat-up truck. "This isn't the same one, is it?" I sniffed deeply. "Yep, I can still smell death."

"Hayley, if you didn't already have a broken arm, I'd hit you. No, this is a new model. The old one was green."

"So, when did you give up the funeral business? Doc didn't say anything. I figured you were in the pit with all your former clients."

Ronnie's hand rested on the stick shift. He jiggled it to force it into reverse. "I reckon I picked up the last one maybe eight or so years ago. Those were fun times. Day and night, whenever one of you failed at your job, I had to pick up the pieces, literally." Ronnie had a wicked sense of humor which was one of the few hints of his remarkable intelligence.

We entered the diner, and the waitresses all hailed Ronnie and asked if he wanted the usual. "No, I'll decide when my date decides. Can we have the booth in the back? I don't want to put off the customers. We'll be discussing the funeral business."

The waitress that served CeeCee and I turned to another and announced she wasn't paid enough for hearing about dead horses, and she was taking a break. The few customers who were seated appeared alarmed. Then they recognized Ronnie's corpulent figure and laughed. He'd always said he was the same size in any direction.

His waist had possibly surpassed his height in recent years. He could see I was assessing his figure, and he pointed his finger at me. "Don't you even dare, Alexander. I get enough of it from my doctor."

"Apparently not." I successfully dodged a swat as I sat down.

We ordered, and after our drinks arrived, Ronnie folded his hands and stared at me. "So, how's Bill?" I was surprised. I didn't know Ronnie was one of the few people in this town that called him by his first name.

I shrugged. "Not great right now, but he's hanging in there."

"Don't BS me. I saw him at the oncologist when I took my wife a few months ago. You don't go into that place to read the magazines."

"I don't know. They have Field and Streams from 1915." I glanced at Ronnie and saw he adopted his take-no-prisoner persona. "Lymphoma, usually a slow death, but Doc's is slightly more aggressive. That's why I'm here. I'm writing a book about his life, but I know he'll want you to do the honors when the time comes."

We both laughed at this joke. Ronnie clasped his hands. "I'll charge up my phone when I get home."

"He's had a slight reprieve, so maybe put that on hold for now. So, what's with your wife?"

"Melanoma. Just a checkup. So far, so good, but at twenty-seven years old, you don't want to take chances." Ron was in his late eighties, and if he had remarried a younger model, I would have heard.

"Yeah, she always was a pretty thing. I guess you beat the sex with a minor charge?"

"It was touch and go." He smiled and nodded, remembering his early courting days. I knew she was of legal age, but Ron always called her his child bride.

"Pun intended?" I rolled my eyes.

"We just had our wedding anniversary." Ronnie pulled out a picture from his wallet. He and Mrs. Hughes stood by a cake she had made.

"I wouldn't mind some of that cake."

"I'll ask her. If she's forgiven you for keeping me out all night, she might make one for you."

Our meals arrived. "I heard you need some stories. I have a few, but there is one that I think you may want for this book. It speaks to the man we all admire."

"Do you mind if I record it in case I forget something?"

"I don't mind. It's hell when you get old and can't remember. It happens. Not everyone can be as sharp as me."

I gently kicked him under the table. "Ronnie, I think we may have a few memories ourselves. I would hate for them to get out. Hmm, was it the Morgan's horse you forgot to take to the pit before you arrived to help me? I doubt I will ever get that ugly memory out of my brain. Three days dead and as whiffy as could be."

Ronnie talked while we ate. "Do you remember Michael Holmes? Michael was the guy who had cutting horses. He died last year. They had a massive sendoff for him at the fairgrounds."

"Oh, yeah. Didn't he stand the stallion Doc's Durango or Doc's Derangement or something like that?" Ronnie laughed at the play on words.

"It was Doc's Durango," he agreed, then continued his story.

Maybe ten years after you left, the market got pretty saturated. The need for the stallion's semen dropped from over ten mares per semen collection to one.

Michael paid for the semen collections and shipping. Since this colt was in the prime of his life, let's just say many potential cutting horses went down the drain that year, and Michael was paying more than he could afford.

Bill saw a chance to learn how to freeze semen, so he asked Michael if he could use the stallion's unused semen to practice the technique. He said it would help them both as he would only charge a nominal fee to do the collections. The deal was struck. Bill and the partners decided not to charge at all for the semen collections, and they would own the frozen semen. That summer, Bill perfected the technique and amassed a fortune in frozen semen. The stallion became a hot item the following year when one of the stallion's first progeny won the finals down in Texas.

"Ronnie, sorry to interrupt, but how do you know all this?"

"I was the silent half owner. Not even Bill knew this at the time. Didn't you know I dabbled in cutting horses? In my youth, I was a 'contenda' as they used to say."

"Wow. Go on." Ronnie had more avenues of income than I had toes and fingers.

So, the next year Mike and I were sitting in tall clover waiting for the requests to come in. They surely did. He could not accommodate everyone. Our boy was as fertile as possible, but we shipped almost fifteen lots per collection. Bill never was able to have enough left over for his little enterprise that year.

I will never forget when I received the call. Our stallion was as good as dead. He fractured his pastern bone, you know, the top one, out playing in the paddock. Bill raced out and, without even an x-ray, confirmed the worst. I was summoned for funeral duties, while Bill still was unaware I was a part-owner. He explained that the fracture was most likely in multiple pieces and that surgery probably wasn't an option. I refused to take him away for burial, and that's when Bill found out about my partnership with Mike as a half-owner.

"Never say never." I don't know how many times I heard Bill say that. Funny, but as the guy who picked up the "never agains," you'd have thought I would be the last person to hear that from Bill. He explained how unlikely this fracture would heal, and he told me that it would be a rather expensive procedure. Bill said he'd probably get laminitis in the other leg.

I asked him to try. We decided to take him to the clinic, and the radiograph showed that the first bone was shattered. Bill suggested it might be a good thing, and he cast the leg with the stallion standing up. It was amazing to see the horse walk out of the padded room into a stall. It was like he wasn't even lame. He stayed at the clinic for a week.

Ron asked for the dessert menu. He chose chocolate cake and then resumed his story.

"Hayley, what's the name for that bone? I can never remember it."

"The first phalanx." I wonder why I hadn't heard about this story.

Yeah, well anyway, the breeding season was a bust. Then we all remembered the frozen semen. The semen belonged to the clinic, and Mike suggested we buy some from Bill to try on a mare that had come from interstate and was close to ovulating. Bill agreed, and we called the mare owner, and he was all for it.

In those days, very few clinics were handling frozen semen, so the owner told us to give it a single try, ship the mare back, and he would have her checked at sixteen days. Bill had the mare at the clinic. He checked her for ovulation every few hours day and night. Poor Bill was exhausted.

I interrupted his story. "You know, these days, it's a lot easier. They can give injections or slip pellets under the skin to make mares ovulate, and usually, the number of times you have to check for ovulation is reduced. But, go on with the story."

Anyway, the mare got in foal, so if people wanted to breed that year, they could buy the frozen semen. Not many vets were set up to do this frozen semen protocol or even knew how, so mares started to arrive, and there wasn't enough room at the clinic.

Mike had all the mares come to his place, and he kept all the records. We did sixty mares, and I think most got in foal. Bill said he would only do younger mares, and the owners had to pay upfront for the semen. Then he charged them a fee for the work it took to inseminate the mares as they ovulated. Bill could have made a fortune on the deal. He sure as hell worked hard enough on it.

Bill was coming and going all hours every day and night for months. He began to sleep at Michael's on a cot in the barn. Michael and his wife were having their first baby. They made a setup, so Bill could get the mare, put her in the chute, and do it all by himself. If the mare was a problem, I came and helped.

In the end, we took care of as many as possible. Of course, we didn't own the semen, so the clinic made a killing, but Mike got the board money, and of course, Bill saved our stallion's life.

"That's a great story. Thanks for sharing it." I eyed Ronnie's cake, and he saw me. He tossed me an extra fork, so I tried a piece.

"That's not the end." Ronnie motioned for the waitress.

The day the final cast came off our stallion, or as we now called him, Bill Junior, Bill sat down with us and went over the final account. We owed him four thousand and some change. We bred two of our mares as well.

Mike and I thought that was beyond fair, but Bill wrote off half of the account. He admitted he and the partners had learned so much that they would start offering frozen semen preservation and insemination as a regular service. They would be ahead of their time.

I was in awe. I didn't know any of this. I knew the clinic was an early entrant into the frozen semen business, but I never knew Ronnie's role in it all.

"So, what happened to Bill Junior?"

"He lived until he was twenty-four. Then we had another colt that took over, and now Michael's son runs the program. I got out after the first ten years, which gave me the option to retire."

"But you didn't, did you, Ronnie?" I took one more bite of the cake and asked the waitress for a piece to go with a meal for Bill when he arrived after his shift.

"Hayley, about then, the partners began taking on a lot more vets, and you know when you have young, inexperienced vets, well, my business went up. Besides, if I were at home with my darling bride's penchant for making cake, I'd be twice as round today as I am. Say, I better get home. She's liable to get suspicious."

"Tell her thanks for sharing you tonight."

Ronnie dropped me off at the motel. He hugged and kissed me. I suggested we all get together when the current drama was over. I was dead to the world in short order. I woke when Bill entered the room. He said there was no change with Myrna. I pointed to the food, but he wasn't hungry and got into bed.

I quickly recounted the story and mentioned the potential get-together with Ronnie and Mrs. Hughes. Bill put his hand on my shoulder and leaned toward me.

"That would be interesting. Ronnie's wife died several years ago."

CHAPTER 35

I woke around fivish. It took all my strength not to eat the cake. I sat in the one stuffed chair, reread what I had written, and then added Ronnie's story to the book. It was now beginning to take shape. If I ended it as written, it would at least be a novella. I wondered how I would include Daniel's story. I could see no reason to leave it out. I wouldn't mention Myrna had barred him from living with the family.

I began to write more about Daniel's parents and Tammy's death when there was a knock at the door. Hmm, so how was this going to work? The room had one bed which contained the sleeping husband of a dying woman and me. I stared at Bill, who I could see was thinking along the same lines.

The knocking persisted, and Bill decided to get up, threw on some pants, and went to the door while I conveniently went into the bathroom. The next thing I heard sounded like a gunshot. That was all I heard, and I raced out to see Bill slumped by the door with a large amount of blood coming from his abdomen. The door was closed, and I heard a car retreating.

Bill gazed up at me and said, "Jake." His face was pale, and he began to breathe in sharp gasps.

I took my phone, called 911, and then the number CeeCee gave me. The ambulance was on its way, as were several other emergency personnel. I held Bill as the blood oozed from a hole in his abdomen. I kept telling him that help was on the way and to hang on and all the other things you would expect a person to say. He smiled and leaned into me. "Hayley?"

"I'm here. Don't talk. I see the ambulance. Don't worry, you'll be fine. Here they are." The ambulance with paramedics and several onlookers gathered around the door to the room where I sat holding Bill.

"Hayley, don't leave me." The first paramedic was by Bill's side and assessed him quickly. The second had a stretcher, and within seconds, they had him strapped in. While they loaded Bill into the ambulance, the driver radioed the hospital to say they were coming in with a man with an abdominal gunshot wound. He asked to have the emergency room on standby and a possible surgical team. Their ETA was six minutes.

The paramedic asked who I was, and as I began to explain, CeeCee ran up and told him I was his partner, and they let me go on the ambulance with Bill. I glanced at her and quietly mouthed, "Thank you."

I was still in my bloody pajamas and did not even have a bathrobe. I sat in the corner where Bill could see me. At the same time, the paramedics worked on Bill, placing an intravenous catheter and oxygen mask onto his now ashen face.

We arrived at the emergency entrance. Bill was stretchered into the room where many people stood ready and waiting. Two women gasped, and their hands flew up to their mouths. "It's Doc, oh my God." His blood type was quickly ascertained, and he was taken away for imaging to determine if surgery was indicated.

I was given a hospital bathrobe and sent to the admission area. CeeCee joined me and helped me fill in the admission form. She said Bill's children were called, and they would arrive in the next few minutes. I didn't remember if I told anyone what Bill told me. "He said it was Jake, Daniel's father."

"Okay, let me radio that in." She stepped out but returned and asked if I saw him.

I explained I was in the bathroom. "I thought Bill's kids might be coming to inform him about Myrna. Bill had arrived sometime after midnight and wanted to be close to Briarwood. He felt that his wife's time might be near, and he was only sharing the bed. It's not what you think, CeeCee."

"Hayley, I don't think anyone would care what was happening. So, you didn't see anything at all?"

"No, but don't they have security cameras?"

"I don't know. I expect they do. Anyway, stay here, and I'll see what's happening." I was in a small room off the main lobby. As I waited, I heard a commotion and saw Jessica and another man run into the entrance. They saw me in a hospital bathrobe with blood on my hands and face.

I rose from my chair, but they ignored me and sped through the foyer to the emergency department.

CeeCee returned after a long while. "Let's take you to the police station and get you processed."

"I should stay. Are they going to do surgery? Is Bill okay?"

"Bill's daughter said you should be examined as a person of interest and removed from the hospital."

My heart sank. Daniel was dead. Bill was in critical condition, and now I would be accused of Bill's murder. I knew that the video footage from the security cameras would exonerate me. The motel was searched, but no weapon was found. I had no motive, but I was the only person at the incident's location.

I had to admit, I was in love with Bill, and it was returned. It was different from the heady young love I'd experienced in my youth. We cared deeply for one another. We were two older people who counted on one another in difficult times. Ours would be a short-term affair. Bill might last another year, but it was doubtful it would go on any longer, and that was only in the remote chance he survived the gunshot. I wanted to be with him before and hopefully after any surgery to correct the damage. Oh, God, please let him live.

"Hayley, I have orders. We can get you processed, take a statement, and you can get showered and back here in no time."

Well, if four hours was no time. They found a small amount of gun residue, which they felt was from me holding Bill. The motel's security camera was not working, and the interview took forever. I kept asking for an update, and all they would say was there had been no verified word from the hospital. Finally, I was informed that the immediate family was not releasing any information. I was being shut out.

I was hurt, disappointed, and, of course, furious. I suspected this was retribution for "consorting" with Bill over the last few weeks. There was nothing I could do. I could only pray that Bill would wake up and have someone call me. I was free to leave, and CeeCee took me back to the motel. I was still in my bloody pajamas.

Her brother said that the family would not pay for my room anymore. Richard and his sister assumed control of Bill's assets. I would have to move anyway, as it was a crime scene. I asked for my clothes, but they were part of the evidence. Could this get any worse?

They had taken my phone and computer, searching for any evidence that would implicate me in the shooting. CeeCee took me to a clothing store, and while I sat in the car, she ran in and bought me some clothes. She took me back to her brother's motel, and while I waited in the car, she went in and spoke with her brother. She emerged from the motel's office and dangled a key. I was given a room behind the building, and she left saying she would get an update one way or another.

I entered a small dingy room, showered, and dressed. At least I was clean. I had no toiletries, food, or money. I sat down on the bed and cried. I decided to turn on the television. This was the first good news I received. Bill had survived the surgery and was en route to Denver for intensive care. A reporter interviewed the family. Richard said that they were uncertain who had shot his father. He mentioned that two people of interest were under investigation. One was interviewed by the police and was under surveillance. The other was either on the run or unaware of the crime—what a load of crap.

He went on to say that his mother was in the final stages of dying, and so they were not releasing any information at this time. "My parents have been married for over fifty years and are very close. If either dies in the next twenty-four hours, we are worried for the remaining parent. There will be no further updates at this time."

I closed my eyes. Yes, it could get worse. I had no means to fill my short-term needs. I had no money or way to contact anyone. There was a knock at my door. I was wary, so I asked who it was.

"It's me, Lorna. Can I come in?"

I cautiously cracked the door and kept my foot at the base if she pushed it forward. She didn't attempt to enter my motel room and instead put a one-hundred-dollar bill in the door's crack. "Hayley, I'm not here to bother you. I know what's going on. You may be a shameless hussy, but I know you didn't shoot Bill."

That made me laugh. I opened the door and asked Lorna to come in. "Do you know anything? They won't even tell me Bill's status." I knew she could see my desperation.

"He's alive. It's touch and go. Bill's in an induced coma. They want to wake him up as soon as they think it's safe, but it might be another twenty-four hours. Bill saw the kids just before he went into surgery, and he thanked them for com-ing. Jessie said he seemed pleased. Myrna is slowly showing fewer and fewer signs that she has any brain function. The kids wanted to put her on a respirator, but Bill said no. There was an outright fight about it."

"Well, thank you for the update. That gives me hope."

Lorna did not mince words. "As I said, I know you and Bill are lovers, but you must remember, Bill's first duty is to Myrna, no matter what she's done. Or how she's treated Bill."

I tried to remain neutral, but my reaction was obvious to Lorna. "Bill knows and has acted accordingly no matter what you think."

"I know what I saw, and I disapprove, but if Bill lives, you'll soon be free to pursue whoever you want. My loyalty is to Myrna. I know it sounds crazy, but it is what it is."

"I admire you and your devotion—no guessing whose side you're on. The thing is, there are no sides. Bill and I support each other when we both have had personal issues. That's where it ends."

"We all know he's dying. He told his kids, and they told me. We know he's afraid to be alone. He concocted the ruse that he asked you to write his story. He knew you were alone and might be the perfect person to care for him. He doesn't care about the story. He's using you to be his nurse with a purse. In your case, it's a nurse with a pen. He'll never stop loving Myrna. He's like an abused puppy, and he can't give up. Myrna knew it and, well, I'm sad to say she used his devotion to her advantage."

"Lorna, why are you really here?" I felt this must be a ploy. No one could do such an about-face in such a short time.

"Hayley, I have my reasons. I know that Myrna may have been unfaithful with someone near and dear to me. We may all be her victims."

I was shocked. "Do you mind if I ask what made you think this?"

"The night I sat with her after her stroke, I saw a phone charging next to her bed. I went through it, and I found several text messages to Trent, my husband. I was sure it was all a mistake. It was around the time of my birthday, and I hoped it might be that they were planning a surprise birthday party for me. Still, the nature of the messages suggested otherwise. I confronted my husband, and he admitted he and Myrna had seen each other off and on over the years."

"I'm sorry." I was sorry. I hated to say it. Myrna was a beautiful woman, but she lacked any attributes that made her worthy of Bill's devotion.

"I probably should have suspected it a few years ago, but I was blind. The truth be told, I was in love with Bill. He never gave me a moment's notice. I thought when Myrna died, he might see beyond Myrna. Maybe he and I could console each other in our grief. Then you showed up, and I knew my chances of us getting together were zero."

I now understood the reason Lorna was so upset with my presence. "You must understand, Bill and I love each other, but like you, I'm second to Myrna, which is a distant second. Our love is more like a brother and sister. Lorna, nothing has ever happened, nor will it. We're supporting each other. That is the sum of it." The problem was that I was lying to Lorna and myself. I don't think I fooled either one of us.

I didn't know the truth about Bill's feelings, but it probably didn't matter. If Bill is incapacitated in any way, I suspected the children would keep him away from me. I knew they would be protecting their assets. Their actions showed little regard for the man who raised them, knowing he was not their biological father. I had to consider my options. I didn't think it would be long before they believed Jake to be the primary person responsible for this attempted murder.

"Hayley, this place is a shitshow. I know you will laugh when you hear this, but would you like to stay with me tonight?" Lorna appeared to be as upset as I was.

"I don't know. I would have to check with the police." Lorna was correct. My current motel room was away from the other rooms and probably had no security camera. How did I know if Jake would return to take more vengeance if he knew Bill was alive? I had one change of clothes and one pair of pajamas. I didn't know when I would get my credit cards back, and one hundred dollars was not enough to sustain me in the next few days. I couldn't call my sister. I knew she was in Europe for the summer.

"What about your husband?" I made the question open-ended. Was I walking into a landmine?

"Oh, Trent's always been on your and Bill's side." This was curious if Trent was one of Myrna's many lovers, why would he take Bill's side?

"Lorna, this whole thing is crazy. I think I'll stay here tonight, and maybe if I don't get anything back, I might take you up on the offer for tomorrow." I could just see myself having a difficult night vocalizing my nightmares, and then what would they think?

"Okay, but the offer is there." Lorna wrote down her number on a notepad in the room and again apologized.

"If you hear anything about Bill, will you let me know? You could leave a message with the motel and ask them to contact me. I'm sick with worry." I was still wary of Lorna's motives.

"I'm in the good books, and the kids think I'm Myrna's greatest friend. I'm sure they'll give me updates on both of them. I heard you stayed with Daniel. I felt so sorry for him when he was a little boy. He was a sweet child."

I nodded and let her out the door. I decided to go to the diner and see if anyone had any updates on the investigation. I was exhausted and starving. I walked down the street and observed a cop car following me. I was relieved. I hoped they would watch my room tonight. I waved to the policewoman and turned into the diner's parking lot.

Two policemen were sitting in a booth. They stared at me and appeared to be surprised to see me. I was warmly greeted by the waitress and the cook behind a wall separating the kitchen from the counter area. I sat down on a stool, and the waitress immediately asked me if I had heard anything about Bill. I almost cried when I replied, "All my reports are secondhand. Bill's family has shut me out."

My back was to the table where the police officers sat. One came over to me and put his hand on my shoulder. "My partner and I want to know if you would like to join us?"

He was about fifty, and he seemed to have a kind manner.

"I don't want to get you in trouble. You could be consorting with a murderer." I smiled, but he saw I was faking my calm, almost humorous mood.

"Let's just say it might be a continuation of your interrogation this morning." He tapped the tabletop, indicating I should join them.

"Can I have this conversation off the record?"

"Uh, no." He smiled and took my good arm. I didn't have the sling, and without the support, my arm was sore. I ordered something easy to eat with juice.

"Thanks. So, I guess you don't know anything about Bill's status?" I asked.

"No. I'm Heath, and this is Mark. If we knew that Doc was maintaining his own and had a good chance to live, we wouldn't be allowed to say. So, we won't say anything. And we won't say that his internal bleeding has stopped, and the bullet didn't harm any vital structures. If we knew for sure, we couldn't say."

I broke down and thanked them for not reporting this. "I take it you know Bill?"

"Oh yeah. Doc's a regular with us. Of course, that's off the record."

"May I ask why he's a regular?" I took a sip of the juice brought to the table, and immediately the sugar seemed to ease my headache.

The men glanced at each other. Mark pointed to Heath. "You tell her."

"Well, first, he had an ongoing issue with the other suspect." Heath used his index and middle fingers to form quotation marks when he said "other." "Then there was his wife and her occasional escapades, but the big reason is he has headed up the benevolent fund for the families in trouble. When we send a person to prison, there is usually a family left to try to make a living, pay the mortgage, and not to mention the emotional support the family needs. He and his friend, Martin, are the go-to men that help these people out."

Our food arrived, and both men took a break to begin eating their dinner. I was not surprised that another aspect of Bill's involvement in the community had not been mentioned. I would have words with Martin when I saw him. He was visiting family interstate, and I didn't know if he knew about Bill's injuries. They were both such quiet achievers. He had mentioned we would speak more when we were alone.

"I didn't know. Did they raise money?"

"We never saw any fundraising activities, so we never knew for sure, but it wasn't thousands. They were clever, and their way of helping was to get them jobs or housing at an affordable rate or even give the family the means to become educated. I know Bill taught one mother how to read. She came into the station this afternoon and wanted to help in any way. Many people called or stopped by the station. I heard about a line out the door with people wanting to donate blood."

Again, I realized Bill's private life, outside veterinary medicine, was complicated. I would kill myself to write this book now. He deserved the recognition even if he was dead by the time it was published.

We finished the meal, and once again, my money was rejected. The police officers escorted me to the motel. I thanked them, and they hung around. "It's okay. You can leave."

"Not a chance. We're tailing you. You never know. You might be the perp. If you aren't the perp, your life might be in danger. You're under guard, so have a good night's sleep. If we hear anything about Doc, we won't let you know. You know we aren't allowed to discuss this."

I woke to a knock on the door. It must have been around three or so in the morning. "Who is it?"

"Dr. Alexander, it's me, Heath. You have a phone call."

I knew the voice, and was sure it really was Heath. I opened the door after throwing a jacket over my pajamas. He handed me the phone. I was praying it was Martin or maybe Lorna with news about Bill.

I could barely understand the voice. "Hayles, are you alright?"

"Bill? Is it you?" I nearly collapsed.

"Yes, the reports of my demise," whispered Bill, but he coughed and didn't finish the sentence.

I finished it for him. "Greatly exaggerated. Oh, Bill—" I couldn't finish the sentence. I broke down.

Heath took the phone. "Doc, I think she's happy, but she's rather emotional. What can we do?"

I couldn't hear the conversation. I was instructed to get dressed. I was going to Denver.

CHAPTER 36

We stopped and got a to-go breakfast roll and coffee. My first stop was the police station, where a clerk returned my property and phone. The battery was dead. I was escorted to a police car, and CeeCee walked up and announced she would be my chauffeur.

I hugged her. "So, how are things? Any word on finding Jake Jensen?"

"No, but we think he's fled and probably headed for the border. How about you?"

"Never better." Of course, I was a basket case.

"Hell of a twenty-four, hey Hayley?" CeeCee smiled. "He's not out of the woods, but all the signs suggest he'll make it. He asked for you as soon as he was awake. His son is with him, and Richard now believes you're innocent. I think he's had a bit of a talking to from his father."

My jaw tightened. "I don't want to upset Bill, but in all of what has happened, I should cut the kids some slack. Not that I want to, mind you."

"Hayley, look at it from their side. Their mother is dying, and their father is embroiled in a custody battle with a psychopath. At his side is a much younger model moving in and poised to take the lot. At least they don't have to share the spoils with Daniel. They knew that if Daniel and Bill died, they were free to claim the properties and investments."

I couldn't talk about what I knew without Bill's permission. I wondered if Bill's close call with death would make him want to clear the air. CeeCee turned on the lights and the siren for a short time. It helped to get us on the interstate, and then she may have broken a few of the traffic laws on the way to Denver, but I didn't see anything. We talked about her family and her parents.

CeeCee's mother was still alive and living at the old homestead. They no longer had horses, and she had begun to raise guinea pigs, which got out of hand several years ago. They became overrun with the little rodents, and dogs were brought to depopulate the farm. "Hayley, my mother asked me if it was okay if she grew a little grass. I was in the police academy. We all got out of our parents' home, and no one went to jail, which is a miracle."

"So, you think I should cut them some slack?" I was dubious.

"No, but deep down, they've got to be devastated. Richard and Jessica appear so successful and happy on the outside. Still, honestly, I'll bet they hate what has happened to them, and now they'll lose both of their parents." CeeCee was wise beyond her years. She understood human nature and motivation, which I suspected resulted from her years on the force.

"Yeah, I guess. I don't mind most of this, but they had to know I wouldn't have shot Bill."

"We all did, but we had to go through the motions. I'm just happy Bill's going to survive. Our town needs more Bills."

I need more Bill. We drove on in silence, and I dozed. We finally entered the parking lot of the hospital. I was surprised to see a small gathering of reporters. CeeCee drove up to the entrance, dropped me off, and went to park the car.

The reporters stared at me, and one person must have recognized me from the police reports. She called out, "Dr. Alexander, are you here to see Dr. O'Neal? Do you have anything to say? Have you been officially cleared?" And then the one I hoped I would not hear, "Were you in the motel room with Dr. O'Neal when he was shot?"

I smiled and, through gritted teeth, said, "I'm here to see my former boss and old friend. He's in critical condition, and I want to respect the family's wishes. Therefore, it's best to thank you for your interest and kindness, but you may know more than I do. Excuse me." I walked into the hospital foyer and was greeted by a nurse waiting for me.

She smiled and knew who I was. "Hi, I'm supposed to take you to the intensive care unit. Dr. O'Neal is waiting for you."

I followed her down a hallway and then up an elevator and down another corridor. "Can I use the bathroom?"

The nurse probably realized I wanted to clean my face and comb my hair before Bill saw me. She pointed to the bathroom. "Hurry, he's going crazy asking when you will arrive."

I entered the bathroom and looked into the mirror. Who the hell is that? An old lady stared back from the mirror. Gray roots had mysteriously grown in the last few days. My face was pale, and I swear there were new wrinkles. I was a mess. I used cold water on my face and a paper towel to clean my teeth. It was a rough job.

How did this happen? It wasn't the aging that dismayed me so much as the fact I cared. Before this week, I had not been concerned about my advancing age, but somehow now I did. I was over ten years younger than Bill, but he was like an aging rock star. When does the downward spiral of my self-esteem end? "Now. It ends now." I said that out loud, and I realized someone was in the cubicle behind me.

The older woman emerged. She might be a relative of some poor sick ICU patient. I then smiled at her, and she acknowledged me. She probably thinks the same about me. She washed her hands and gazed into the mirror. "Oh, damn. He's going to dump me for one of those nurses."

I laughed, and she turned to me. "It's hell up here. They want my husband to relax, and then in walks a twenty-something nurse, and I can see his heart monitor go crazy. Thank God they moved that vet out of the main ICU area. At least now my husband can get some rest."

I exited the bathroom, and the nurse announced we were going to another ward. Bill was now in a separate room with a guard sitting at his door. The woman shook her head. "The staff say the man who tried to kill him might be around. My husband doesn't need that kind of excitement."

We turned a corner, and I observed a uniformed guard sitting on a chair outside a door. I could feel my heart racing.

It was like a first date. I knew what I was going to say. I would not gush. I suspected his son was in the room.

I entered the room. Bill lay on a bed with intravenous tubes and wires emerging from every direction under a single sheet. He was pale but appeared to be comfortable. We stared at one another, and I walked up to the bed. Richard was sitting next to the bed, and he smiled. I nodded to him. I bent down and kissed Bill on the cheek.

His thin, gnarled hand took mine. It was weak, but he would not let go. He mouthed, "I'm sorry."

I began to cry. It was short, but I could not help it. As I regained my composure, CeeCee also entered the room. I finally was able to say what I had planned.

"Knock, knock." I waited for a response. Bill looked at me curiously. I repeated, "Knock, knock." I then shrugged my shoulders.

He weakly replied, "Who's there?"

"Yes, 'who's there,' Bill. From now on, try to remember your lines before you open a door. Jesus, you scared me. You aren't paying me enough for this shit." I began to cry again, and Bill began to laugh, which brought on a spasm of pain. He pulled me to him, and once he had control, he replied, "If you're asking for another raise, forget it. Some women are not worth it. I have my limits."

CHAPTER 37

Bill would not let go of my hand. He turned to Richard and asked him to get me a chair. Bill saw CeeCee, who had tears in her eyes. He waved and, with his finger, asked her to come to the bed. He did let me go, and he kissed her as well and thanked her for bringing me. She said she was going out and wondered if she could get anything for anyone. She stared at Richard, who asked to go with her.

When they left, I leaned over and kissed Bill on the lips. I then told him how much I loved him. I was officially out of the closet. "I'm not going to pretend anymore, Billy Boy. I was sure this was only a job, that I was helping you, but I can't fool myself any longer. I know it's a short-term thing, but that's the sum of it, and damned if I will let another day go by without you knowing you have options. I'm not the love of your life, but I'm here in the long-term in whatever capacity you need. My love doesn't have to be returned, but you must know you are loved."

Bill squeezed my hand and nodded. I was crushed. I hoped he would say something similar, but he didn't. I was a complete idiot. Why did I do that? Oh, earth, swallow me. I pretended everything was all good. At least he was alive. Suck it up, get the job done, and let him go.

Bill fell asleep and didn't wake for an hour. CeeCee and Richard returned. We sat in silence, watching the rhythmic rise and fall of Bill's chest, electrocardiogram, blood pressure, and oxygen saturation on the screen displaying his vitals. We didn't talk, and after an hour, Bill woke again for a few minutes. He appeared to be disoriented, and then he recognized where he was.

Bill smiled at us all and he again thanked us for coming. He asked about Myrna and nodded when Richard said there had been no change. I felt like a knife was in my abdomen, and the blade was skewering me. God, I'm good at faking it. No one had a clue about how I felt.

All I have to do is act naturally. Thank God for Buck Owens. Eventually, CeeCee said she needed to get back. I said I would leave as well. That surprised everyone, especially Richard, who asked me to stay. I considered my options. My suitcase and laptop were in the police car. He offered to follow CeeCee and retrieve them. He said there was a motel near the hospital. He wanted to get back to be with his mom, and now that I was here, he felt it was more important to return to his mother's side.

The two left, and once again, I was alone with Bill. He smiled and suggested I get in bed with him. I think not. He was demented and so inappropriate.

"Not gonna happen, Dr. O'Neal. I almost got busted for attempted murder yesterday. I'm not interested in causing a heart attack."

"Oh, I won't have a heart attack. That's one of my few organs that is doing well."

"Not you. Richard would have one when he returns and finds us canoodling." I wanted to know if Bill had said anything, but now was not the time to ask painful questions.

Bill gazed around the room. "I want to go home. I need to get out of this joint. You know Hayley, my greatest risk is now an iatrogenic complication."

"Bill, no one is going to make a mistake. You'll be fine." I wanted to comfort him, but then again, he had ignored my confession of love. Well, that wouldn't happen again. I would play my nursing and author role, then get on with my life.

A nurse came in and asked to speak to me. I excused myself as Richard brought in my possessions from CeeCee's car. I said I would be back in a few minutes. Martin, Bill's neighbor, was on the phone at the nurses' station.

"Hey, it's Hayley."

"Oh good, how's Bill? Jesus, how did that happen? You must be in shock."

"He's weak, and he's slightly disoriented. I haven't talked to a doctor. I only got here an hour or so ago. He sleeps a lot. I've watched his vitals on a monitor, and they look pretty good."

"Oh, good. I'm headed home tonight. What were you doing in a motel? That sounds kind of kinky."

I explained about Myrna and Daniel. He hadn't heard about Daniel's passing, and he asked me to pass on his condolences to Bill. I gave him my number.

"Hayley, I'll come to the hospital tomorrow. I don't get in until late. Where are you staying?"

I wasn't sure of the motel's name. "If you call my phone, I'll get it charged and text you the address. I know it's within walking distance of the hospital. Richard is here, and it's a little awkward right now. I'll tell you about it when I see you."

"Be careful, Hayley. I know how Bill feels. Don't let anything happen to you. It would kill Bill."

Uh, I don't think so, but a girl can dream.

I returned to Bill's room. "That was Martin, Bill. He said to tell you how sorry he is about it all and especially Daniel. He plans to stop by in the morning."

"Oh, good." Bill had been given something for pain, and he was becoming groggy.

Richard stood at the door. "Hayley, can we talk for a moment?"

"Sure?" What did Richard want to say?

"Let's step outside. I want to apologize on behalf of Jessie and me. Dad set me straight. I understand he's counting on you to help him over the next few months, and he said you were only here to help. Dad explained your inability to sleep and how just sleeping in the same room since your abduction has made it easier for you. Dad says you've been a great help, and he doesn't want to lose you. He knows he'll need real help toward the end, and he doesn't want to end up at a facility. Jessie and I need to get home. So, we decided that we'll let you hang around with our father. We want you to understand that we disapprove of the arrangement, but if it makes our father happy in his last few months, well, we think if you're discreet, we can live with it."

I was somewhere between flummoxed and furious. "Gee, thanks." I could not imagine a more insulting conversation. I barely hid my actual reaction. I felt like walking out on the entire family. I had to contain myself.

With all the stories I had gathered about Bill, I couldn't understand how he had let these twits grow up in his house. My kids lived their own lives, and they were not perfect angels, but holy shit, I would kick their donkeys from here to Christmas if any of my kids talked to my friends like I had just experienced.

I took a deep breath and reentered Bill's room. He was asleep, and I quietly resumed my seat next to his bed. I watched the screen, and everything appeared to be as expected. I dozed as well and woke to find him staring at me. Bill smiled as he reached for my hand. "You okay?"

"I'm fine, but how are you? Can I get you anything?" As I asked, a nurse entered the room. She said the doctor was on her way. She announced I would have to leave when Bill's dressing was changed.

"No," Bill shouted, scaring the nurse and me. Bill's monitor went off. "No, she stays. Hayley, I mean, Dr. Alexander is the only person allowed to have any information, and I want her here with me."

"I'm sorry." The nurse examined the chart. "It says here your son is the designated person responsible for any decisions or allowed to have any information."

I watched Bill's expression. He was beyond angry.

"Bill, I mean Dr. O'Neal, calm down. This will not help you get better. You have every right to choose who's in charge. You were unconscious when you came in, and your son assumed the responsibility. We can change it."

"Damn right you will. The only person I want to have any information is sitting right here. Where do I sign? I want it changed right now." Bill began to cough, and his oxygen level went down briefly. I thought I saw a quick ventricular tachycardia trace on his ECG, but it might have been from his swift attempt to raise himself.

Two nurses rushed into the room and examined Bill and his monitoring device. The poor nurse who had been in the room was flustered but explained that Bill wanted to change his designated person of care and decision-making.

The nurse took the chart and glanced back at me. "I'll be back in a moment."

I shrugged.

"Bring me the damn papers." Bill was almost shouting.

I don't ever remember seeing Bill so mad. I can never recall him yelling at anyone before. He lay back in his bed and took my hand. "Sorry, I think my filter's off. It happens when you get old, you know."

I shook my head. "I guess." Holy heck. There was no way I would tell him what his son had said to me in the hallway. He'd have a heart attack for sure.

The nurse and a doctor returned a few minutes later. The doctor observed me and extended her hand. "Hi, I'm Dr. Ventura, and you?"

Before I could answer, Bill replied, "She's my partner, Dr. Alexander."

Partner? That was interesting.

"Well, so pleased to meet you." Dr. Ventura saw my sling and asked if I was injured in the shooting.

Bill wasted no time. "Hayley had her own adventure. She's a hero. She stopped a man from kidnapping a little girl near Jackson. It was in all the papers and on television. We live together, and she will be my designated person to receive any information about my progress from this moment on."

"Oh my God, you are a hero. I saw the story on the news. May we drop the formalities? I'm Barbara." She extended her hand to shake mine.

I took hers. "I'm Hayley. Thanks for all your efforts to save this cranky bastard. On behalf of my partner," and I emphasized the words, my partner. "I promise he will behave himself from now on." I laughed.

Bill relaxed but replied, "Like hell."

"Your partner is one lucky man. What area of medicine do you practice, Hayley?"

Bill answered for me. "The highest. She was a horse vet, like me."

I rolled my eyes and laughed. "Yep, between the two of us, we have enough human medical information to be half dangerous. I'm sure Bill and I will allow you to make most of the decisions necessary to help Bill recover. Mind you, doctor. Bill won't go down easy."

This time the surgeon rolled her eyes. "Well, how about we compromise, and if there are any decisions to make, we can discuss them together, and then I will do what I think is best anyway. Here is one. Bill, do you want green or red jello?"

CHAPTER 38

That afternoon, the nurses had Bill sit up and then stand. Bill's urinary catheter was removed, much to his satisfaction. He took a few steps and then slumped. I helped the nurses ease him back into his bed.

"Not quite ready for prime time, Billy Boy."

He grimaced and mentioned my first walk following surgery for my arm. "Turnabout is fair play, kid." The attempt to walk later in the evening was successful. He needed help returning to the bed. After he had settled, I stepped out of the room and noticed a new guard.

I thought I recognized the older gentleman and stared at him. He returned my gaze and then smiled. He stood to shake my hand. "Dr. Alexander? I'm Louisa's father. You took care of my pony so long ago."

I tried to remember and, like I have done so many times, pretended to remember him.

"Oh, yes. How is Louisa?"

"She's been dead for twenty-five years. I guess you were gone by then."

He was being polite as I frantically searched my mind for the pony's name and the case. "I am busting, so I'll be back in a second." I sat in the bathroom cubical, trying to remember the case. I could not, and I had to admit defeat. I returned, and he stood up as I walked down the hall toward Bill's room.

"It's okay. I know you don't remember. It's been so long. Your part wasn't that much anyway. It was really Doc who was the hero. I'm Troy Smothers. Our pony was Checkers, and he ended up dying."

Bingo. No wonder I didn't remember. It was a case I wanted to forget. It was the kind where there were no winners—a humbling moment in my career. I hugged the man and said sorry I had forgotten his name. I remember this story. I didn't know Louisa had died, but I did know she was ill at the time. "I think it was a brain tumor?"

"Yes, it was a glioblastoma. We lost Louisa a few years later. You were gone by then. We never blamed you. No one would save Checkers, just like no one would save Louisa. Life isn't fair sometimes."

"Mr. Smothers. I'm sure Doc would love to know you're guarding him. Let me step inside and see if he's decent."

I walked into the room; he was eating green Jell-O. I grinned. "I thought you ordered red?"

"The doctor was messing with me. They only have green today." But he did laugh. "Hayles, promise me when the end is near, you'll let me have red Jell-O."

"I'll consider it, old man. More importantly, the man out guarding you is a former client. Do you remember Troy Smothers?"

"Troy? Oh yeah. Whenever you are feeling sorry for your-self, think of this man. Hayley, despite everything that had happened to us in our whole lifetime combined, that man's had it five times worse. I'd love to talk to him."

"Okay. I'll take over the guarding while you two talk. Let me at that gun."

Bill rolled his eyes. "On second thought."

I leaned out the door and invited Troy into Bill's room. He smiled and thanked me. He entered and walked over to Bill, and they shook hands.

"Troy, you old bugger, it's so good to see you. Man, you have slimmed down, buddy. How many years? Are you living in Denver?"

I noticed he didn't ask how anyone was. I stood outside the door and nervously watched the hallway. It was thirty minutes before Troy emerged. He hugged me briefly and thanked me for helping Bill at this time. "I owe him more than I can say. He saved my life. I would take a bullet for him. He asked for me to tell you that he wants you to go get him a milkshake."

"Did he say what flavor?" Already breaking the rules. That's my old boss.

"No, he fell asleep. Dr. Alexander, thank you so much for allowing me to talk to him."

"Hayley to my friends. I saw a fast food across the street. What can I get you?"

"Really? Are you sure?" He seemed so pleased at the small gesture. I took his order and went across the street to the Golden Arches and bought Troy and Bill what they ordered. As I crossed the street to return to the hospital, I thought I recognized Jake's car. He could not have seen me. It might be a similar car or color, but I was frightened, and I hurried across the four-lane road and ran into the hospital.

I handed Troy his order and told him what I saw. He immediately called his station and asked me to stay in the room and not answer the phone. He agreed it might be mistaken identity, but there was no room for complacency. I decided not to tell Bill for fear it would cause further worry. He sipped on the milkshake, and as a knock came at the door, he quickly handed it to me before Troy entered.

All Troy said was, "False alarm." I gave him the thumbs up and turned to Bill, who had his hand out for the shake.

"What was that about?"

"I saw a car that resembled Jake's, but it wasn't." I reached in the bag that had hidden the shake when I entered the hospital and found a fry.

"When were you going to tell me?" His eyes bore down on me, and I could see he was displeased.

I shrugged. "I guess I better head over to the motel I saw. It looks nice."

"No," he shouted. The monitor went crazy, and I took the drink as we knew it would be seconds until the nurses would enter.

This was a new group of nurses. They surveyed the scene, adjusted the wires, and straightened Bill's bed as Troy peered into the room.

"I want my partner to stay by my bed tonight. Is there a recliner or something she can have to be comfortable?"

"Yes, of course." An older nurse gazed at us and casually announced, "You know there are no conjugal visits here?"

As if it was a regular everyday event, Bill asked if she had read the doctor's orders.

"Yes, it says explicitly, no hanky panky, Dr. O'Neal." She pointed to the page without showing it to anyone. The second nurse laughed and nodded. "You know we have you on a video camera. All these intensive care rooms are equipped with cameras. Need I say more?"

I shook my head and quietly mentioned, "You don't pay me nearly enough for this."

"Are you asking for another raise?" Bill laid back sharply, and I could see it hurt him.

"You okay, honey?" I asked.

That made him laugh, which also pained him. "When can I leave the hospital?"

Oh boy, how many times a day will I hear this question?

"Dr. O'Neal, we are so honored and happy to have you here, and it hurts our feelings for you to be asking to leave. I'm personally offended, and my nursing sister here is as well. Aren't you as well, Melodie?"

The older nurse turned to the younger one, who nodded. "Totally offended."

The older nurse continued. "So, I suggest you suck it up and enjoy being waited on by our wonderful nursing staff, or I see an uncharted enema in your future. Okay, poopsie?"

I tried to hide it, but I could not stop laughing. It was painful, so I turned away from Bill as he took this all in. Was this a sign of things to come? Everyone left the room, and when we were alone, I asked him on a scale of one to ten what was his pain level.

"Eight, but if we were in bed together, it might be a five. When we get out, there will be no more sleeping alone. Do you agree?"

I was confused. Earlier in the day, I had laid my heart on the line, and he had not even replied. Now he wants to sleep with me?

"I guess." It was the best I could do for a response.

"You guess? That's all? You just guess?"

"Bill, I'm a little confused." I turned to him, but he was asleep. I suspected the pain medication had kicked in.

A few minutes later, an orderly wheeled in a recliner chair. He set it up on the far side of the bed and quietly showed me how to move the chair to various positions. I mouthed, "Thank you."

I stepped out, and Troy was still sitting on the chair outside Bill's room. I went to the bathroom, took my toothbrush, and prepared to sleep. I thanked him. I wondered about his story. "How long are you here for, Troy?"

"I have one more hour. I don't live far, so I'll get some sleep and return tomorrow afternoon. I usually hate these assignments, but not for Doc. I owe him so much."

I needed this story, and despite my exhaustion, things might change, and I would never get it. "Troy, any chance you'd want to tell me your story?" I explained I was writing a book, and if he didn't want it included, I would not go further.

"No, it's a tribute to the man, and everyone knows anyway. Well, it's kind of long. You're in a part of it."

"I know. I missed the diagnosis. It's okay. I learned and went on, but it was a huge blow to my ego."

I pulled up a chair to observe Bill as he slept while Troy whispered, "Do you remember our pony, Checkers, who had diarrhea and began to lose weight? You did every test known to man, and we were getting nowhere. My wife was frantic. Our daughter had been diagnosed with a brain tumor, and the pony was very important to her. My wife asked me to seek a second opinion, and I was embarrassed to ask you to step aside."

"Troy, I was young and proud, but I was over my head on that case. I had asked all the partners if they had any suggestions. Maybe Bill was away then. I don't remember. When Bill approached me about the case, I explained all the symptoms and tests I'd performed and the results. Bill asked me to accompany him to your ranch. You had asked him for a second opinion."

"He brought you to do a rectal exam on Checkers, and you found the mass. I think Bill said his arm was too big to enter Checkers' backside and mentioned that is why they now allowed girls into vet school."

Bill's arm was not too big, and his joke was to take the pressure off the situation. The pony had cancer or a sizeable internal abscess. Still, Bill and I knew it was the big C. Here was a family with a dying young daughter, and her precious pony would also die.

When Bill and I returned to the car, he put his hand on my shoulder and thanked me. I had felt pretty useless, embarrassed, and distraught. I had failed to do one of the essential exams that should have been done on the very first appointment. A simple rectal exam might not have delineated the problem then. The tumor, or as it turned out, tumors as was the case, may have been too small in the initial exam.

I remembered he stopped along the road where there was river access and went to the back of his truck and retrieved his fishing rod. He scrambled down a narrow path to the small river and began to fly fish while I sat in the car, bawling my eyes out, knowing the horrible time this family would soon experience.

I finally walked down to the river and washed my face in the cool water. I observed Bill casting and retrieving the small fly on the end of an invisible line. Bill turned to me, and I saw he had also been crying. He smiled and shrugged. "Some days are hard, Hayley. Damn hard."

"Yeah?" I didn't want his pity. I was sure he was trying to make me feel better.

"Learn to forgive yourself. It's what will save you. This job could eat you up, but most of the time, you will use your skills and save lives or make horses more comfortable. You'll be a hero. Take those moments and revisit them when things don't go well."

He continued to cast and, with a sudden jerk, had a fish on his line. He played it until the fish tired, and then he brought it to shore. Bill unhooked it and let it go.

He turned to me and said, "Life as a vet is like this. I have come to this spot many times. Some days, I get lucky and catch a fish, but some days, I don't. Hayley, have you ever fly-fished?"

I shook my head, still trying to contain my tears. Bill waved me over and handed me the rod. He stood behind me, held my right arm, and showed me the motion necessary to get a fly out onto the river. I was pathetic. I had no skills to do this. After a minute, he let me go, and I finally got the fly into the area where Bill said there were fish. Wham, a trout hit the fly, and Bill watched me set the hook, play the fish, and eventually bring it to shore and return it to the water. I was captivated. For several minutes, I forgot my failures and the devastating news Bill and I gave this struggling family.

Troy continued his story.

Doc said there were no cures, but we may extend Checker's life with steroids. We put him on the powder that I remember was expensive. We had to feed it or syringe it into Checkers every day. One day, Bill stopped in and brought a large box of the powder and said the drug rep had given it to the clinic as it was short-dated. It was several hundred dollars' worth of steroids. A few days later, Checkers was not doing well, and I thought it might be because of the out-of-date medicine. I studied the packet, and it showed it would not expire for another year.

I think you left a few weeks after that. I hope it wasn't from missing the diagnosis. My wife and I knew the delay in diagnosis would not have hurt Checkers. The steroids didn't help much anyway after a few months. Checkers was euthanized, but our daughter was too far gone to realize he was no longer there. She died sixteen months later.

I put my hand on Troy's shoulder and said I was sorry. I got up and said I needed to see if Bill was okay. I had tears. I used his sheet to wipe my eyes and then returned to Troy. "Thanks for sharing your story."

"That's just the beginning." Troy stood and allowed me to sit in his chair.

When our daughter died, Bill came to the funeral, and then he would periodically visit us over the next year. We had two boys, and he took them fishing. Bill had his personal dramas then, as well. The poor nurse who worked for him was killed, and then he was saddled with the Downs' boy.

"Whatever happened to him?" he asked.

"Daniel died a few days ago of heart failure." I checked my phone to make sure I was recording this story.

"Oh, I didn't know. When Doc wakes up, please tell him how sorry I am."

Anyway, Bill began to take the two boys fishing with his son. Then my wife decided I was too sad and asked to move to Denver with the kids. I agreed, but then she told me she wanted a divorce. Cassie wanted to make a new start.

Bill stepped in when I wasn't at the house. He had no idea about Cassie's plan, and when she told him, he asked her to reconsider and let Bill talk to me. He took me to his friend, Dr. Goodman. It helped for a while, but you know depression is a tough gig. Cassie left, and then I did something very foolish.

I didn't have to guess. Suicide attempts were common among parents who lost children, as was divorce. Again, I put my hand on Troy's shoulder. He stopped talking for a moment and then resumed.

Well, that's about it. Bill got me to a hospital. Between him and Dr. Goodman, I was hospitalized and eventually moved to Denver myself. I see my boys almost every day. They're grown and have families of their own. Cassie got remarried and had another daughter. We settled our differences, and I went to her wedding. I remarried as well to a wonderful woman who had two daughters. Life goes on.

We sat in silence until Troy's replacement arrived. "Hey, thanks for the chat. I'll be back tomorrow unless they let Doc out." Troy stood and had a quiet word with the new guard.

I re-entered the room, and Bill stirred for a moment, smiled, and mumbled he loved me. He was asleep in seconds. So was I.

CHAPTER 39

Two nurses and a guard rushed into the room as we slept. There had been an intruder. A man wearing a security badge and uniform had entered the hospital from the emergency room when an ambulance arrived.

The hospital's internal security team realized that there was an unauthorized person when he tried to enter a restricted area. He quickly moved to the general admission lobby. There was an influx of people from a homicide and an automobile accident with multiple injuries. He may have changed into his regular street clothes and left the building, or the man, who everyone assumed was Jake Jensen, may be hiding in the hospital somewhere.

An orderly in surgical scrubs spoke to everyone. "The police are on their way with more personnel to assist in finding him. We need you to stay where you are, and we are handling the situation." The policeman who was assigned to guard duty appeared young and inexperienced. He'd been told that he was to stay in Bill's room. The window was quickly covered with a surgical drape to prevent anyone from seeing us inside the room.

Bill was sitting up. "Should you bring the chair inside? Isn't that a red flag?"

The chair was brought into the room, and the door to the hallway was barricaded. I felt safe. I needed to use the bathroom, and I stepped into the bathroom off Bill's room. As I stepped in, I realized the bathroom was also linked to the room next door. I tried to lock it from Bill's side, but it was broken. I quickly relieved myself, and as I zipped up my jeans, the door opened, and there was Jake dressed in an orderly's uniform.

Jake put his finger to his lips, indicating for me to be quiet. He had a revolver. He pointed to the door, and we stepped into the adjoining room, where he motioned for me to sit down as he locked the door to the bathroom. His back was to the door leading to the hallway. I saw an officer move past the room without glancing through the window. My heart sank. He placed a doorstop against the door leading to the hallway, preventing anyone from entering the room.

Jake spoke in a whisper, "Hayley, we need to stop meeting like this. It would have been so pleasant had you visited me at the lake. You see, now I have nothing to lose. I'm going down one way or another. So, if you do anything that messes with my plan to kill your friend, I'll kill you too. Plain and simple." He pulled a knife out, and I could see he would stab me if I didn't follow his orders.

"Jake, please think about this. What are you going to get out of all this? Tammy and Daniel are dead. Bill has incurable cancer and won't live out the year, and his wife is dying. She may be dead now. There's no point. You won't make it out of the hospital alive. I've done this once before. I'm not even afraid. You aren't half as scary as the other guy."

"Shut up!" Jake lunged at me, and the knife grazed my neck. I felt blood and touched my neck. It was only a scrape, but it was a warning.

"I'll do whatever you want. Please don't kill me. I'm begging you." I wanted him to think I was scared to death and would comply with his every wish. I was, and I would, but my recent experience told me to satisfy his demands and wait for a chance to escape or for someone to see the monitor and overpower him.

Jake now positioned himself to see the door. I knew my only hope was that someone was looking at this room. We both heard the communal bathroom door open, and then there was knocking on the door, and someone attempted to open the door.

I heard the guard ask if I was in there. Jake put the gun barrel to his lips, indicating for me to be quiet. I sat silently. The door jiggled again, and then there was no more noise from the other side.

Invoking Buck Owens, I tried to be casual and "act naturally." "Jake, this is a fool's errand. It won't resolve anything."

"I've spent my whole adult life trying to make everyone understand that fucking bastard was not my child. Now the world is going to know."

"It's pretty simple these days. You can get a DNA paternity test kit and sort it out in a few weeks. I can help you and order one right here from my phone." I reached for my mobile phone in my pocket, but Jake told me to stop and cocked the hammer.

"Stop. I don't need to prove it. I know."

"Well, if you already did the test, I could help you show everyone. Do you have the results?"

"I didn't do a test. I don't need to. There is no way I would have a stupid kid like that."

"Jake, there are plenty of intelligent people who have children born with Down's syndrome."

"Not me." He waved the gun around in a circle.

"Okay, you may be correct. If you shoot me, there is no way you will ever know. You won't get out alive."

"You don't get it, bitch. I don't need to prove it. I already know. Just shut up. I gotta figure this out."

I sat while he stared out the window next to me and back to the gun. I thought I would die when I saw Bill peer into the window. I tried to divert Jake's attention, but Bill knocked on the door and held up both hands, indicating he was unarmed.

Jake hadn't noticed him. I stared at the window and shook my head vehemently. I mouthed "no," and gave him the meanest stare I could muster. He knocked again, and Jake seemed to arouse from a trance. He saw Bill and pointed the gun toward me. I shook my head and shouted, "No, it's okay."

Jake moved the doorstop as Bill began to open the door. He entered with just a hospital gown on. Once more, I cried, "Get out. Jake and I are talking."

But it was too late. Jake stood and aimed at Bill. Bill had his hands in the air. "Jake, wait. Let her go. She's not part of this. It should be between you and me. You know you'll be dead too, don't you? Let her go, for God's sake. Please, I'm begging you."

"Why should I?" Jakes swung the revolver from Bill to me and then back to Bill.

"Hayley works for me. She's helping me, but that's it. Hayley doesn't deserve to die. She's just an employee—a caregiver. I'm dying, Jake. I was glad when you shot me. My death will happen over the next few months. It's a painful, slow death. Shoot me, and I won't even care. A quick death is a good death, eh Jake?"

"Why do you care if she's just an employee? Is she another one of your employees you're screwing, Doc?"

Bill didn't answer, but once again, he asked Jake to let me go.

Jake sat for a long time with his revolver trained on me. "Tell me, what's it to you, old man?"

"Jake, she's innocent. It's not like Tammy and me. I'll admit Tammy and I had been lovers but not this woman. Let her go. I'm the one you want."

I knew Bill was lying. He no more fathered that child or had a relationship with Tammy than he had with me. I felt I had a better shot at stopping Jake than Bill did. I suspected Jake planned to do a murder-suicide.

Bill turned to me and then back to Jake. "Hayley, get up and leave now. Jake, you will let her go, then you can kill me, and I won't put up any resistance."

Jake pointed the gun at the door and said, "You have three seconds."

I stood and stared at Bill. I whispered, "Thank you," and hugged him. I mouthed, "I love you." As I did, I felt a protective bulletproof vest under his gown. I glanced at his face, but Bill's eyes were trained on Jake. I opened the door and exited the room, stepping away from the door where any misaligned gunfire might penetrate the wall.

I was quickly grabbed by a policeman and rushed down the hall. The nurses in Bill's room took me and wanted to know if I was all right. I was unable to speak. The tears were flowing; we all moved and sat in a room several doors down the hall.

Two police snipers would take Jake out if he tried to leave the room. One policeman had a walkie-talkie and asked me to describe where Jake and Bill were positioned in the room. It seemed like a lifetime as I listened to the police tactical squad that arrived after being whisked into a more distant room. I heard a commotion and then gunfire. Was it one shot or two?

I tried to leave the room, but I was not allowed. I heard a man yell, "He's down. Go, go, go, now."

I watched the police run into the room where I had left Bill and Jake. The two nurses supported me. Several minutes passed before Bill emerged, standing and slowly walking down the hallway supported by two police in armored masks and chest protectors. They turned to escort him to his room, and I was allowed to enter the room.

A multitude of doctors, nurses, and paramedics prevented me from approaching Bill. I stood along the wall, watching and waiting for the all-clear. I was unsure what had happened, and I could see the hallway with no sign of Jake—alive or dead.

Bill eventually glanced my way and smiled. He gave me a thumbs up while answering questions. Finally, it seemed like everyone was convinced Bill was uninjured, and he motioned for me to come over to his bed. He was shaking, but his color wasn't too bad. I leaned over and kissed him on the cheek.

Bill pulled me closer. "I almost took a bullet for you, Hayles. I want a proper kiss."

"You mean lip lock, old man? I'm not sure you deserve it." But I caved and kissed him full on the lips. Everyone waited, and as I straightened up, they realized we were both crying. "I normally detest public displays of emotionalism." I winked and smiled so only Bill could see.

We held hands as the monitors were replaced. My phone rang, and I recognized the number. "I think it's Richard. Do you want to take it or me?"

He signaled for me to hand him the phone. "Richard, it's me, your father." I could only hear half the conversation.

Bill frowned. "Well, that was my doing. Hayley's in charge of everything now. I'm going to let her handle my affairs from now on. Hayley's the person you need to call for updates on my health and medical decisions." Bill nodded. "I'm sorry you feel that way, Son. How is your mother?"

I watched Bill as he grimaced into the phone. "Hang in there. It sounds like it won't be too long, then. Make sure your mother isn't in pain. Tell Jessie I need my house back as soon as I'm discharged. You'll all need to leave unless you want to stay with Hayley and me."

There was a long pause. "You're going to have to get used to it, Richard. That's the way it's going to be until I die."

Again, a pause. "I don't know how long I have. Listen, Richard, the police want to interview me. I'll talk to you later. I love you both." Another pause. "Take care, son. I'm sorry I'm not there to help you, but it will be a few days before I'm allowed to leave. I love you."

He handed me the phone. "Clearly, I failed to instill courtesy in raising these two kids."

"One out of three isn't a complete failure." Bill knew I was referring to Daniel as the courteous child, which reminded us of his passing.

Bill quickly told me that a sniper had shot Jake through the window. Bill had a gun taped to his side, but he could never get to it fast enough. Jake didn't have a chance to shoot.

Bill's surgeon arrived and immediately wanted to examine Bill's incision. There was a slight increase in exudate, and it had a bloody tinge to it. His temperature was below a range that would be considered suspicious of sepsis.

She peered at Bill and tapped her pen against a clipboard. "I guess I need to be more specific about what you can and cannot do. I think we'll strike off the use of a loaded firearm for a few more days. No more rescuing damsels, and if I hear about any breaches of the hanky-panky embargo, I'll have to ban Hayley from the hospital. Now, red or yellow Jell-O today?"

"I am partial to a red, doctor." He smiled weakly.

"No promises, Dr. O'Neal, but how about I allow you a chocolate shake? Wouldn't that be nice for a change? Not." Barbara Ventura winked at me as she left the room. I could hear her mumble, "It's always the oldies that give me the most trouble."

Martin Goodman arrived and was able to get past security to see Bill. He and I hugged. "I'll let you gentlemen male bond, spit, and punch. I'm going to call my kids, and then

I'll see if I can find a place to clean up." I hugged Martin and left.

The hospital was swarming with police, reporters, and family members of hospitalized patients. The siege lasted for over forty minutes, but it would be hours before things would return to normal if they ever did. Few people knew me or recognized me as playing a role.

The hospital director saw me and asked if I needed anything. He took me to a private area, and I called and reassured my children that I was all right, and then he allowed me to use his personal bathroom. I returned to Bill's room, where Bill and Martin were sitting and discussing or probably debriefing one another. Jake's body was on its way to the morgue. Cleaners and hospital maintenance personnel were coming and going. The area was cordoned off with red and white tape.

"I can come back." I wanted Bill to have as much time as possible. He had just observed a man being shot. I knew how difficult it must be for Bill.

"No, come in. Please stay, Hayley. We'll need some counseling, and Martin wants to help us."

"I can go find a pony, but he might slip on the floors here." I smiled at Bill and Martin.

Martin had heard about the psychologist who suggested that equine therapy might help with my PTSD. "I think you two will need a heard of ponies by the sounds of what went down."

Bill patted the bed, and I walked over and sat on the edge. Bill put his hand on my back and rubbed it. Martin could see things had progressed from that interaction. He raised his eyebrows and cocked his head.

Bill smiled. "It took a while, but I think she's a stayer." The obvious was that I would only be a short-timer. What this trauma did to Bill's temporary reprieve from lymphoma would not be known for a while.

Martin finally left, and I lay down on the bed with my head next to Bill's chest but away from his gunshot wound. The staff let us stay like that for an hour or more before they returned to do observations on Bill and restart his intravenous fluids laced with antibiotics. I returned to the recliner and opened my laptop. I began writing the story about Checkers, the pony with cancer.

Bill was about to fall asleep and asked what I was writing. I told him about Checkers and my failure to diagnose her condition. Bill turned to me and, in all seriousness, said, "I have a new requirement. You know what I said about nothing bad about Myrna and the kids?"

"Yes?" I wondered if he was going to rescind that caveat.

"Well, nothing that makes you look bad either."

"Nope, not in this story. Young vets must know they will not be perfect. I remember that an old geezer once told me that he had made mistakes, and it's essential that we learn to forgive ourselves. Remember the triumphs and use those memories to help get past the mistakes. Learn from the mistakes, but don't linger on them."

"That guy must have been very worldly."

"Buck Owens, yep, he was. Ow, that hurt." I pretended to feign pain when Bill kicked me with his foot.

"I would prefer you not write the book now. I think you know I only used it as a ruse to get you to come up and stay for a while. I never really cared. It's too much." Bill adjusted himself, and I knew he needed to sleep.

"Other than your family being off-limits and adding the shameful hussy you shack up with, I kind of think it's out of your hands, Billy Boy. Get some sleep while I write up your legacy. We'll have some rough seas ahead, and I want you to take advantage of the pain meds while you are allowed. I'm not letting you get hooked on anything at this stage. Remember, you are no longer in charge. You answer to me now, Dr. O'Neal."

CHAPTER 40

Myrna died that night. Jessica was by her side and said it was a peaceful death. Myrna never talked and eventually stopped breathing. Jessica called my number and asked to speak to her father. Bill talked to her and told her how sorry he was for her loss. I left the room and didn't come back for an hour. I noted he had said "her," not their loss.

When I returned with a breakfast roll and coffee, it was apparent Bill had cried again. I asked him if he wanted to be alone, if I could get anything, or arrange something on his and the children's behalf.

"No, thanks. They have it covered. They'll have Myrna cremated and leave for home and return for the memorial service in two weeks so that I can attend." I hugged Bill again and told him how sorry I was. He was somewhat distant, and I wanted to give him time to sort out his feelings.

CHAPTER 41

Bill and I returned to the lake house a week later. He was weak and leaned on me as we walked up the steps to the house. Martin came over and helped me get Bill showered and onto the couch. Martin left right after and said he was a shout away. Bill didn't bother removing any pictures or memorabilia from Myrna. He knew his time here at the lake was limited. The house would go to his children.

He asked me how I felt. "Bill, I'm heading back to my place when…" I had to find a way to discuss the inevitable.

"When I die. It's okay to say it, Hayles. Neither of us will escape it in the end. Let's not try to pretend it isn't going to happen. I wish it would be you that passed first, and I was the one helping you, but that's not going to happen."

Dr. Cotter's wedding was postponed until Bill could walk her down the aisle. I still had to wear a damn dress. I did get a few more stories during the wedding reception, so it wasn't a wasted evening. Bill introduced me as his partner to everyone, which raised eyebrows as Myrna had been dead less than a month.

Bill's children returned for Myrna's memorial service. They were allowed to stay at the house, but they were warned not to say anything that would upset me. I was not allowed to leave. I didn't attend the service, and I didn't care. Martin said it was not a joyful experience. "You didn't miss anything."

My arm continued to improve, and shortly before the season ended and winter set in, Bill and I went out once in the kayak and had a quick fish. As we paddled past Lorna's house, she saw us and waved to us. "Hey, you two. I'm expecting you for dinner on Friday."

Lorna had been over several times and helped me with meal preparations and casseroles for the family when they came for the memorial. She later reported that it was not well attended. Several men they didn't know had arrived and appeared particularly sad. She and her husband were getting counseling, and things had improved. "You know, at our age, it's not like we need to have sex every day anymore."

I stared at her. "Wait a minute. You had sex every day? For how long?"

She stared at me and shook her head. "Well, until recently. You know he's still under punishment. Of course, guess who's really suffering here?" She pointed to herself. She had to be at least sixty.

I shook my head. "Don't tell Bill any of this. Sheesh, he doesn't pay me enough."

At first, she thought I was serious. She observed me trying not to laugh, and then we both had one of those laughs that became viral. If one stopped, the laughter of the other incited the other to restart. We had tears from laughing so much.

Bill walked into the kitchen, saw us crying, and quickly excused himself which restarted the contagious laughter. "Stop, Hayley. I'm going to wet my pants."

"Too late for me," I responded, and then it began again. Finally, my sides ached, and I asked Lorna to leave before I needed resuscitation. That was how it was for us the rest of my time at the lake. I would see her for coffee or dinner, and we would glance at one another and then start laughing again. We were the only two who knew what started the laughter. It was our little secret. My comment to her was that she was my new inspiration. Her husband was back in her good graces, full-time, shortly after Myrna's funeral.

Martin and I became closer, and his support in helping me with Bill was my greatest strength. He said he would visit me yearly when I moved back to my home and expected me to come out at least once a year. "Scouts honor, Marty. Pinky promise." We locked little fingers often. We knew what it meant without the words.

Bill lived for another year and a half. We went back up to Montana. He decided to hell with all his family's wishes. He wanted his ashes taken to the cabin up in the mountains. That would be my last act. "I'll need a bonus for that, darling. I'm still waiting for a raise."

"Hayley, I know the young vets see our lives as unbalanced. I know you feel the same, but I never thought about what I was missing. I loved what I did. I could hardly wait to start the day. It was never work to me. I felt so blessed to have a profession where I was paid to do what I did. That's why I'm so glad it is you telling my story. My balance was right where I wanted it. Call me Dr. Michener. It was work, and it was play, and I never could decide which was which. Was my life perfect? No, but it was damn close, and like my son always said, I did my best."

Bill asked me to end the book with a poem by Emily Dickinson.

<u>Because I could not stop for Death</u>
By Emily Dickinson
Because I could not stop for Death—
He kindly stopped for me—
The Carriage held but just Ourselves—
And Immortality.

We slowly drove—He knew no haste
And I had put away
My labor and my leisure too,
For His Civility—

We passed the School, where Children strove
At Recess—in the Ring—
We passed the Fields of Gazing Grain—
We passed the Setting Sun—

Or rather—He passed us—
The Dews drew quivering and chill—
For only Gossamer, my Gown—
My Tippet—only Tulle—

We paused before a House that seemed
A Swelling of the Ground—

The Roof was scarcely visible—
The Cornice—in the Ground—

Since then—'tis Centuries—and yet
Feels shorter than the Day
I first surmised the Horses' Heads
Were toward Eternity—

"So, when you ask me was it worth it? Yes, it was."
I smiled to myself. So worth it.

EPILOGUE

Bill never paid me a dime. I lived like a queen during my time with him. The book had been accepted for publication. The proceeds would be divided between a respite care facility for families with children with disabilities and The Foundation for the Horse, managed by the American Association of Equine Practitioners.

Four months after I returned, Bill's red truck arrived at my cabin. Martin smiled when he approached my driveway as I worked in the garden.

My new dog, Mister Bossy Boots, wagged his tail in circles as Martin pulled up and exited the truck.

"Boots, you're not even a hint of a guard dog."

Inside the vehicle were all Bill's books, albums of his correspondence, poetry, and photos. His fly-fishing equipment and kayak were in the truck bed.

On the passenger seat was an envelope. Inside was a check, a deed to the Montana ranch, and a card. I would wait to open it when I was alone.

Later that night, I sat on my bed and reminded Boots that his job was to protect me. He lay on his back and expected me to scratch his belly. Belly scratching completed, I reached for the envelope.

My darling wife,
Please be kind to the young vets who you meet and mentor.
They will never have it as easy as we did. For us it was never work.
All ya gotta do is act naturally.
Love,
Bill and Buck

Yes, we had married and never told anyone. One day, Bill was staring at me and just announced he could no longer live in sin. I was perfectly happy with sin, but he wasn't. "Suit yourself, Billy Boy." No one knew besides Martin and us.

Until now.

ACKNOWLEDGMENTS

Mimi Schrumpf, Mary Smith, Candace Fox, Dr. Ann Dwyer, Dale McKinney Dr. Sharon Spier, and others have read the various drafts. Valuable edits were completed by Chris Hall and her team at The Editing Hall.

I am indebted to the many veterinarians who have influenced my practice and personal life. They include but are not limited to the named vets. The early years: Drs. J.D. Wheat, B. Richards, D. Meagher, J.T. Vaughan, J. Humberg, P. Kennedy, J. Hughes, and my father J. Woolsey. The later years include C. Ragle, R. Estes, T. Crocker, P. Wilkins, M. McAllister, M.B. Whitcomb, W. Moyer, J. Madigan, M. Aleman, H. Mortimer, G. Norwood, B. Brock, D. Thal, A. Cuddy, S. Harbison, and J. Meyer. These veterinarians influenced what I attempted to portray in Dr. Bill O'Neal. He is a composite of all of these practitioners.

While most of the veterinary stories included in this book were from my personal experience, some are from stories

I have heard. So, if I stole your story, or you think I did, thanks.

Thanks to April Cox for her advice and guidance in this publication and Holly Moore for her cover design. Special thanks to Jan Dappen for her artistic contribution to the cover. More of her artwork can be found at https://jandappen.com/

ELIZABETH WOOLSEY DVM

Elizabeth Woolsey DVM grew up in postwar California. Sure she was the daughter of Roy Rogers, she spent her youth emulating him. Sadly, DNA evidence has proved her wrong. Thus, she followed in her other father's footsteps into equine veterinary practice. She subsequently migrated to Australia, where she practiced equine veterinary medicine near Adelaide, South Australia, until her retirement in December 2020. She began writing about her experiences as a horse vet and published her first book, Horse Doctor An American Vet's Life Down Under in 2005. A few years before her father's death, she discovered a treasure trove of personal and historically significant letters. She knew this would make a great book not only for her family but also for WWII enthusiasts. She published Jack's War, Letters to Home from an American WII Navigator in 2015.

While veterinary medicine has been her passion, fly-fishing, horseback riding, and writing occupy her leisure time. Her new books include stories about women in equine practice. Small Town Secrets: Horse Doctor Adventures 2021 is her latest book. She now resides in North Georgia, where she follows her passions.

She loves to hear from her readers! You can write to her at:

ewoolseydvm@gmail.com

https://www.facebook.com/elizabeth.woolseydvm

https://elizabethwoolsey.com/

https://amzn.to/3dPAoGc

Catch and Release
Catch and Keep
https://amzn.to/3eoPHWH

Also by Elizabeth Woolsey (Herbert)
Horse Doctor: An American Vet's Life Down Under
Jack's War: Letters Home from an American WII Navigator